1

M^CBAIN

Nocturne

A Novel of the 87th Precinct

COMPASS PRESS
· OXFORD · MELBOURNE ·

Compass Press Large Print Book Series; an imprint of ISIS Publishing Ltd, Great Britain, and Bolinda Press, Australia.

Published in Large Print in 1998 by ISIS Publishing Ltd, 7 Centremead, Osney Mead, Oxford, OX2 0ES, and Australian Large Print Audio & Video Pty Ltd, 17 Mohr Street, Tullamarine, Victoria 3043, with the permission of Hodder & Stoughton Ltd.

Australian Cataloguing in Publication Data

McBain, Ed, 1926–

Nocturne / Ed McBain. – (Compass Press large print book series).

ISBN 1863407855

1. Large print books.

2. Detective and mystery stories, American.

I. Title

813.54

British Library Cataloguin in Publication Data

McBain, Ed, 1926–

Nocturne. – Large print ed.

1. 87th Precinct (Imaginary place) – Fiction

2. Detective and mystery stories

3. Large type books

I. Title

813.5'4 [F]

ISBN 1-86340-785-5 (ALPAV Pty Ltd)

ISBN 0-7531-5840-X (ISIS Publishing Ltd)

This is for

Rachel and Avrum Ben-Avi

The city in these pages is imaginary.
The people, the places are all fictitious.
Only the police routine is based on established investigatory technique.

1

The phone was ringing as Carella came into the squadroom. The clock on the wall read 11:45 P.M.

"I'm out of here," Parker said, shrugging into his overcoat.

Carella picked up. "Eighty-seventh Squad," he said. "Detective Carella."

And listened.

Hawes was coming into the squadroom, blowing on his hands.

"We're on our way," Carella said, and hung up the phone. Hawes was taking off his coat. "Leave it on," Carella said.

The woman was lying just inside the door to her apartment. She was still wearing an out-of-fashion mink going orange. Her hair was styled in what used to be called finger waves. Silver-blue hair. Orange-brown mink. It was twelve degrees Fahrenheit out there in the street tonight, but under the mink she was wearing only a flowered cotton housedress. Scuffed French-heeled shoes on her feet. Wrinkled hose. Hearing aid in her right ear. She must have been around eighty-five or so. Someone had shot her twice in the chest. Someone had also shot and killed her cat, a fat female tabby with a bullet hole in her chest and blood in her matted fur.

The Homicide cops had got here first. When Carella and Hawes walked in, they were still speculating on what had happened.

"Keys on the floor there, must've nailed her the minute she come in the apartment," Monoghan said.

"Unlocks the door, blooie," Monroe said.

It was chilly in the apartment; both men were still wearing their outer clothing, black overcoats, black fedoras, black leather gloves. In this city, the appearance of Homicide Division detectives was mandatory at the scene, even though the actual investigation fell to the responding precinct detectives. Monoghan and Monroe liked to think of themselves as supervisory and advisory professionals, creative mentors so to speak. They felt black was a fitting color, or lack of color, for professional Homicide Division mentors. Like two stout giant penguins, shoulders hunched, heads bent, they stood peering down at the dead old woman on the worn carpet. Carella and Hawes, coming into the apartment, had to walk around them to avoid stepping on the corpse.

"Look who's here," Monoghan said, without looking up at them.

Carella and Hawes were freezing cold. On a night like tonight, they didn't feel they needed either advice or supervision, creative or otherwise. All they wanted to do was get on with the job. The area just inside the door smelled of whiskey. This was the first thing both cops registered. The second was the broken bottle in the brown paper bag, lying just out of reach of the old

6

woman's bony arthritic hand. The curled fingers seemed extraordinarily long.

"Been out partying?" Monoghan asked them.

"We've been here twenty minutes already," Monroe said petulantly.

"Big party?" Monoghan asked.

"Traffic," Hawes explained, and shrugged.

He was a tall, broad-shouldered man wearing a woolen tweed overcoat an uncle had sent him from London this past Christmas. It was now the twentieth of January, Christmas long gone, the twenty-first just a heartbeat away—but time was of no consequence in the 87th Precinct. Flecks of red in the coat's fabric looked like sparks that had fallen from his hair onto the coat. His face was red, too, from the cold outside. A streak of white hair over his left temple looked like glare ice. It was the color his fear had been when a burglar slashed him all those years ago. The emergency room doctor had shaved his hair to get at the wound, and it had grown back white. Women told him they found it sexy. He told them it was hard to comb.

"We figure she surprised a burglar," Monroe said. "Bedroom window's still open." He gestured with his head. "We didn't want to touch it till the techs got here."

"*They* must be out partying, too," Monoghan said.

"Fire escape just outside the window," Monroe said, gesturing again. "Way he got in."

"Everybody's out partying but us," Monoghan said.

"Old lady here was planning a little party, that's for sure," Monroe said.

"Fifth of cheap booze in the bag," Monoghan said.

7

"Musta gone down while the liquor stores were still open."

"It's Saturday, they'll be open half the night," Monroe said.

"Didn't want to take any chances."

"Well, she won't have to worry about taking chances anymore," Monroe said.

"Who is she, do you know?" Carella asked.

He had unbuttoned his overcoat, and he stood now in an easy slouch, his hands in his trouser pockets, looking down at the dead woman. Only his eyes betrayed that he was feeling any sort of pain. He was thinking he should have asked Who *was* she? Because someone had reduced her to nothing but a corpse afloat on cheap whiskey.

"Didn't want to touch her till the M.E. got here," Monroe said.

Please, Carella thought, no par—

"*He's* probably out partying, too," Monoghan said.

Midnight had come and gone without fanfare.

But morning would feel like night for a long while yet.

To no one's enormous surprise, the medical examiner cited the apparent cause of death as gunshot wounds. This was even before one of the crime scene techs discovered a pair of spent bullets embedded in the door behind the old woman, and another one in the baseboard behind the cat. They looked like they might be thirty-eights, but not even the creative mentors were willing to guess. The tech bagged them and marked them for transport to the lab. There were no latent fingerprints on the windowsill, the sash, or the fire escape outside. No latent footprints, either. To everyone's great relief, the tech who'd been out there came back in and closed the window behind him.

The coats came off.

The building superintendent told them the dead woman was Mrs. Helder. He said he thought she was Russian or something. Or German, he wasn't sure. He said she'd been living there for almost three years. Very quiet person, never caused any trouble. But he thought she drank a little.

This was what was known as a one-bedroom apartment. In this city, some so-called one-bedrooms were really L-shaped studios, but this was a genuine one-bedroom, albeit a tiny one. The bedroom faced the street side, which was unfortunate in that the din of automobile horns was incessant and intolerable, even at this early hour of the morning. This was not a particularly desirable section of the city or the precinct. Mrs. Helder's building was on Lincoln Street, close to the River Harb and the fish market that ran dockside, east to west, for four city blocks.

The team had relieved at a quarter to twelve and would in turn be relieved at seven forty-five A.M. In some American cities, police departments had abandoned what was known as the graveyard shift. This was because detective work rarely required an immediate response except in homicide cases, where any delay in the investigation afforded the killer an invaluable edge. In those cities, what they called Headquarters, or Central, or Metro, or whatever, maintained homicide hotlines that could rustle any

9

detective out of bed in a minute flat. Not this city. In this city, whenever your name came up on the rotating schedule, you pulled a month on what was accurately called the *morning* shift even though you worked all through the empty hours of the night. The graveyard shift, as it was familiarly and unaffectionately called, threw your internal clock all out of whack, and also played havoc with your sex life. It was now five minutes past midnight. In exactly seven hours and forty minutes, the day shift would relieve and the detectives could go home to sleep. Meanwhile, they were in a tiny one-bedroom apartment that stank of booze and something they realized was cat piss. The kitchen floor was covered with fish bones and the remains of several fish heads.

"Why do you suppose he shot the cat?" Monroe said.

"Maybe the cat was barking," Monoghan suggested.

"They got books with cats in them solving murders," Monroe said.

"They got books with all *kinds* of amateurs in them solving murders," Monoghan said.

Monroe looked at his watch.

"You got this under control here?" he asked.

"Sure," Carella said.

"You need any advice or supervision, give us a ring."

"Meanwhile, keep us informed."

"In triplicate," Monoghan said.

There was a double bed in the bedroom, covered with a quilt that looked foreign in origin, and a dresser that definitely was European, with ornate pulls and painted drawings on the sides and top. The dresser drawers were stacked with underwear and socks and hose and sweaters and blouses. In the top drawer, there was a painted candy tin with costume jewelry in it.

There was a single closet in the bedroom, stuffed with clothes that must have been stylish a good fifty years ago, but which now seemed terribly out of date and, in most instances, tattered and frayed. There was a faint whiff of must coming from the closet. Must and old age. The old age of the clothes, the old age of the woman who'd once worn them. There was an ineffable sense of sadness in this place.

Silently, they went about their work.

In the living room, there was a floor lamp with a tasseled shade.

There were framed black-and-white photographs of strange people in foreign places.

There was a sofa with ornately carved legs and worn cushions and fading lace antimacassars.

There was a record player. A shellacked 78 rpm record sat on the turntable. Carella bent over to look at the old red RCA Victor label imprinted with the picture of the dog looking into the horn on an old-fashioned phonograph player. The label read:

Albums of 78s and 33 1/3s were stacked on the table beside the record player.

Against one wall, there was an upright piano. The keys were covered with dust. It was apparent that no one had played it for a long while. When they lifted the lid of the piano bench, they found the scrapbook.

There are questions to be asked about scrapbooks.

Was the book created and maintained by the person who was its subject? Or did a second party assemble it?

There was no clue as to who had laboriously and fastidiously collected and pasted up the various clippings and assorted materials in the book.

The first entry in the book was a program from Albert Hall in London, where a twenty-three-year-old Russian pianist named Svetlana Dyalovich made her triumphant debut, playing Tchaikovsky's B-flat Minor Concerto with Leonard Horne conducting the London Philharmonic. The assembled reviews from the London *Times*, the *Spectator* and the *Guardian* were ecstatic, alternately calling her a "great musician" and a "virtuoso," and praising her "electrical temperament," her "capacity for animal excitement" and "her physical genius for tremendous climax of sonority and for lightning speed."

The reviewer from the *Times* summed it all up with, "The piano, in Miss Dyalovich's hands, was a second orchestra, nearly as powerful and certainly as eloquent as the first, and the music was spacious, superb, rich enough in color and feeling, to have satisfied the composer himself. What is to be recorded here is the wildest welcome a pianist has received in many seasons in London, the appearance of a new pianistic talent which cannot be ignored or minimized."

There followed a similarly triumphant concert at New York's Carnegie Hall six months later, and then three concerts in Europe, one with the La Scala Orchestra in Milan, another with the Orchestre Symphonique de Paris and a third with the Concertgebouw Orchestra in Holland. In rapid succession, she gave ten recitals in Sweden, Norway and Denmark, and then went on to play five more in Switzerland, ending the year with concerts in Vienna, Budapest, Prague, Liège, Anvers, Brussels, and then Paris again. It was not surprising that in March of the following year, the then twenty-four-year-old musical genius was honored with a profile in *Time* magazine. The cover photo of her showed a tall blond woman in a black gown, seated at a grand piano, her long, slender fingers resting on the keys, a confident smile on her face.

They kept turning pages.

Year after year, review after review hailed her extraordinary interpretive gifts. The response was the same everywhere in the world. Words like "breathtaking talent" and "heaven-storming octaves" and "conquering technique" and "leonine sweep and power" became commonplace in anything anyone ever wrote about her. It was as if reviewers could not find vocabulary rich enough to describe this phenomenal woman's artistry. When she was thirty-four, she married an Austrian impresario named Franz Helder . . .

"There it is," Hawes said. "Mrs. Helder."

"Yeah."

. . . and a year later gave birth to her only child, whom they named Maria, after her husband's mother. At the age of forty-three, when Maria was eight, exactly twenty years after a young girl from Russia had taken the town by storm, Svetlana returned to London to play a commemorative concert at Albert Hall. The critic for the London *Times*, displaying a remarkable lack of British restraint, hailed the performance as "a most fortunate occasion" and went on to call Svetlana "this wild tornado unleashed from the Steppes."

There followed a ten-year absence from recital halls— "I am a very poor traveler," she told journalists. "I am afraid of flying, and I can't sleep on trains. And besides, my daughter is becoming a young woman, and she needs more attention from me." During this time, she devoted herself exclusively to recording for RCA Victor, where she first put on wax her debut concerto, the Tchaikovsky B-flat Minor, and next the Brahms D Minor, one of her favorites. She went on to interpret the works of Mozart, Prokofieff, Schumann, Rachmaninoff, Beethoven, Liszt, always paying strict attention to what the composer intended, an artistic concern that promoted one admiring critic to write, "These recordings reveal that Svetlana Dyalovich is first and foremost a consummate musician, scrupulous to the nth degree of the directions of the composer."

Shortly after her husband's death, Svetlana returned triumphantly to the concert stage, shunning Carnegie Hall in favor of the venue of her first success, Albert Hall in London. Tickets to the single comeback performance were sold out in an hour and a half. Her daughter was eighteen. Svetlana was fifty-three. To thunderous standing ovations, she played the Bach-Busoni Toccata in C Major, Schumann's Fantasy in C, Scriabin's Sonata No. 9 and a Chopin Mazurka, Etude and Ballade. The evening was a total triumph.

But then . . .

Silence.

After that concert thirty years ago, there was nothing more in the scrapbook. It was as if this glittering, illustrious artist had simply vanished from the face of the earth.

Until now.

When a woman the super knew as Mrs. Helder lay dead on the floor of a chilly apartment at half past midnight on the coldest night this year.

They closed the scrapbook.

The scenario proposed by Monoghan and Monroe sounded like a possible one. Woman goes down to buy herself a bottle of booze. Burglar comes in the window, thinking the apartment is empty. Most apartments are burglarized during the daytime, when it's reasonable to expect the place will be empty. But some "crib" burglars, as they're called, are either desperate junkies or beginners, and they'll go in whenever the mood strikes them, day *or* night, so long as they think they'll score. Okay, figure the guy sees no lights burning, he jimmies open the window—though the techs hadn't found any jimmy marks—goes in, is getting accustomed to the dark and acquainted with the pad when he hears a key sliding in the keyway and the door opens and all at once the lights come on, and there's this startled old broad standing there with a brown paper bag in one hand and a pocketbook in the other. He panics. Shoots her before she can scream. Shoots the cat for good measure. Man down the hall hears the shots, starts yelling. Super runs up, calls the police. By then, the burglar's out the window and long gone.

"You gonna want this handbag?" one of the techs asked.

Carella turned from where he and Hawes were going through the small desk in the living room.

"Cause we're done with it," the tech said.

"Any prints?"

"Just teeny ones. Must be the vic's."

"What was in it?"

"Nothing. It's empty."

"Empty?"

"Perp must've dumped the contents on the floor, grabbed whatever was in it."

Carella thought this over for a moment.

"Shot her first, do you mean? And then emptied the bag and scooped up whatever was in it?"

"Well . . . yeah," the tech said.

This sounded ridiculous even to him.

"Why didn't he just run off with the bag itself?"

"Listen, they do funny things."

"Yeah," Carella said.

He was wondering if there'd been money in that bag when the lady went downstairs to buy her booze.

"Let me see it," he said.

The tech handed him the bag. Carella peered into and then turned it upside down. Nothing fell out of it. He peered into it again. Nothing.

"Steve?"

Cotton Hawes, calling from the desk.

"A wallet," he said, holding it up.

In the wallet, there was a Visa card with a photo ID of the woman called Svetlana Helder in its left-hand corner.

There was also a hundred dollars in tens, fives and singles.

Carella wondered if she had a charge account at the local liquor store.

They were coming out into the hallway when a woman standing just outside the apartment down the hall said, "Excuse me?"

Hawes looked her over.

Twenty-seven, twenty-eight, he figured, slender dark-haired woman with somewhat exotic features spelling Middle Eastern or at least Mediterranean. Very dark brown eyes. No makeup, no nail polish. She was clutching a woolen shawl around her. Bathrobe under it. Red plaid, lambskin-lined bedroom slippers on her feet. It was slightly warmer here in the hallway than it was outside in the street. But only slightly. Most buildings in this city, the heat went off around midnight. It was now a quarter to one.

"Are you the detectives?" she asked.

"Yes," Carella said.

"I'm her neighbor," the woman said.

They waited.

17

"Karen Todd," she said.

"Detective Carella. My partner, Detective Hawes. How do you do?"

Neither of the detectives offered his hand. Not because they were male chauvinists, but only because cops rarely shook hands with so-called civilians. Same way cops didn't carry umbrellas. See a guy with his hands in his pockets, standing on a street corner in the pouring rain, six to five he was an undercover cop.

"I was out," Karen said. "The super told me somebody killed her."

"Yes, that's right," Carella said, and watched her eyes. Nothing flickered there. She nodded almost imperceptibly.

"Why would anyone want to hurt her?" she said. "Such a gentle soul."

"How well did you know her?" Hawes asked.

"Just to talk to. She used to be a famous piano player, did you know that? Svetlana Dyalovich. That was the name she played under."

Piano player, Hawes thought. A superb artist who had made the cover of *Time* magazine. A piano player.

"Her hands all gnarled," Karen said, and shook her head.

The detectives looked at her.

"The arthritis. She told me she was in constant pain. Have you noticed how you can never open bottles that have pain relievers in them? That's because America is full of loonies who are trying to hurt people. Who would want to hurt *her*?" she asked again, shaking her head. "She was in so much pain already. The arthritis. *Osteo*arthritis, in fact, is what her doctor called it. I

18

went with her once. To her doctor. He told me he was switching her to Voltaren because the Naprosyn wasn't working anymore. He kept increasing the doses, it was really so sad."

"How long did you know her?" Carella asked.

Another way of asking How *well* did you know her? He didn't for a moment believe Karen Todd had anything at all to do with the murder of the old woman next door, but his mama once told him everyone's a suspect till his story checks out. Or *her* story. Although the world's politically correct morons would have it "Everyone's a suspect until *their* story checks out." Which was worse than tampering with the jars and bottles on supermarket shelves—and ungrammatical besides.

"I met her when I moved in," Karen said.

"When was that?"

"A year ago October. The fifteenth, in fact."

Birthdate of great men, Hawes thought, but did not say.

"I've been here more than a year now. Fourteen months, in fact. She brought me a housewarming gift. A loaf of bread and a box of salt. That's supposed to bring good luck. She was from Russia, you know. They used to have the old traditions over there. We don't have any traditions anymore in America."

Wrong, Carella thought. Murder has become a tradition here.

"She was a big star over there," Karen said. "Well, here, too, in fact."

Bad verbal tic, Hawes thought.

"She used to tell me stories of how she played for royalty all over the world, in fact. She had a lot of memories."

"When did she tell you these stories?"

"Oh, in the afternoons. We had tea together every now and then."

"In her apartment?"

"Yes. It was another tradition. Tea time. She had a lovely tea set. I had to pour because of her hands. We used to sit and listen to records she'd made when she was famous. And sip tea in the late afternoon. It reminded me of T. S. Eliot somehow."

Me, too, Hawes thought, but again did not say.

"So when you said you knew her just to talk to," Carella said, "you were including these visits to her apartment . . ."

"Oh, yes."

" . . . when you listened to music together."

"Yes. Well, my apartment, too. Some nights, I invited her in. We had little dinner parties together. She was alone and lonely and . . . well, I didn't want her to start drinking too early. She tended to drink more heavily at night."

"By heavily . . . ?"

"Well . . . she started drinking as soon as she woke up in the morning, in fact. But at night . . . well . . . she sometimes drank herself into a stupor."

"How do you know that?" Hawes asked.

"She told me. She was very frank with me. She knew she had a problem."

"Was she doing anything about it?"

20

"She was eighty-three years old. What could she do about it? The arthritis was bad enough. But she wore a hearing aid, you know. And lately, she began hearing ringing in her head, and hissing, like a kettle, you know? And sometimes a roaring sound, like heavy machinery? It was really awful. She told me her ear doctor wanted to send her to a neurologist for testing, but she was afraid to go."

"When was this?" Hawes asked.

"Before Thanksgiving. It was really so sad."

"These afternoon teas," Carella said, "these little dinner parties . . . was anyone else at them? Besides you and Miss Dyalovich?"

Somehow he liked that better than Mrs. Helder. Cover of *Time* magazine, he was thinking. You shouldn't end up as Mrs. Helder.

"No, just the two of us. In fact, I don't think she had any other friends. She told me once that all the people she'd known when she was young and famous were dead now. All she had was me, I guess. And the cat. She was very close to poor Irina. What's going to happen to her now? Will she go to an animal shelter?"

"Miss, he killed the cat, too," Hawes said.

"Oh dear. Oh dear," Karen said, and was silent for a moment. "She used to go out early every morning to buy fresh fish for her, can you imagine? No matter how cold it was, arthritic old lady. Irina *loved* fish."

Her brown eyes suddenly welled with tears. Hawes wanted to take her in his arms and comfort her. Instead, he said, "Did she have any living relatives?"

People to inform, Carella thought. He almost sighed.

21

"A married daughter in London."

"Do you know her name?"

"No."

"Anyone here in this country?"

"I think a granddaughter someplace in the city."

"Ever meet her?"

"No."

"Would you know *her* name?"

"No, I'm sorry."

"Did Miss Dyalovich ever mention any threatening phone calls or letters?"

"No."

Run her through the drill, Carella was thinking.

"Had she ever seen anyone lurking around the building . . . ?"

"No."

"Following her . . . ?"

"No."

"Do you know of any enemies she may have had?"

"No."

"Anyone with whom she may have had a continuing dispute?"

"No."

"Anyone she may have quarreled with?"

"No . . ."

"Even anyone on unfriendly terms with her?"

"No."

"Did she owe anyone money?"

"I doubt it."

"Did anyone owe *her* money?"

"She was an old woman living on welfare. What money did she have to lend?"

Toast of six continents, Hawes thought. Ends up living on welfare in a shithole on Lincoln. Sipping tea and whiskey in the late afternoon. Listening to her own old 78s. Her hands all gnarled.

"This granddaughter," he said. "Did you ever see her?"

"No, I never met her. I told you."

"What I'm asking is did you ever *see* her? Coming out of the apartment next door. Or in the hall. Did she ever come here to *visit*, is what I'm asking?"

"Oh. No. I don't think they got along."

"Then there *was* someone on unfriendly terms with her," Carella said.

"Yes, but family," Karen said, shrugging it off.

"Was it Miss Dyalovich who told you they didn't get along?"

"Yes."

"When was this?"

"Oh, two or three months ago."

"Came up out of the blue, did it?"

"No, she was lamenting the fact that her only daughter lived so far away, in London . . ."

"How'd that lead to the granddaughter?"

"Well, she said if only she and Priscilla could get along . . ."

"Is *that* her name?" Hawes asked at once. "The granddaughter?"

"Oh. Yes. I'm sorry, I didn't remember it until it popped out of my mouth."

"Priscilla what?"

"I don't know."

"Maybe it'll come to you."

23

"No, I don't think I *ever* knew it."

"The obit will tell us," Carella said. "Later this morning."

It was now exactly one A.M.

The man who owned the liquor store told them Saturdays were his biggest nights. Made more in the hour before closing on Saturday nights than he did the rest of the entire year. Only thing bigger was New Year's Eve, he told them. Even bigger than that was when New Year's Eve fell on a Saturday night. Couldn't beat it.

"*Biggest* night of the year," he said. "I could stay open all night New Year's Eve and sell everything in the store."

This was already Sunday, but it still felt like Saturday night to the guy who owned the store. It must have still felt like Christmas, too, even though it was already the twenty-first of January. A little Christmas tree blinked green and red in the front window. Little cardboard cutouts, hanging across the ceiling, endlessly repeated HAPPY HOLIDAYS. Gift-packaged bottles of booze sat on countertops and tables.

The store owner's name was Martin Keely. He was maybe sixty-eight, sixty-nine, in there, a short stout man with a drunkard's nose and wide suspenders to match it. He kept interrupting their conversation, such as it was, to make yet another sale. This hour of the night, he was selling mostly cheap wine to panhandlers who straggled in with their day's take. This became a different city after midnight. You saw different people in the streets and on the sidewalks. In

24

the bars and clubs that were open. In the subways and the taxicabs. An entirely different city with entirely different people in it.

One of them had killed Svetlana Dyalovich.

"What time did she come in here, would you remember?" Hawes asked.

"Around eleven o'clock."

Which more or less tied in. Man down the hall said he heard the shots at about eleven-twenty. Super called 911 five minutes after that.

"What'd she buy?"

"Bottle of Four Roses."

Exactly the brand that had dropped to the floor when someone shot her.

"How much did it cost?"

"Eight dollars and ninety-nine cents."

"How'd she pay for it?"

"Cash."

"Exact?"

"What do you mean?"

"Did she hand you *exactly* eight dollars and ninety-nine cents."

"No, she handed me a ten-dollar bill. I gave her change."

"Where'd she put the change?"

"In this little purse she was carrying. Took a ten out of the purse, handed it to me. Gave her one dollar and one cent in change. Put that in the purse."

"The dollar was in change, too?"

"No, the dollar was a bill."

"And you say she put the change in her handbag?"

"No, she put it in this *purse*. A little purse. A change purse. With the little snaps on top you click open with your thumb and forefinger. A purse, you know?" he said, seeming to become inappropriately agitated. "You know what a purse is? A purse ain't a handbag. A purse is a purse. Doesn't anybody in this city speak English anymore?"

"Where'd she put this purse?" Carella asked calmly.

"In her coat pocket."

"The pocket of the mink," he said, nodding.

"No, she wasn't wearing a mink. She was wearing a cloth coat."

The detectives looked at him.

"Are you sure about that?" Hawes asked.

"Positive. Ratty blue cloth coat. Scarf on her head. Silk, I think. Whatever. Pretty. But it had seen better days."

"Cloth coat and a silk scarf," Carella said.

"Yeah."

"You're saying that when she came in here at eleven o'clock last night . . ."

"No, I'm not saying that at all."

"You're not saying she was wearing a cloth coat and a silk scarf?"

"I'm not saying she came in at eleven last night."

"If it wasn't eleven, what time *was* it?"

"Oh, it was eleven, all right. But it was eleven yesterday morning."

They found the change purse in the pocket of a blue cloth coat hanging in the bedroom closet.

There was a dollar and a penny in it.

2

In the year 1909, There used to be forty-four morning newspapers in this city. By 1929, that figure had dropped to thirty. Three years later, due to technological advances, competition for circulation, standardization of the product, managerial faults, and, by the way, the Great Depression, this number was reduced to a mere three. Now there were but two.

Since there was a killer out there, the detectives didn't want to wait till four, five A.M., when both papers would hit the newsstands. Nor did they think a call to the morning tabloid would be fruitful, mainly because they didn't think it would run an obit on a concert pianist, however famous she once may have been. It later turned out they were wrong; the tabloid played the story up big, but only because Svetlana had been living in obscurity and poverty after three decades of celebrity, and her granddaughter—but that was another story.

Hawes spoke on the phone to the obituary editor at the so-called quality paper, a most cooperative man who was ready to read the full obit to him until Hawes assured him that all he wanted were the names of Miss Dyalovich's surviving kin. The editor skipped to the last paragraph, which noted that Svetlana was survived by a daughter, Maria Stetson, who lived in London, and a granddaughter, Priscilla Stetson, who lived right here in the big bad city.

"You know who she is, don't you?" the editor asked.

Hawes thought he meant Svetlana.

"Yes, of course," he said.

"We couldn't mention it in the obit because that's supposed to be exclusively about the deceased."

"I'm not following you," Hawes said.

"The granddaughter. She's Priscilla Stetson. The singer."

"Oh? What kind of singing does she do?"

"Supper club. Piano bar. Cabaret. Like that."

"You wouldn't know *where*, would you?" Hawes asked.

In this city, many of the homeless sleep by day and roam by night. Nighttime is dangerous for them; there are predators out there and a cardboard box offers scant protection against someone intent on robbery or rape. So they wander the streets like shapeless wraiths, adding a stygian dimension to the nocturnal landscape.

The streetlamps are on. Traffic lights blink their intermittent reds, yellows and greens into the empty hours of the night, but the city seems dark. Here and there, a bathroom light snaps on. In the otherwise blank face of an apartment building, a lamp burns steadily in the bedroom of an insomniac. The commercial buildings are all ablaze with illumination, but the only people in them are the office cleaners, readying the spaces for the workday that will begin at nine Monday morning. Tonight—it still feels like night even though the morning is already an hour and a half old—the cables on the bridges that span the city's river are festooned with bright lights that reflect in the black waters below. Yet all seems so dark, perhaps because it is so empty.

At one-thirty in the morning the theater crowd has been home and in bed for a long time, and many of the hotel bars have been closed for a half hour already. The clubs and discos will be open till four A.M., the outside legal limit for serving alcoholic beverages, at which time the delis and diners will begin serving breakfast. The underground clubs will grind on till six in the morning. But for now and for the most part, the city is as still as any tomb.

Steam hisses up from sewer lids.

Yellow cabs streak like whispered lightning through deserted streets.

A black-and-white photograph of Priscilla Stetson was on an easel outside the entrance to the Cafe Mouton at the Hotel Powell. Like an identifying shot in a home movie, the script lettering above the photo read *Mrs Priscilla Stetson*. Below the photo, the same script lettering announced:

Now Appearing
9:00 P.M. - 2:00 A.M.

The woman in the photo could have been Svetlana Dyalovich on the cover of *Time* magazine. The same flaxen hair falling straight to her shoulders and cut in bangs on her forehead. The same pale eyes. The same high Slavic cheekbones. The same imperial nose and confident smile.

The woman sitting at the piano was perhaps thirty years old, dressed in a long black gown with a risky décolletage. A creamy white expanse of flesh from bosom to neck was interrupted at the throat by a silver choker studded with black and white stones. She was singing "Gently, Sweetly" when the detectives came in and took stools at the bar. There were perhaps two dozen people sitting at tables scattered around the smallish candlelit room. It was twenty minutes to two in the morning.

Here with a kiss
In the mist on the shore
Sip from my lips
And whisper
I adore you . . .
Gently,
Sweetly,
Ever so completely,
Take me,
Make me
Yours.

Priscilla Stetson struck the final chord of the song, bent her head, and looked reverently at her hands spread on the keys. There was a spatter of warm applause. "Thank you," she whispered into the piano mike. "Thank you very much." Raising her head, tossing the long blond hair. "I'll be taking a short break before the last set, so if you'd like to order anything before closing, now's your chance." A wide smile, a wink. She played a lithe signature riff, rose, and was walking toward a table where two burly men

30

sat alone, when the detectives came off their stools to intercept her.

"Miss Stetson?" Carella said.

She turned, smiling, the performer ready to greet an admirer. In high-heeled pumps, she was perhaps five-eight, five-nine. Her blue-grey eyes were almost level with his.

"Detective Carella," he said. "This is my partner, Detective Hawes."

"Yes?"

"Miss Stetson," he said. "I'm sorry to have to tell you this, but . . ."

"My grandmother," she said at once, looking certain rather than alarmed.

"Yes. I'm sorry. She's dead."

She nodded.

"What happened?" she asked. "Did she fall in the bathtub again?"

"No, she was shot."

"Shot? My grandmother?"

"I'm sorry," Carella said.

"Jesus, shot," Priscilla said. "Why would . . . ?" She shook her head again. "Well, this city," she said. "Where'd it happen? On the street someplace?"

"No. In her apartment. It may have been a burglar."

Or maybe not, Hawes thought, but said nothing, just allowed Carella to continue carrying the ball. This was the hardest part of police work, informing the relatives of a victim that something terrible had happened. Carella was doing a fine job, thanks, no sense interrupting him. Not at a quarter to two in the morning, when the whole damn world was asleep.

31

"Was she drunk?" Priscilla asked.

Flat out.

"There hasn't been an autopsy yet," Carella said.

"She was probably drunk," Priscilla said.

"We'll let you know," Carella said. It came out more harshly than he'd intended. Or maybe it came out exactly as he'd intended. "Miss Stetson," he said, "if this is what it looks like, a burglar surprised during the commission of a felony, then we're looking for a needle in a haystack. Because it would've been a random thing, you see."

"Yes."

"On the other hand, if this is someone who wanted your grandmother dead, who came into the apartment with the express purpose of killing her . . ."

"Nobody wanted her dead," Priscilla said.

"How do you know that?"

"She was already dead. No one even knew she existed. Why would anyone go to the trouble of shooting her?"

"But someone did, you see."

"A burglar then. As you said."

"The problem with that is nothing was stolen."

"What was there to steal?"

"You tell us."

"What do you mean?

"There didn't seem to be anything of value in the apartment—but was there? Before he broke in?"

"Like what? The Imperial Czar's crown jewels? My grandmother didn't have a pot to piss in. Whatever she got from welfare, she spent on booze. She was drunk morning, noon and night. She was a pathetic, whining

32

old bitch, a has-been with nothing of value but her memories. I hated her."

But tell us how you really feel, Carella thought.

He didn't much like this young woman with her inherited good looks and her acquired big-city, wiseass manner. He would just as soon not be here talking to her, but he didn't like burglaries that turned into murders, especially if maybe they weren't burglaries in the first place. So even if it meant pulling teeth, he was going to learn something about her grandmother, anything about her grandmother that might put this thing to rest one way or another. If someone had wanted her dead, fine, they'd go looking for that someone till hell froze over. If not, they'd go back to the squadroom and wait until a month from now, a year from now, five years from now, when some junkie burglar got arrested and confessed to having killed an old lady back when you and I were young, Maggie. Meanwhile . . .

"Anyone else feel the way you do?" he asked.

"How do you mean?"

"You said you hated her."

"Oh, what? Did *I* kill her? Come on. Please."

"You okay, Priss?"

Carella turned at once, startled. The man standing at his elbow was one of the two Priscilla had been heading to join when they'd intercepted her. Even before he noticed the gun in a holster under the man's jacket, Carella would have tapped him for either a bodyguard or a mobster. Or maybe both. Some six-four and weighing in at a possible two-twenty, he stood balanced on the balls of his feet, hands dangling

33

half-clenched at his sides, a pose that warned Carella he could take him out in a minute if he had to. Carella believed it.

"I'm fine, Georgie" Priscilla said.

Georgie, Carella thought, and braced himself when he saw the other man getting up from the table and moving toward them. Hawes was suddenly alert, too.

"Because if these gentlemen are disturbing you . . ."

Carella flashed the tin, hoping to end all discussion.

"We're police officers," he said.

Georgie looked at the shield, unimpressed.

"You got a problem here, Georgie?" the other man said, approaching. Georgie's twin, no doubt. Similarly dressed, down to the hardware under the wide-shouldered suit jacket. Hawes flashed *his* shield, too. It never hurt to make the same point twice.

"Police officers," he said.

Must be an echo in this place, Carella thought.

"Is Miss Stetson in some kind of trouble?" Georgie's twin asked. Two hundred and fifty pounds of muscle and bone draped in Giorgio Armani threads. No broken nose, but otherwise the stereotype was complete.

"Miss Stetson's grandmother was killed," Hawes said calmly. "Everything's under control here. Why don't you just go back to your table, hm?"

A buzz was starting in the room now. Four big guys surrounding the room's star, looked like there might be some kind of trouble here. One thing people in this city didn't much care for was trouble. First whiff of trouble, people in this city picked up their skirts and ran for the hills. Even out-of-towners in this city (which some of the people in the room looked like),

34

even foreigners in the city (which some of the other people in the room looked like), the minute they caught that first faint whiff of trouble brewing, they were out of here, man. *Miss Priscilla Stetson, Now Appearing* 9:00 P.M.-2:00 A.M. was in imminent danger of playing her last set to an empty room. She suddenly remembered the time. "I'm on," she said. "We'll talk later," and left the four men standing there with their thumbs up their asses.

Like most macho fools who display their manhood to no avail, the men stood glaring at each other a moment longer, and then mentally flexed their muscles with a few seconds of eyelock before the two cops went back to the bar and the two gun-toting whatever-they-weres went back to their table. Priscilla, professionally aloof to whatever masculine urges were surfacing here, warmly sang a set consisting of "My Funny Valentine," "My Romance," "If I Loved You" and "Sweet and Lovely." A woman sitting at one of the tables asked her escort why they didn't write love songs like that anymore, and he said, "Because now they write hate songs."

It was 2:00 A.M.

Either Georgie (or his twin brother Frankie or Nunzio or Dominick or Foongie) asked Priscilla why she hadn't played the theme song from *The Godfather* tonight. She sweetly told them no one had requested it, kissed them both on their respective cheeks and simultaneously kissed them off. Big detectives that they were, neither Carella nor Hawes yet knew whether they were bodyguards or wiseguys. Priscilla came to the bar.

35

"Too late for a glass of champagne?" she asked the bartender.

He knew she was kidding; he poured one in a flute. Dispersing guests came over to tell Priscilla how terrific she'd been. Graciously, she thanked them all and sent them on their early morning way. Priscilla wasn't a star, she was just a good singer in a small café in a modest hotel, but she carried herself well. They could tell by the way she merely sipped at the champagne that she wasn't a big drinker. Maybe her grandmother had something to do with that. Which brought them back to the corpse in the shabby mink coat.

"I told you," Priscilla said. "All her friends are dead. I couldn't give you their names if I wanted to."

"How about enemies?" Carella asked. "All of them dead, too?"

"My grandmother was a lonely old woman living alone. She had no friends, she had no enemies. Period."

"So it had to be a burglar, right?" Hawes asked.

Priscilla looked at him as if discovering him for the first time. Looked him up and down. Red hair with white streak, size twelve gunboats.

"That's your job, isn't it?" she asked coolly. "Determining whether it was a burglar or not?"

"And, by the way, she did have a friend," Carella corrected.

"Oh?"

"Woman down the hall. Played her old records for her."

"Please. She played those old 78s for anyone who'd listen."

"Ever meet her?"

"Who?"

"Woman named Karen Todd. Lived down the hall from your grandmother."

"No."

"When's the last time you saw her alive?" Hawes asked.

"We didn't get along."

"So we understand. When did you see her last?"

"Must've been around Eastertime."

"Long time ago."

"Yeah," she said, and fell suddenly silent. I guess I'll have to call my mother, huh?" she asked.

"Might be a good idea," Carella said.

"Let her know what happened."

"Mm."

"What time is it in London?"

"I don't know," Carella said.

"Five or six hours ahead, is that it?"

Hawes shook his head, shrugged.

Priscilla fell silent again.

The champagne glass was empty now.

"Why'd you hate her?" Carella asked.

"For what she did to herself."

"She didn't cause the arthritis," Hawes said.

"She caused the alcoholism."

"Which came first?"

"Who knows? Who cares? She was one of the greats. She ended up a nobody."

"Enemies," Carella said again.

"I don't know of any."

"So it had to be a burglar," Hawes said again.

"Who cares what it was?" Priscilla asked.

"We do," Carella said.

It was time to stop the clock.

Time was running by too fast, someone out there had killed her, and time was on his side, her side, whoever's side. The faster the minutes went by, the greater would become the distance between him, her, whomever and the cops. So it was time to stop the clock, hardly a difficult feat here in the old Eight-Seven, time to pause for a moment, and reflect, time to make a few phone calls, time to call time out.

Carella called home.

When he'd left there at eleven last night, his son Mark was burning up with a hundred-and-two-degree fever and the doctor was on the way. Fanny Knowles, the Carella housekeeper, picked up on the third ring.

"Fanny," he said, "hi. Did I wake you?"

"Let me get her," Fanny said.

He waited. His wife could neither speak nor hear. There was a TDD telephone answering device in the house, but typing out long messages was time-consuming, tedious, and often frustrating. Better that Teddy should sign and Fanny should translate. He waited.

"Okay," Fanny said at last.

"What'd the doctor say?"

"It's nothing serious," Fanny said. "He thinks it's the flu."

"What does Teddy think?"

"Let me ask her."

There was a silence on the line. Fanny signing, Teddy responding. He visualized both women in their nightgowns. Fanny some five feet five inches tall, a stout Irish woman with red hair and gold-rimmed eyeglasses, fingers flying in the language Teddy had taught her. Teddy an inch taller, a beautiful woman with raven-black hair and eyes as dark as loam, fingers flying even faster because she'd been doing this from when she was a child. Fanny was back on the line.

"She says what worried her most was when he started shakin like a leaf all over. But he's all right now. The fever's come down, she thinks the doctor's right, it's only the flu. She's going to sleep in his room, she says, just in case. When will you be home, she wants to know."

"Shift's over at eight, she knows that."

"She thought, with the lad sick and all . . ."

"Fanny, we've got a homicide. Tell her that."

He waited.

Fanny came back on the line.

"She says you've always got a homicide."

Carella smiled.

"I'll be home in six hours," he said. "Tell her I love her."

"She loves you too," Fanny said.

"Did she say that?"

"No, I said it," Fanny said. "Its two in the mornin, mister. Can we all go back to bed now?"

"Not me," Carella said.

Hawes was talking to a Rape Squad cop named Annie Rawles. Annie happened to be in his bed. He was telling her that since he'd come to work tonight, he'd met a beautiful Mediterranean-looking woman and also a beautiful piano player with long blond hair.

"Is the piano player a woman, too? "Annie asked.

Hawes smiled.

"What are you wearing?" he asked.

"Just a thirty-eight in a shoulder holster," Annie said.

"I'll be right there," he said.

"Fat Chance Department," she said.

The clock began ticking again. '

Every hour of the day looks the same inside a morgue. That's because there are no windows and the glare of fluorescent light is neutral at best. The stench, too, is identical day in and day out, palpable to anyone who walks in from the fresh air outside, undetectable to the assistant medical examiners who are carving up corpses for autopsy.

Dr. Paul Blaney was a shortish man with a scraggly black mustache and eyes everyone told him were violet, but which he thought were a pale bluish-grey. He was wearing a bloodstained blue smock and yellow rubber gloves, and was weighing a liver when the detectives walked in. He immediately plopped the organ into a stainless-steel basin, where it sat looking like the Portnoy family's impending dinner. Yanking off one of the gloves, presumably to shake hands, he remembered where the hand had recently been, and pulled it back abruptly. He knew why the detectives were here. He got directly to the point.

"Two to the heart," he said. "Both bull's-eyes, and not a bad title for a movie."

"I think there was one," Hawes said.

"*Bull's-Eyes*?"

"No, no . . ."

"You're thinking of *One-Eyed Jacks*."

"No, *Two to the Heart*, something like that."

"*Two for the Road*, you're thinking of," Blaney said.

"No, that was a song," Hawes said.

"That was, 'One for the Road.' "

"This was a movie. *Two from the Heart*, maybe."

"Cause *Two for the Road* was very definitely a movie."

Carella was looking at them both.

"This had the word 'heart' in the title," Hawes said.

Carella was still looking at them. Everywhere around them were bodies or body parts on tables and countertops. Everywhere around them was the stink of death.

"Heart, heart," Blaney said, thinking out loud. "*Heart of Darkness*? Because that became a movie, but it was called *Apocalypse Now*."

"No, but I think you're close."

"Is it Coppola?"

"Carella," Carella said, wondering why Blaney, whom he'd known for at least a quarter of a century, was getting his name wrong.

"Something Coppola directed?" Blaney asked, ignoring him.

"I don't know," Hawes said. "Who's Coppola?"

"He directed the *Godfather* movies."

Which reminded Carella of the two hoods in the hotel bar. Which further reminded him of Svetlana's granddaughter. Which brought him full circle to why they were here.

"The autopsy," he reminded Blaney.

"Two to the heart," Blaney said. "Both of them in a space the size of a half-dollar. Which didn't take much of a marksman because the killer was standing quite close."

"How close?"

"I'd say no more than three, four feet. All the guy did was point and fire. Period."

"Was she drunk?" Carella asked.

"No. Percentage of alcohol in the brain was point-oh-two, well within the normal range. Urine and blood percentages were similarly normal."

"Can you give us a PMI?"

"Around eleven, eleven-thirty last night. Ballpark."

No postmortem interval was entirely accurate. They all knew that. But Blaney's educated guess coincided with the time the man down the hall had heard shots.

"Anything else we should know?" Hawes asked.

"Examination of the skull revealed a schwannoma arising from the vestibular nerve, near the porus acusticus, extending into both the internal auditory meatus . . ."

"In English, please," Carella said.

"An acoustic neuroma . . ."

"Come on, Paul."

"In short, a tumor on the auditory nerve. Quite large and cystic, probably causing hearing loss, headache, vertigo, disturbed sense of balance, unsteadiness of gait, and tinnitus."

"Tinnitus?"

"Ringing of the ears."

"Oh."

"Liquid chromatography of the coagulated blood disclosed a drug called diclofenac, in concentrations indicating therapeutic doses. But the loose correlation between dosage and concentration is a semi-quantitative process at best. All I can say for certain is that she was *taking* the drug, not *why* she was taking it.

"Why do you *think* she was taking it?"

"Well, we don't normally examine joints in a post, and I haven't here. But a superficial look at her fingers suggest what I'm sure a vertebral slice would reveal."

"And what's that?"

"Lipping on the anterior visible portion."

"What's lipping?"

"Knobby, bumpy, small excrescences of bone. In short, smooth, asymmetric swellings on the body of the vertebrae."

"Indicating what?"

"Arthritis?"

"Are you asking?"

"Do you know whether or not she was arthritic?"

"She was."

"Well, there," Blaney said.

Hawes was still trying to remember the title of that movie. He asked Sam Grossman if he remembered seeing it.

"I don't go to movies," Grossman said.

He was wearing a white lab coat, and standing before a counter covered with test tubes, graduated cylinders, beakers, spatulas, pipettes and flasks, all of

43

which gave his work space an air of scientific inquiry that seemed in direct contrast to Grossman himself. A tall, angular man with blue eyes behind dark-framed glasses, he looked more like a New England farmer worried about drought than he did the precise police captain who headed up the lab.

Some ranking E-flat piano player in the department had undoubtedly decided that the death of a once-famous concert pianist rated special treatment, hence the dispatch with which Svetlana's body and personal effects had been sent respectively to the Chief Medical Examiner's Office and the lab. The mink coat, the cotton housedress, the pink sweater, the cotton panty hose, and the bedroom slippers were all on Grossman's countertop, dutifully tagged and bagged. At another table, one of Grossman's assistants sat with her head bent over a microscope. Hawes looked her over. A librarian type, he decided, which he sometimes found exciting.

"Why do you ask?" Grossman said.

"Cause of death was two to the heart," Carella said.

"Plenty of blood to support that," Grossman said, nodding. "All of it hers, by the way. Nobody else bled all over the sweater and dress. The dress is a cheap cotton *schmatte* you can pick up at any Woolworth's. The house slippers are imitation leather, probably got *those* in a dime store, too. But the sweater has a designer label in it. And so does the mink. Old, but once worth something."

Which could have been said of the victim, too, Carella thought.

"Anything else?"

"I just *got* all this stuff," Grossman said.

"Then when?"

"Later."

"When later?"

"Tomorrow afternoon."

"Sooner."

"A magician I'm not," Grossman said.

They went back to the apartment again.

The yellow CRIME SCENE tapes were still up. A uniformed cop stood on the stoop downstairs, his hands behind his back, peering out at the deserted street. It was bitterly cold. He was wearing earmuffs and a heavy-duty overcoat, but he still looked frozen to death. They identified themselves and went upstairs. Another of the blues was on duty outside the door to apartment 3A. A cardboard CRIME SCENE card was taped to the door behind him. The door was padlocked. He produced a key when they identified themselves.

Hidden under a pile of neatly pressed and folded, lace-trimmed silk underwear at the back of the bottom drawer in her dresser, they found another candy tin.

There was a savings account passbook in it.

The book showed a withdrawal yesterday of an even one hundred and twenty-five thousand dollars, leaving a balance of sixteen dollars and twelve cents. The withdrawal slip was inserted in the passbook at the page that recorded the transaction. The date and time on the slip were January 20, 10:27 A.M.

This would have been half an hour before Svetlana Dyalovich went downstairs to buy a fifth of Four Roses.

According to Blaney and the man down the hall, she was killed some twelve hours later.

The man in apartment 3D did not enjoy being awakened at ten minutes to three in the morning. He was wearing only pajamas when he grumblingly unlocked the door for them, but he quickly put on a woolen robe, and, still grumbling, led the detectives into the apartment's small kitchen. A tiny window over the sink was rimed with frost. Outside, they could hear the wind howling. They kept on their coats and gloves.

The man, whose name was Gregory Turner, went to the stove, opened the oven door, and lighted the gas jets. He left the door open. In a few moments, they could feel heat beginning to seep into the kitchen. Turner put up a pot of coffee. A short while later, while he was pouring for them, they took off the coats and gloves.

He was sixty-nine years old, he told them, a creature of impeccable habit, set in his ways. Got up to pee every night at three-thirty. They'd got him out of bed forty minutes early, he didn't like this break in his routine. Hoped he could fall back asleep again after they were done with him here and he had his nocturnal pee. For all his grumbling, though, he seemed cooperative, even hospitable. Like buddies about to go on an early morning fishing trip, the three men sat around the oil cloth covered kitchen table sipping coffee. Their hands were warm around the steaming cups. Heat poured from the oven. Springtime didn't seem all that far away.

"I hated those records she played day and night," he told them. "Sounded like somebody *practicing*. All classical music sounds that way to me. How can anyone make any sense of it? I like swing, do you know what swing is? Before your time, swing. I'm sixty-nine years old, did I tell you that? Get up to pee regular every night at three-thirty in the morning, go back to sleep again till eight, get up, have my breakfast, go for a long walk. Jenny used to go with me before she died last year. My wife. Jenny. We'd walk together in the park, rain or shine. Settled a lot of our problems on those walks. Talked them out. Well, I don't have any problems now she's gone. But I miss her like the devil."

He sighed heavily, freshened the coffee in his cup.

"More?" he asked.

"Thank you, no," Carella said.

"Just a drop," Hawes said.

"Benny Goodman, Glenn Miller, that was swing. Harry James, the Dorsey Brothers, wonderful stuff back then. You had a new song come out, maybe six, seven bands covered it. Best record usually was the one made the charts. 'Blues in the Night' came out, there must've been a dozen different big-band versions of it. Well, that was some song. Johnny Mercer wrote that song. You ever hear of Johnny Mercer?"

Both detectives shook their heads.

"He wrote that song," Turner said. "Woody Herman had the best record of that song. That was some song." He began singing it. His voice, thin and frail, filled the stillness of the night with the sound of train whistles echoing down the track. He stopped abruptly. There were tears in his eyes. They both wondered if he'd been singing it to Jenny. Or for Jenny.

47

"People come and go, you hardly get a chance to say hello to them, no less really know them," he said. "Woman who got killed tonight, I don't think I even knew her name till the super told me later on. All I knew was she irritated me playing those damn old records of hers. Then I hear three shots and first thing I wonder is did the old lady shoot herself? She seemed very sad," he said, "glimpses I got of her on the stairs. Very sad. All bent and twisted and bleary-eyed, a very sad old lady. I ran out in the hall . . ."

"When was this?"

"Right after I heard the shots."

"Do you remember what time that was?"

"Around a quarter past eleven."

"Did you see anyone in the hall?"

"No."

"Or coming out of her apartment?"

"No."

"Was the door to the apartment open or closed?"

"Closed."

"What'd you do, Mr. Turner?"

"I went right downstairs and knocked on the super's door."

"You didn't call the police?"

"No, sir."

"Why not?"

"Don't trust the police."

"What then?"

"I stayed in the street, watched the show. Cops coming, ambulances coming. Detectives like you. A regular show. I wasn't the only one."

"Watching, do you mean?"

48

"Watching, yes. Is it getting too hot in here for you?"

"A little."

"If I turn this off, though, we'll be freezing again in five minutes. What do you think I should do?"

"Well, whatever you like, sir," Hawes said.

"Jenny liked it warm," Turner said. He nodded. He was silent for several moments, staring at his hands folded on the kitchen table. His hands looked big and dark and somehow useless against the glare of the white oilcloth.

"Who else was there?" Carella asked. "Watching the show?"

"Oh, people I recognized from the building mostly. Some of them leaning out their windows, others coming downstairs to see things firsthand."

"Anyone you didn't recognize?"

"Oh, sure, all those cops."

"*Aside* from the cops or the ambulance peop—"

"Lots of others, sure. You know this city. Anything happens, a big crowd gathers."

"Did anyone you didn't recognize come *out* of the building? Aside from cops or . . ."

"See what you mean, yeah. Just let me think a minute."

The gas jets hissed into the stillness of the apartment. Somewhere in the building, a toilet flushed. Outside on the street, a siren doo-wah, doo-wahed to the night. Then all was still again.

"A tall blond man," Turner said.

As he tells it, he first sees the man when he comes out of the alleyway alongside the building. Comes out and stands there with the crowd behind the police lines, hands in his pockets. He's wearing a blue overcoat and a red muffler. Hands in the pockets of the coat. Black shoes. Blond hair blowing in the wind.

"Beard? Mustache?"

"Clean-shaven."

"Anything else you remember about him?"

He just stands there like all the other people, behind the barricades the police have set up, watching all the activity, more cops arriving, plainclothes cops, they must be, uniformed cops, too, with brass on their hats and collars, the man just stands there watching, like interested. Then the ambulance people carry her out of the building on a stretcher, and they put her inside the ambulance and it drives off.

"That's when he went off, too," Turner said.

"You watched him leave?"

"Well, yes."

"Why?"

"There was a . . . a sort of sad look on his face, I don't know. As if . . . I don't know."

"Where'd he go?" Hawes asked. "Which direction?"

"Headed south. Toward the corner. Stopped near the sewer up the street . . ."

Both detectives were suddenly all ears.

"Bent down to tie his shoelace or something, went on his way again."

Which is how they found the murder weapon.

3

The gun they'd fished out of the sewer was registered to a man named Rodney Pratt, who—on his application for the pistol permit—had given his occupation as "security escort" and had stated that he needed to carry a gun because his business was "providing protection of privacy, property, and physical wellbeing to individuals requiring personalized service." They figured this was the politically correct way of saying he was a private bodyguard.

In the United States of America, no one is obliged to reveal his race, color, or creed on any application form. They had no way of knowing Rodney Pratt was black until he opened the door for them at five minutes past three that morning, and glowered out at them in undershirt and boxer shorts. To them, his color was merely an accident of nature. What mattered was that Ballistics had already identified the gun registered to him as the weapon that had fired three fatal bullets earlier tonight.

"Mr. Pratt?" Hawes asked cautiously.

"Yeah, *what*?" Pratt asked.

He did not have to say This is three o'fucking clock in the morning, why the fuck are you knocking my door down? His posture said that, his angry frown said that, his blazing eyes said that.

"May we come in, sir?" Hawes asked. "Few questions we'd like to ask you."

"What *kind* of questions?" Pratt asked.

The "sir" had done nothing to mollify him. Here were two honkie cops shaking him out of bed in the middle of the night, and he wasn't buying any sirs, thank you. He stood barring the door in his tank top undershirt and striped boxer shorts, as muscular as any prizefighter at a weigh-in. Hawes now saw that the tattoo on his bulging right biceps read *Semper Fidelis*. An ex-Marine, no less. Probably a sergeant. Probably had seen combat in this or that war the United States seemed incessantly waging. Probably drank the blood of enemy soldiers. Three o'clock in the morning. Hawes bit the bullet.

"Questions about a .38 Smith & Wesson registered to you, sir."

"What about it?"

"It was used in a murder earlier tonight, sir. May we come in?"

"Come in," Pratt said, and stepped out of the door frame, back into the apartment.

Pratt lived in a building on North Carlton Street, at the intersection of St. Helen's Boulevard, across the way from Mount Davis Park. The neighborhood was mixed—black, white, Hispanic, some Asians—the rents price-fixed. These old prewar apartments boasted high ceilings, tall windows and parquet floors. In many of them, the kitchens and bathrooms were hopelessly outdated. But as they followed Pratt toward a lighted living room beyond, they saw at a glance that his kitchen was modern and sleek, and an open-door glimpse of a hall bathroom revealed marble and polished brass. The living room was furnished in teakwood and nubby fabrics, throw pillows everywhere, chrome-framed prints on the white walls. An upright piano stood against the wall at the far end of the room, flanked by windows that overlooked the park.

"Have a seat," Pratt said, and left the room. Hawes glanced at Carella. Carella merely shrugged. He was standing by the windows, looking down at the park four stories below. At this hour of the night, it appeared ghostly, its lampposts casting eerie illumination on empty winding paths.

Pratt was back in a moment, wearing a blue robe over his underwear. The robe looked like cashmere. It conspired with the look of the apartment to create a distinct impression that the "security escort" business paid very well indeed these days. Hawes wondered if he should ask for a job recommendation. Instead, he said, "About the gun, Mr. Pratt."

"It was stolen last week," Pratt said.

They had seen it all and heard it all, of course, and they had probably heard *this* one ten thousand, four hundred and thirteen times. The first thing any criminal learns is that it is not his gun, his dope, his car, his burglar's tools, his knife, his mask, his gloves, his bloodstains, his semen stains, his *anything*. And if it is his, then it was either lost or stolen.

Catch a man red-handed, about to shoot his girlfriend, a gun in his fist, the barrel in the woman's mouth, and he will tell you first that it isn't his gun, hey, what kind of individual do you think I am? Besides, we're only rehearsing a scene from a play

53

here. Or if they won't quite appreciate that one in Des Moines, then how about she was choking on a fish bone, and I was trying to hook it out with the gun barrel while we were waiting for the ambulance to take her to the hospital? Or if that sounds a bit fishy, how about she *asked* me to put the barrel in her mouth in order to test her mettle and her courage? Anyway, this isn't even my gun, and if it is my gun, it was stolen or lost. Besides, I'm a juvenile.

"Stolen," Carella said, turning from the windows. No intonation in his voice, just the single unstressed word, spoken softly, and sounding like a booming accusation in that three A.M. living room.

"Yes," Pratt said. "*Stolen*."

Unlike Carella, he did stress the word.

"When did you say this was?" Hawes asked.

"Thursday night."

"That would've been . . ."

Hawes had taken out his notebook and was flipping to the calendar page.

"The eighteenth," Pratt said. "A hoodoo jinx of a day. First my car quits dead, and next somebody steals my gun from the glove compartment."

"Let's back up a little," Hawes said.

"No, let's back up a *lot*," Pratt said. "Reason you're putting me through this shit three A.M. in the morning is I'm black. So just do your little ritual dance and get the hell out, okay? You've got the wrong party here."

"We may have the wrong party," Carella said, "but we've got the right *gun*. And it happens to be yours."

"I don't know anything about what that gun was doing earlier tonight. You say it killed somebody, I'll

54

take your word for it. I'm telling you the gun has not been in my possession since Thursday night, when my car quit and I stopped at an all-night gas station to have it looked at."

"Where was that?"

"Just off the Majesta Bridge."

"Which side of it?"

"This side. I'd driven a diamond merchant home and was coming back to the city."

The locution marked him as a native. This sprawling city was divided into five separate distinct geographical zones, but unless you'd just moved here from Mars, only one of these sectors was ever referred to as "the city."

"Started rattling on the bridge," Pratt said. "Time I hit Isola, she quit dead. Brand-new limo. Less than a thousand miles on it." He shook his head in disgust and disbelief. "Never buy a fuckin American car," he said.

Carella himself drove a Chevrolet that had never given him a moment's trouble. He said nothing.

"What time was this?" Hawes asked.

"Little before midnight."

"This past Thursday."

"Hoodoo jinx of a day," he said again.

"Remember the name of the gas station?"

"Sure."

"What was it?"

"Bridge Texaco."

"Now that's what I call inventive," Hawes said.

"You think I'm *lying*?" Pratt said at once.

"No, no, I meant . . ."

"When did you discover the gun was missing?" Carella asked.

Get this thing back on track, he thought. Pratt wasn't quite getting all this. He thought two white cops were here hassling him only because he was black when instead they were hassling him only because he owned a gun used in a murder. So let's hear about the *gun*, okay?

"When I picked the car up," Pratt said, turning to him. He still suspected a trap, still figured they were setting him up somehow.

"And when was that?"

"Yesterday morning. There weren't any mechanics on duty when I pulled in Thursday night. The manager told me they'd have to work on it the next day."

"Which they did, is that right?"

"Yeah. Turned out somebody'd put styrene in my fuckin crankcase."

Carella wondered what styrene in the crankcase had to do with buying an American car.

"Broke down the oil and ruined the engine," Pratt said. "They had to order me a new one, put it in on Friday."

"And you picked the car up yesterday?"

"Yes."

"What time?"

"Ten o'clock in the morning."

"So the car was there all night Thursday and all day Friday."

"Yeah. And two hours yesterday, too. They open at eight."

"With the gun in the glove compartment."

"Well, it *disappeared* during that time."

"When did you realize that?"

"When I got back here. There's a garage in the building. I parked the car, unlocked the glove compartment to take out the gun, and saw it was gone."

"Always take it out of the glove compartment when you get home?"

"Always."

"How come you left it at the garage?"

"I wasn't thinking. I was pissed off about the car quitting on me. It's force of habit. I get home, I unlock the box, reach in for the gun. The garage wasn't home. I just wasn't thinking."

"Did you report the gun stolen?"

"No."

"Why not?" Hawes asked.

"I figured somebody steals a piece, I'll never see it again, anyway. So why bother? It's not like a TV set. A piece isn't gonna turn up in a hockshop. It's gonna end up on the street."

"Ever occur to you that the gun might be used later in the commission of a crime?"

"It occurred to me."

"But you still didn't report its theft?"

"I didn't report it, no."

"How come?"

This from Hawes. Casually. Just a matter of curiosity. How come your gun is stolen and you know somebody might use it to do something bad, but you don't go to the cops? How come?

Carella *knew* how come. Black people were beginning to believe that the best way to survive was to keep their distance from the police. Because if they didn't, they got set up and framed. That was O.J.'s legacy. Thanks a lot Juice, we needed you.

"I talked privately to the day manager," Pratt said. "Told him somebody'd ripped of the piece. He said he'd ask around quietly."

"*Did* he ask around? Quietly."

"None of his people knew anything about it."

Naturally, Carella thought.

Hawes was thinking the same thing.

"And you say the glove compartment was locked when you got back home here?"

"I think so, yeah."

"What do you mean, you *think* so?"

"Why do you guys think everything I say is a lie?"

Carella sighed in exasperation.

"Come on, was it locked or wasn't it?" he said. "That isn't a trick question. Just tell us yes or no."

"I'm telling you I don't *know*. I put the key in the lock and turned it. But whether it was locked or not ..."

"You didn't try to thumb it open *before* you put the key in?"

"No, I always leave it locked."

"Then what makes you think it may have been unlocked this time?"

"The fucking gun was missing, wasn't it?"

"Yes, but you didn't know that before you opened the compartment."

"I know it *now*. If it was already unlocked when I turned the key, then what I was doing was locking it all over again. So I had to turn the key back again to *un*lock it."

"*Is* that in fact what you did?"

"I don't remember. I might have. A glove compartment isn't like your front door, you know, where you lock it and unlock it a hundred times a day, and you know *just* which way to turn the key to open it."

"Then what you're saying now, in retrospect, is that it might have been *un*locked."

"Is what I'm saying in retrospect. Because the gun was missing. Which means somebody had already got in there."

"Did you leave a valet key with the car, or . . . ?"

"I lost the valet key."

"So the key you left in the ignition could have unlocked the glove compartment, is that it?"

"That's it."

"So you're saying someone at the garage unlocked it and stole the gun."

"Is exactly what I'm saying."

"You don't think whoever put styrene in the crankcase might have stolen the gun, do you?"

"I don't see how."

"You didn't notice the hood open, did you?"

"*Yeah*, the hood was open. How would they get at the engine without lifting the hood?"

"I mean, *before* you took it to the garage."

"No, I didn't see the hood open."

"Tell us where you went with the car that Thursday. *Before* somebody did the styrene job."

"I don't *know* when the styrene job was done."

"Tell us where you went, anyway, okay? Help us out here, willya?"

"First, I drove an actress over to NBC for a television interview that morning . . ."

"NBC where?"

"Downtown. Off Hall Avenue."

"When was that?"

"Six-thirty in the morning."

"Did you go inside with her?"

"No, I stayed with the car."

"Then what?"

"Drove her back to her hotel, waited downstairs for her."

"Leave the car?"

"No. Well, wait a minute, yeah. I got *out* of the car to have a smoke, but I was standing right by it."

"Gun still in the glove compartment?"

"Far as I know. I didn't look."

"You said you waited for her downstairs . . ."

"Yeah."

"What time did she come back down?"

"Twelve-fifteen."

"Where'd you go then?"

"To J. C. Willoughby's for lunch. She was meeting her agent there."

"And then?"

"Picked her up at two, drove her to . . ."

"Were you with the car all that time?"

"Come to think of it, no. I went for a bite myself. Parked it in a garage."

"Where?"

"Near the restaurant. On Lloyd."

"So somebody *could* have lifted the hood and poured that styrene in."

"I guess."

"Did you leave the key in the car?"

"Of course. How else could they drive it?"

"Then someone could have unlocked the glove compartment, too."

"Yeah, but . . ."

"Yeah?"

"I *still* think somebody at the gas station swiped that piece."

"What makes you think that?"

"Just a feeling. You know how you get a feeling something's wrong? I had the feeling those guys knew something about the car I *didn't* know."

"Like what?"

"I don't know what."

"Which guys?"

"All of them. The day manager when I went to pick it up, all the guys working . . ."

"When did you pick up your diamond merchant?"

"What?"

"You said . . ."

"Oh, yeah, Mr. Aaronson. I was with the actress all day, stayed with her while she shopped Hall Avenue. She was doing some shopping before she went back to L.A. Drove her to meet some friends for dinner, took her back to the hotel afterward."

"Stayed with the car all that time?"

"Didn't budge from it. Picked up Mr. Aaronson at ten-thirty, drove him home. He was heavy that night."

"Heavy."

"Lots of gems in his suitcase."

"What'd you do then?"

"Started back over the bridge, heard the car starting to conk out."

"Would you remember where you parked the car while you were having lunch?"

"I told you. Place on Lloyd, just off Detavoner. Only one on the block, you can't miss it."

"You wouldn't know who *parked* it, would you?"

"All those guys look the same to me."

"Can you think of anyone who might've put that styrene in your crankcase?"

"No."

"Or stolen the gun?"

"Yeah. Somebody at the fuckin gas station."

"One last question," Carella said. "Where were you tonight between ten and midnight?"

"Here it comes," Pratt said, and rolled his eyes.

"Where were you?" Carella asked again.

"Right here."

"Anyone with you?"

"My wife. You want to wake *her* up, too?"

"Do we have to?" Carella asked.

"She'll tell you."

"I'll bet she will."

Pratt was beginning to glower again.

"Let her sleep," Carella said.

Pratt looked at him.

"I think we're finished here. Sorry to have bothered you. Cotton? Anything?"

"One thing," Hawes said. "Do you know who worked on your car?"

"Yeah, somebody named Gus. He's the one who signed the service order, but he wasn't there when I picked the car up yesterday."

"Do you know if the day manager asked *him* about the gun?"

"He says he did."

"What's *his* name?"

"The day manager? Jimmy."

"Jimmy what?"

"I don't know."

"How about the night manager? The one you left the car with?"

"Ralph. I don't know Ralph what. They have their names stitched on the front of their coveralls. Just the first names."

"Thanks," Hawes said. "Good night, sir, we're sorry to have bothered you."

"Mm," Pratt said sourly.

In the hallway outside, Carella said, "So now it becomes the tale of a gun."

"I saw *that* movie, too," Hawes said.

Bridge Texaco was in the shadow of the Majesta Bridge, which connected two of the city's most populous sectors, creating massive traffic jams at either end. Here in Isola—simply and appropriately named since it was an island and Isola meant "island" in Italian—the side streets and avenues leading to the bridge were thronged with taxis, trucks and passenger vehicles from six A.M. to midnight, when things began slowing down a bit. At three-thirty in the morning, when the detectives got there, one would never have guessed that just a few hours earlier the surrounding streets had resonated with the din of honking horns and shouted epithets, the result of a stalled truck in the middle of the bridge.

There were two city statutes, both of them punishable by mere fines, that made the blowing of horns unlawful. Using profanity in public was also against the law. The pertinent section in the Penal Law was 240.20, and it was titled Disorderly Conduct. It read: "A person is guilty of disorderly conduct when, with intent to cause public inconvenience, annoyance or alarm, or recklessly creating a risk thereof, he uses abusive or obscene language, or makes an obscene gesture." Disorderly conduct was a simple violation, punishable by not more than a term of fifteen days in jail. The two statutes and the Penal Law section only defined civilization. Perhaps this was why a uniformed cop on the street corner had merely scratched his ass at midnight while an angry motorist leaned incessantly on his horn, yelling "*Move* it, you fuckin cocksucker!"

Now, at 3:30 A.M., all the horn-blowing had stopped, all the profanity had flown on the wind. There was only the bitter cold of the January streets, and a gas station with fluorescent lights that seemed to echo winter's chill. A yellow taxicab was parked at one of the pumps. Its driver, hunched against the cold, jiggling from foot to foot, was filling the tank. The paneled doors opening on the service bays were closed tight against the frigid air. In the station's warmly lighted office, a man wearing a brown uniform and a peaked brown hat sat with his feet up on the desk, reading a copy of *Penthouse*. He looked up when the detectives came in. The stitched name on the front of his uniform read *Ralph*.

Carella showed the tin.

"Detective Carella," he said. "My partner, Detective Hawes."

"Ralph Bonelli. What's up?"

"We're trying to trace a gun that . . ."

"*That* again?" Bonelli said, and looked heavenward.

"Any idea what happened to it?"

"No. I told Pratt nobody here knew anything about it. That hasn't changed."

"Who'd you ask?"

"The mechanic who worked on it. Gus. He didn't see it. Some of the other guys who were working on Friday. None of them saw any gun."

"How *many* other guys?"

"Two. They're not mechanics, they just pump gas."

"So Gus is the only one who worked on the car."

"Yeah, the only one."

"Where'd he work on it?"

"One of the service bays in there," Bonelli said, and gestured with his head. "Had it up on the hydraulic lift."

"Key in it?"

"Yeah, he had to drive it in, didn't he?"

"How about when he was finished with it? Where'd the key go then?"

"Key box there on the wall," Bonelli said, indicating a grey metal cabinet fastened to the wall near the cash register. A small key was sticking out of a keyway on the door.

"Do you ever lock that cabinet?"

"Well . . . no."

"Leave the key in it all the time?"

"I see where you're going, but you're wrong. Nobody who works here stole that gun."

"Well, it was in the glove compartment when Mr. Pratt drove the car in . . ."

"That's what *he* says."

"You don't think it was, huh?"

"Did *I* see it? Did *anybody* see it? We got only the jig's word for it."

"Why would he say there was a gun in the glove compartment if there wasn't one?"

"Maybe he wanted me to write off the repair job, who knows?"

"What do you mean?"

"A trade, you know? He forgets the gun, we forget the bill."

"You think that's what he had in mind, huh?"

"Who knows?"

"Well, did he actually *suggest* anything like that?"

"No, I'm just saying."

"So, actually," Hawes said, "you have no reason to believe there *wasn't* a gun in that glove compartment?"

"Unless the jig had some other reason to be lying about it."

"Like what?"

"Maybe he had some use for it later on. Claim it was stolen, build an alibi in advance, you follow?"

"Can you write down the names of everyone who was working here while the car was in the shop?" Carella asked.

"Sure."

"Would anyone else have access to that key cabinet? Aside from your people?" Hawes asked.

"Sure. Anybody walking in and out of the office here. But there's always one of us around. We would've seen anybody trying to get in the cabinet."

"Addresses and phone numbers, too," Carella said.

Despite the cold, the blonde was wearing only a brief black miniskirt, a short red fake-fur jacket, gartered black silk stockings and high-heeled, red leather, ankle-high boots. A matching red patent-leather clutch handbag was tucked under her arm. Her naked thighs were raw from the wind, and her feet were freezing cold in the high-heeled boots. Shivering, she stood on the corner near the traffic light, where any inbound traffic from Majesta would have to stop before moving into the city proper.

The girl's name was Yolande.

She was free, white, and nineteen years old, but she was a hooker and a crack addict, and she was here on the street at this hour of the morning because she hoped to snag a driver coming in, and spin him around the block once or twice while she gave him a fifty-dollar blow job.

Yolande didn't know it, but she would be dead in three hours.

The detectives coming out of the gas station office spotted the blonde standing on the corner, recognized her for exactly what she was, but didn't glance again in her direction. Yolande recognized them as well, for exactly what they were, and watched them warily as they climbed into an unmarked, dark blue sedan. A white Jaguar pulled to the curb where she was standing. The window on the passenger side slid noiselessly down. The traffic light bathed the car and the sidewalk and Yolande in red. She waited until she saw a plume of exhaust smoke billow from the tailpipe of the dark sedan up the street. Then she leaned into the window of the car at the curb, smiled and said, "Hey, hiya. Wanna party?"

"How much?" the driver asked.

The changing traffic light suddenly turned everything to green.

A moment later, the two vehicles moved off in opposite directions.

The night was young.

They found Gus Mondalvo in an underground club in a largely Hispanic section of Riverhead. This was now a little past four in the morning. His mother, who refused to open the door of her apartment despite repeated declarations that they were police, told them they could find her son at the Club Fajardo "up dee block," which is where they were now, trying to convince the heavyset man who opened the chain-held door that they weren't here to bust the place.

The man protested in Spanish that they weren't serving liquor here, anyway, so what was there to bust? This was just a friendly neighborhood social club having a little party, they could come in and see for themselves, all of this while incriminating bottles and glasses were being whisked from behind the bar and off the tabletops. By the time he took off the chain some five minutes later, you would have thought this was a teenage corner malt shop instead of a joint selling booze after hours to a clientele that included

68

underage kids. The man who let them in told them Gus Mondalvo was sitting at the bar drinking . . .

"But nothing alcoholic," he added hastily.

. . . and pointed him out to them. A Christmas tree still stood in the corner near the bar, elaborately decorated, extravagantly lighted. The detectives made their way across a small dance floor packed with teenagers dancing and groping to Ponce's Golden Oldies, moved past tables where boys and girls, men and women alike were all miraculously drinking Coca-Cola in bottles, and approached the stool where Gus Mondalvo sat sipping what looked like a lemonade.

"Mr. Mondalvo?" Hawes asked.

Mondalvo kept sipping his drink.

"Police," Hawes said, and flipped a leather case open to show his shield.

There are various ways to express cool when responding to a police presence. One is to feign total indifference to the fact that cops are actually *here* and may be about to cause trouble. Like "I've been through this a hundred times before, man, and it don't faze me, so what can I do for you?" Another is to display indignation. As, for example, "Do you realize who I am? How dare you embarrass me this way in a public place?" The third is to pretend complete ignorance. "Cops? Are you *really* cops? Gee. What business on earth could cops possibly have with *me*?"

Mondalvo turned slowly on his stool.

"Hi," he said, and smiled.

They had seen it all and heard it all.

This time around, it would be pleasant indifference.

"Mr. Mondalvo," Hawes said, "we understand you worked on the engine of a Cadillac belonging to a Mr. Rodney Pratt on Friday, would you remember having done that?"

"Oh, sure," Mondalvo said. "Listen, do you think we'd be more comfortable at a table? Something to drink? A Coke? A ginger ale?"

He slid off the stood to reveal his full height of five-six, five-seven, shorter than he'd looked while sitting, a little man with broad shoulders and a narrow waist, sporting a close-cropped haircut and mustache. Carella wondered if he'd acquired the weight lifter's build in prison, and then realized he was prejudging someone who was, after all, gainfully employed as an automobile mechanic. They moved to a table near the dance floor. Hawes noticed that the club was discreetly and gradually beginning to clear out, people slipping into their overcoats and out the door. If a bust was in the cards, nobody wanted to be here when it came down. Some foolhardy couples, enjoying the music and maybe even the sense of imminent danger, flitted past on the dance floor, trying to ignore them, but everyone knew The Law was here, and eyes sideswiped them with covert glances.

"We'll get right to the point," Carella said. "Did you happen to notice a gun in the glove compartment of that car?"

"I didn't go in the glove compartment," Mondalvo said. "I had to put in a new engine, why would I go in the glove compartment?"

"I don't know. Why would you?"

"Right. Why would I? Is that what this is about?"

70

"Yes."

"Because I already told Jimmy I didn't know anything about that guy's gun."

"Jimmy Jackson?"

"Yeah, the day manager. He asked me did I see a gun, I told him *what* gun? I didn't see no gun."

"But you did work on the Caddy all day Friday."

"Yeah. Well not *all* day. It was a three-, four-hour job. What it was, somebody put styrene in the crankcase."

"So we understand."

"Styrene is what they use to make fiberglass. It's this oily shit you can buy at any marine or boat supply store, people use it to patch their fiberglass boats. But if you want to fuck up a guy's engine, all you do you mix a pint of it with three, four quarts of oil and pour it in his crankcase. The car'll run maybe fifty, sixty miles, a hundred max, before the oil breaks down and the engine binds. Pratt's engine was shot. We had to order a new one for him. Somebody didn't like this guy so much, to do something like that to his car, huh? Maybe that's why he packed a gun."

Maybe, Carella was thinking.

"Anybody else go near that car while you were working on it?"

"Not that I saw."

"Give us some approximate times here," Hawes said. "When did you start working on it?"

"After lunch sometime Friday. I had a Buick in needed a brake job, and then I had a Beamer had something wrong with the electrical system. I didn't get to the Caddy till maybe twelve-thirty, one o'clock. That's when I put it up on the lift."

"Where was it until then?"

"Sitting out front. There's like a little parking space out front, near where the air hose is?"

"Was the car locked?"

"I don't know."

"Well, were you the one who drove it into the bay and onto the lift?"

"Yeah."

"So, was the car locked when you . . . ?"

"Come to think of it, no."

"You just got into it without having to unlock the door."

"That's right."

"Was the key in the ignition?"

"No, I took it from the cabinet near the cash register."

"And went to the car . . ."

"Yeah."

". . . and found it unlocked."

"Right. I just got in and started it."

"What time did you finish work on it?"

"Around four, four-thirty."

"Then what?"

"Drove it off the lift, parked it outside again."

"Did you lock it?"

"I think so."

"Yes or no? Would you remember?"

"I'm pretty sure I did. I knew it was gonna be outside all night, I'm pretty sure I would've locked it."

"What'd you do with the key after you locked it?"

"Put it back in the cabinet."

"You weren't there on Thursday night when Mr. Pratt brought the car in, were you?" Carella asked.

"No, I go home six o'clock. We don't have any mechanics working the night shift. No gas jockeys, either. It's all self-service at night. There's just the night manager there. We mostly sell gas to cabs at night. That's about it."

"What time did you get to work on Friday morning?"

"Seven-thirty. I work a long day."

"Who was there when you got there?"

"The day manager and two gas jockeys."

Carella took out the list Ralph had written for him.

"That would be Jimmy Jackson . . ."

"The manager, yeah."

"Jose Santiago . . ."

"Yeah."

". . . and Abdul Sikhar."

"Yeah, the Arab guy."

"See any of *them* going in that Caddy?"

"No."

"Hanging around it?"

"No. But I have to tell you the truth, I wasn't like *watching* it every minute, you know? I had work to do."

"Mr. Mondalvo, the gun we're tracing was used in a homicide earlier tonight . . ."

"I didn't know that," Mondalvo said, and looked around quickly, as if even mere possession of this knowledge was dangerous.

"Yes," Hawes said. "So if you know anything at all . . ."

"Nothing."

". . . about that gun, or who might have taken that gun from the car . . ."

"Nothing, I swear."

" . . . then you should tell us now. Because otherwise . . ."

"I swear to God," Mondalvo said, and made the sign of the cross.

"Otherwise you'd be an accessory after the fact," Carella said.

"What does that mean?"

"It means you'd be as guilty as whoever pulled that trigger."

"I don't know who pulled any trigger."

Both cops looked at him hard.

"I swear to God," he said again. "I don't know."

Maybe they believed him.

4

The three kids were all named Richard.

Because they were slick-as-shit preppies from a New England school, they called themselves Richard the First, Second, and Third, after Richard the Lion-Hearted, Richard the son of Edward, and Richard who perhaps had his nephews murdered in the Tower of London. They were familiar with these monarchs through an English history course they'd had to take back in their sophomore year. The three Richards were now seniors. All three of them had been accepted at Harvard. They were each eighteen years old, each varsity football heroes, all smart as hell, handsome as devils, and drunk as skunks. To coin a few phrases.

Like his namesake Richard Coeur de Lion, Richard Hopper—for such was his real name—was six feet tall and he weighed a hundred and ninety pounds, and he had blond hair and blue eyes, just like the twelfth-century king. Unlike that fearless monarch, however, Richard did not write poetry although he sang quite well. In fact, all three Richards were in the school choir. Richard the First was the team's star quarterback.

The real Richard the Second had ruled England from 1377 to 1399 and was the son of Edward the Black Prince. The present-day Richard the Second was named Richard Weinstock, and his father was

Irving the Tailor. He was five feet ten inches tall and weighed two hundred and forty pounds, all of it muscle and bruised bones. He had dark hair and brown eyes, and he played fullback on the team.

Richard the Third, whose true and honorable name was Richard O'Connor, had freckles and reddish hair and greenish eyes and he was six feet three inches tall and weighed two-ten. His fifteenth-century namesake was the third son of the duke of York, a mighty feudal baron. Richard's left arm was withered and shrunken, but this did not stop him from being a fierce fighter and a conniving son of a bitch. The king, that is. The present-day Richard was known to cheat on French exams, but he had two strong arms and very good hands and he played wide receiver on the Pierce Academy team.

All three Richards had come down to the city for the weekend. They were not due back at school till Monday morning. All three Richards were wearing the team's hooded parka, navy blue with a big letter P in white on the back. Just below the stem of the P, there was a white logo in the shape of a football, about three inches wide and five inches long. The patch indicated which team they played on. Over the left pectoral on the front of the parka, the name of the school was stitched in white script lettering, *Pierce Academy* ta-ra.

The Richards Three.

At four-thirty on that gelid morning, it was doubtful that any of the three, despite the similarity, knew his own name. Turning back to yell "Fuck you!" and "Go eat *shit*!" at the bouncer who'd told them the club was now closed and then politely but firmly showed them

76

the front door, they came reeling out onto the sidewalk and stood uncertainly toggling their parkas closed, pulling the hoods up over their heads, wrapping their blue and white mufflers, trying to light cigarettes, burping, farting, giggling, and finally throwing their arms around each other and going into a football huddle.

"What we need to do now," Richard the First said, "is to get ourselves laid."

"That's a good idea," Richard the Third said. "Where can we find some girls?"

"Uptown?" Richard the First suggested.

"Then let's go uptown," Richard the Second agreed.

They clapped out of the huddle.

Uptown, Yolande was climbing into another automobile.

The three Richards hailed a taxi.

Jimmy Jackson's kids knew there was a black Santa Claus because they'd seen one standing alongside a fake chimney and ringing a bell outside a department store downtown on Hall Avenue after their mother had taken them to sit on the lap of a white Santa Claus inside. The white Santa apparently hadn't listened all that hard because James Jr. hadn't got the bike he'd asked for, and Millie hadn't got this year's hot doll, and Terrence hadn't got this year's hot warrior. So when the doorbell rang at a quarter to five that Sunday morning, they ran to wake up their father because they figured this might be the black bell ringing Santa coming back to make amends for the white department-store Santa's oversights.

77

Jimmy Jackson was only mildly annoyed to be awakened by his kids so early on a Sunday morning when his mother-in-law was coming to visit, not to mention his sister Naydelle and her two screaming brats. He became singularly *irritated,* however, when he opened the door and found it wasn't no joke but was *really* two honkie dicks, just like they'd said through the wood, standing there with gold and blue badges in they hands. On a Sunday no less, did the motherfuckers have no consideration whatever?

The kids were asking if he would make pancakes, since everybody was up, anyway.

Jackson told them to go ask they mother.

"So whut is it?" he said to the cops.

"Mr. Jackson," Carella said, "we realize it's early in the morning . . ."

"Yeah, yeah, whut is it?"

"But we're investigating a homicide . . ."

"Yeah, yeah."

"And we're trying to track the murder weapon."

Jackson looked at them.

He was a tall, rangy, very dark man, wearing a robe over pajamas, his eyes still bleary from sleep, his mouth pulled into a thin angry line. Man had a right to the sancty of his own home on Sunday morning, he was thinking, thout these motherfuckers comin roun. Murder weapon my ass, he was thinking.

"Is this about that damn gun again?" he asked.

From somewhere in the apartment, a woman asked, "Who is it, James?"

"It's the *po*-lice!" one of the children shouted gleefully. "Can Daddy make pancakes now?"

78

"The police?" she said. "James?"

"Yeah, yeah," he said.

"It's about the gun again, yes," Hawes said.

"I tole Pratt I dinn see no damn gun in his car. *Nobody* seen that damn gun. You want my opinion, that gun is a fiction of Pratt's imagination."

No one had yet invited them into the apartment. Mrs. Jackson came down the hall now in a robe and slippers, a perplexed frown on her face. She was a tall woman with the bearing of a Masai warrior, the pale yellow eyes of a panther. She didn't like cops here scaring her kids, and she was ready to tell them so.

"What's this," she said, "five o'clock in the mornin?"

"Ma'am," Carella said, "we're sorry to be bothering you, but we're working a homicide and . . ."

"What's anybody in this household got to do with a homicide?"

"We're simply trying to find out when the murder weapon disappeared from the owner's car. That's all."

"What car?" she asked.

"Caddy was in for service," her husband explained.

"You work on that Caddy?"

"No. Gus did."

"Then why they botherin you?" she said, and turned to the cops again. "Why you botherin my man?"

"Because an old lady was killed," Carella said simply.

Mrs. Jackson looked into their faces.

"Come in," she said, "I'll make some coffee."

They went into the apartment. Jackson closed the door behind them, double-bolted it, and put on the safety chain. The apartment was cold; in this city, in this building, they couldn't expect heat to start coming up till six-thirty, seven o'clock. The radiators would begin clanging then, loud enough to wake the dead. Meanwhile, all was silent, all was chilly. The children wanted to hang around. This was better than TV. Mrs. Jackson hushed them off to bed again. Husband and wife sat at the small kitchen table with the two detectives, drinking coffee like family. This was five A.M., it was pitch-black outside. They could hear police sirens, ambulance sirens wailing to the night. All four of them could tell the difference; sirens were the nocturnes of this city.

"That car was a headache minute it come in," Jackson said. "I'da been the night man, I'da tole Pratt go get a tow truck, haul that wreck outta here, more trouble'n it's worth. Had to turn away two, three other cars the next day, cause Gus had that damn Caddy up on the lift. When I finely figured we were done with it, I come in yesterday mornin, the car's a mess. Man's coming in to pick it up at ten, it's a mess like I never seen before in my life."

"What do you mean? Was there still trouble with the engine?" Carella asked.

"No, no. This was *inside* the car."

Both detectives looked at him, puzzled. So did his wife.

"Somebody musta left the window open when they moved it outside," Jackson said.

They were still looking at him, all three of them, trying to figure out what kind of mess he was talking about.

"You see *The Birds*?" he asked. "That movie Alfred Hitchcock wrote?"

Carella didn't think Hitchcock had written it.

"Birds tryin'a kill people all over the place?"

"Whut about it?" Mrs. Jackson asked impatiently.

"Musta been birds got in the car," Jackson said. "Maybe cause it was so cold."

"What makes you figure that?" Hawes asked reasonably.

"Bird shit and feathers all over the place," Jackson said. "Hadda put Abdul to cleanin it up fore the man came to claim his car. Never seen such a mess in my life. Birds're smart, you know. I read someplace when they was shootin that movie, the crows used to pick the locks on they cages, that's how smart they are. Musta got in the car."

"How? Did you notice a window down?"

"Rear window on the right was open about six inches, yeah."

"You think somebody left that window open overnight?"

"Had to've been."

"And a bird got in, huh?"

"At least a *few* birds. There was shit and feathers all over the place."

"Where was all this?" Carella asked.

"The backseat," Jackson said.

"And you asked Abdul to clean it up, huh?"

"Directly when he come in Saturday mornin. I seen the mess, put him to work right away."

"Was he alone in the car?"

"Alone, yeah."

81

"You didn't see him going into that glove compartment, did you?"

"Nossir."

"Fiddling around anywhere in the *front* seat?"

"No, he was busy cleanin up the mess in back."

"Did you watch him all the time he was in the car?"

"No, I din't. There was plenty other work to do."

"How long was he in the car?"

"Hour or so. Vacuuming, wiping. It was some mess, you better believe it. Man came to pick it up at ten, it was spotless. Never've known some birds was nestin in it overnight."

"But the birds were already gone when you noticed that open window, huh?"

"Oh yeah, long gone. Just left all they feathers and shit."

"I wish you'd watch your mouth," Mrs. Jackson said, frowning.

"You figure they got out the same way they got in?" Hawes asked.

"Musta, don't you think?"

Hawes was wondering how they'd managed *that* little trick.

So was Carella.

"Well, thank you," he said, "we appreciate your time. If you can remember anything else, here's my. . ."

"Like what?" Jackson asked.

"Like anyone near that glove compartment."

"I already tole you I didn't see anyone near the glove compartment."

"Well, here's my card, anyway," Carella said. "If you think of anything at all that might help us . . ."

"Just don't come around five o'clock again," Jackson said.

Mrs. Jackson nodded.

"What we'd like to do," Carella said on the phone, "is send someone around for the car and have our people go over it."

"What?" Pratt said.

This was a quarter past five in the morning. Carella was calling from a cell phone in the police sedan. Hawes was driving. They were on their way to Calm's Point, where Abdul Sikhar lived.

"When do I get some *sleep* here?" Pratt asked.

"I didn't mean someone coming by right this *minute*. If we can . . ."

"I'm talking about you waking me *up* right this minute."

I'm sorry about that, but we want to check out the car, find out . . ."

"So I understand. Why?"

"Find out what happened inside it."

"What happened is somebody stole my gun."

"That's what we're working on, Mr. Pratt. Which is why we'd like our people to go over the interior."

"What people?"

"Our techs."

"Looking for what?"

Carella almost said feathers and shit.

"Whatever they can find," he said.

"You're lucky it's Sunday," Pratt said.

"Sir?"

"I'm not working today."

The three Richards were beginning to sober up and beginning to get a little surly. They had come all the way up here to Diamondback—which was not such a good idea to begin with—and now they couldn't find any girls on the streets, perhaps because anybody sensible was already asleep at five-twenty in the morning. Richard the First wasn't afraid of black people. He knew that Diamondback was a notoriously dangerous black ghetto, but he'd been up here before, in search of cocaine—not for nothing was he nicknamed Lion-Hearted—and he felt he knew how to deal with African Americans.

It was Richard the First's contention that a black man, or a black woman, for that matter, could tell in a wink whether a person was a racist or not. Of course, the only black men and women he knew were drug dealers and prostitutes, but this didn't lessen his conviction. A black person could look in a white man's eyes and either find those dead blue eyes he'd been conditioned to expect, or else he might discover that the white person was truly color-blind. Richard the First liked to believe he was color-blind, which is why he was up here in Diamondback at this hour, looking for black pussy.

"Trouble is," he told the other two Richards, "we're here too late. Everybody's asleep already."

"Trouble is we're here too *early*," Richard the Second said. "Nobody's awake yet."

"Man, it's fuckin cold out here," Richard the Third said. Up the street, three black men warmed their hands at a fire blazing in a sawed-off oil drum, oblivious to the three preppies in their hooded blue

84

parkas. The lights of an all-night diner across the street cast warm yellow rectangles on the sidewalk. The sun was still an hour and forty-five minutes away.

The three boys decided to urinate in the gutter.

This was perhaps a mistake.

They were standing there with their dicks in their hands—what the hell, this was five-thirty in the morning, the streets were deserted except for the three old farts standing around the oil drum—looking like three monks in their hooded parkas, certainly intending no affront, merely answering the call of nature, so to speak, on a dark and stormless night. It was not perceived in quite this manner by the black man who came out of the night like a solitary guardian of public decency, the sole member of the Pissing in Public Patrol, dressed in black as black as the night, black jeans, black boots, a black leather jacket, a black O.J. Simpson watch cap pulled down over his ears.

He came striding toward them at exactly the same moment Yolande stepped into a taxi a mile and a half downtown.

"Thing I hate about the boneyard shift," Hawes said, "is you just start getting used to it and you're back on the day shift again."

Carella was dialing his home number.

The boneyard shift was the graveyard shift, which was the so-called *morning* shift that kept you up all *night*.

Fanny picked up on the third ring.

"How is he?" Carella asked.

"Better. The fever's gone, he's sleeping like an angel." She paused for the briefest tick of time. "Which is what *I'd* like to be doing," she said.

"Sorry," Carella said. "I won't call again. See you in a few hours."

That's what *he* thought.

"You a working girl?" the cabbie asked.

"You a cop?" Yolande said.

"Sure, a cop," he said.

"Then mind your own business," she said.

"I'm just wondering if you know where you're going."

"I know where I'm going."

"White girl going up to Diamondback . . ."

"I said I . . ."

" . . . this hour of the night."

"I know where I'm going. And it's morning."

"By me, it ain't morning till the sun comes up."

Yolande shrugged. It had been a pretty good night for her, and she was exhausted.

"Why you going to Diamondback?" the cabbie asked. His name on the plastic-enclosed permit on the dashboard to the right of the meter read MAX R. LIEBOWITZ. Jewish, Yolande thought. Last of a dying breed of big-city cabdrivers. Nowadays, most of your cabbies were from India or the Middle East. Some of them couldn't speak English. None of them knew where Duckworth Avenue was. Yolande knew where it was. She had blown a Colombian drug dealer on Duckworth Avenue in Calm's Point. He had given her a five-hundred-dollar tip. She would never forget

Duckworth Avenue in her life. She wondered if Max Liebowitz knew where Duckworth Avenue was. She wondered if Max Liebowitz knew she herself was Jewish.

"I didn't hear your answer, miss," he said.

"I live up there," she said.

"You live in *Diamondback*?" he said, and shot a glance at her in the rearview mirror.

"Yes."

Actually *Jamal* lived in Diamondback. All *she* did was live with Jamal. Jamal Stone, no relation to Sharon, who had built a career by flashing her wookie. Yolande flashed her wookie a thousand times a day. Too bad she couldn't act. Then again, neither could a lot of girls who were good at flashing their wookies.

"How come you live up there?" Liebowitz asked.

"I like paying cheap rent," she said.

Which wasn't exactly true. *Jamal* paid the rent. But he also took every penny she earned. Kept her in good shit, though. Speaking of which, it was getting to be about that time. She looked at her watch. Twenty-five to six. Been a hard day's night.

"Worth your life, a white girl living up there," Liebowitz said.

Nice Jewish girl, no less, Yolande thought, but did not say because she couldn't bear seeing a grown man cry. A nice Jewish girl like you? Giving blow jobs to passing motorists at fifty bucks a throw. A *Jewish* girl? Suck your *what*? She almost smiled.

"So what are you then?" Liebowitz asked. "A dancer?"

"Yeah," she said, "how'd you guess?"

"Pretty girl like you, this hour of the night, I figured a dancer in one of the topless bars."

"Yeah, you hit it right on the head."

"I'm not a mind reader," Liebowitz said, chuckling. "You were standing in front of the Stardust when you hailed me."

Which was where she'd given some guy from Connecticut a twenty-dollar hand job while the girls onstage rattled and rolled.

"Yep," she said.

Tipped the manager two bills a night to let her freelance in the joint. Pissed the regulars working there, but gee, tough shit, honey.

"So where you from originally?" Liebowitz asked.

"Ohio," she said.

"I knew it wasn't here. You don't have the accent."

She almost told him her father owned a deli in Cleveland. She didn't. She almost told him her mother had once been to Paris, France. She didn't. Yolande Marie was her mother's idea. Yolande Marie Marx. Known in the trade as Groucho, just kidding. Actually known in the trade as Marie St. Claire, which Jamal had come up with, lot of difference it made to the johns on wheels. My name is Marie St. Claire, case you're interested. Nice to meet you, Marie, take it deeper.

She had nightmares about a john pulling up in a blue station wagon and she leans in the window and says, "Hey, hiya. Wanna party?" and she gets in the car and unzips his fly and it's her father. Dreamt that on average twice a week. Woke up in a cold sweat every time. *Dear Dad, I am still working here in the toy shop, it's a shame you never get out of Cleveland now*

88

that Mom's bedridden, maybe I'll be home for Yom Kippur. Sure. Take it deeper, hon.

"So do you have to do anything *else* at that bar?"

"How do you mean?"

"You know," Liebowitz said, and looked at her in the rearview mirror. "Besides dancing?"

She looked back at him. He had to be sixty years old, short bald-headed little fart could hardly see over the steering wheel. Hitting on her. Next thing you knew he'd offer to barter. Fare on the meter was now six dollars and thirty cents. He'd agree to swap it for a quickie in the backseat. Nice Jewish man. Unzip his fly, out would pop her father.

"So do you?"

"Do what?"

"Other things beside dancing topless."

"Yeah, I also *sing* topless," she said.

"Go on, they don't sing in those places."

"I do."

"You're kidding me."

"No, no. You want to hear me sing, Max?"

"Nah, you don't sing."

"I sing like a bird," Yolande said, but did not demonstrate. Liebowitz was thinking this over, trying to determine whether or not she was putting him on.

"What else do you *really* do?" he asked. "Besides sing and dance? Topless."

She was beginning to think it might not be a bad idea to turn another trick on the way home. But not for the six-ninety now on the meter. How much cash you carrying, Zayde? she wondered. Want a piece of nineteen-year-old Jewish-girl ass you can tell your

89

grandchildren about next Hanukkah? She thought of her father again, decided no. Still, talk old Max here into a hundred for a quick blow job, might be worth it. Twice the going price for a street girl, but oh such tender goods, what do you say, Granpa?

"What'd you have in mind?" she asked coyly.

The black man in the black jeans, black leather jacket, black boots, and black watch cap appeared in front of them like an avenging angel of death. They almost all three of them peed on his boots, he was standing that close.

"Now what do you call *this*?" he asked rhetorically.

"We call it pissing in the gutter," Richard the Second said.

"I call it disrespect for the neighborhood," the black man said. "That what the letter P stand for? Pissing?"

"Join us, why don't you?" Richard the Third suggested.

"My name is Richard," Richard the First said, zipping up and extending his hand to the black man.

"So is mine" Richard the Second said.

"Me, too," Richard the Third said.

"As it happens," the black man said, "*my* name is Richard, too."

Which now made four of them.

Bloody murder was only an hour and sixteen minutes away.

Abdul Sikhar lived in a two-bedroom Calm's Point apartment with five other men from Pakistan. They had all known each other in their native town of

Rawalpindi, and they had all come to the United States at different times over the past three years. Two of the men had wives back home. A third had a girlfriend there. Four of the men worked as cabdrivers and were in constant touch by CB radio all day long. Whenever they babbled in Urdu, they made their passengers feel as if a terrorist act or a kidnapping was being plotted. The four cabbies drove like the wind in a camel's mane. None of them knew it was against the law to blow your horn in this city. They would have blown it anyway. Each and every one of them could not wait till he got out of this fucking city in this fucking United States of America. Abdul Sikhar felt the same way, though he did not drive like the wind. What *he* did was pump gas and wash cars at Bridge Texaco.

When he answered the door at ten to six that morning, he was wearing long woolen underwear and a long-sleeved woolen top. He looked like he needed a shave but he was merely growing a beard. He was twenty years old, give or take, a scrawny kid who hated this country and who would have wet the bed at night if he wasn't sleeping in it with two other guys. The detectives identified themselves. Nodding, Sikhar stepped out into the hallway, closing the door behind him, whispering that he did not wish to awaken his "mates," as he called them, an archaic term from the days of British rule back home, *those* bastards. When he learned what their business here was, he excused himself and went back inside for a moment, stepping into the hallway again a moment later, wearing a long black overcoat over his long johns, unlaced black shoes on his feet. They stood now beside a grimy hall window that sputtered orange neon from someplace outside. Sikhar lighted a cigarette. Neither Carella nor Hawes smoked. They both wished they could arrest him.

"So what is this about a pistol?" he asked. "Everyone wishes to know about this pistol."

"The feathers, too," Carella said.

"And the bird shit," Hawes said.

"Such a mess," Sikhar agreed, nodding, puffing on the cigarette, holding it the way Peter Lorre did in *The Maltese Falcon*. He himself looked something of a mess, but perhaps that was because the developing beard looked like a smudge on his face.

"What kind of feathers were they, would you know?" Hawes asked.

"Pigeon feathers, I would say."

"Why would you say that?"

"There are many pigeons near the bridge."

"And you think some of them got in the car somehow, is that it?"

"I think so, yes. And panicked. Which is why they shit all over everything."

"Pretty messy in there, huh?" Carella said.

"Oh yes."

"How do you suppose they got out again?" Hawes asked.

"Birds have ways," Sikhar said.

He looked at the men mysteriously.

They looked back mysteriously.

"How about the gun?" Carella said.

"What gun?"

"You know what gun."

92

Sikhar dropped the cigarette to the floor, ground it out under the sole of one black shoe, and took a crumpled package of Camels from the right-hand pocket of the long black coat. "Cigarette?" he asked, offering the pack first to Carella and next to Hawes, both of whom refused, each shaking his head somewhat violently. Sikhar did not get the subtle message. He fired up at once. Clouds of smoke billowed into the hallway, tinted orange by the sputtering neon outside the window. For some peculiar reason, Carella thought of Dante's *Inferno*.

"The gun," he prompted.

"The famous missing pistol," Sikhar said. "I know nothing about it."

"You spent an hour or so in that car, didn't you? Cleaning up the mess?"

"A terrible mess," Sikhar agreed.

"Did the birds get anywhere near the glove compartment?"

"No, the mess was confined exclusively to the backseat."

"So you spent an hour or so in the backseat of the car."

"At least."

"Never once went into the front seat?"

"Never. Why would I? The mess was in the backseat."

"I thought, while you were cleaning the car . . ."

"No."

". . . you might have gone up front, given the dashboard a wipe . . ."

"No."

93

"The glove compartment door, give everything a wipe up there, too."

"No, I didn't do that."

"Then you wouldn't know whether the glove compartment was unlocked or not, would you?"

"I would not know."

"What time did you start work on the car?"

"When I got there. Jimmy showed me the mess and told me to clean it up. I got immediately to work."

"What time was that?"

"About seven o'clock."

"On Saturday morning."

"Yes, Saturday. I work six days a week," he said pointedly, and looked at his watch. It was now close to six o'clock on Sunday morning. Dawn would come in an hour and fifteen minutes.

"Anybody else come near that car while you were in it?"

"Yes."

"Who?"

"Jose Santiago."

The thing Richard the Fourth did up here in Diamondback was sell crack cocaine to nice little boys like the three Richards he was now leading up the street to an underground bar where he promised them there'd be girls aplenty. Richard's family name was Cooper, and he was sometimes called Coop by people who wanted to get friendly with him, not knowing he despised the name Coop. This was the same as some jackass coming up to some dude and slamming him on the back and yelling in his face, "Hey, remember me,

Sal?" Only his fuckin name ain't *Sal*, dig? Richard's name was Richard, and that was what he preferred being called, thank you. Certainly not Coop, nor Rich or Richie neither, nor even Ricky or Rick. Just plain *Richard*. Like the three Richards with him now, who he was telling about these quite nice jumbo vials he happened to have in his pocket, would they care for a taste at fifteen a pop?

The crack and the money were changing hands, black to white and white to black, when the taxi pulled up to the curb, and a long-legged white girl in a fake-fur jacket and red leather boots stepped out. The driver's window rolled down. The driver looked somewhat dazed, as if he'd been hit by a bus. "Thanks, Max," the girl said, and blew him a kiss, and was swiveling onto the sidewalk, a slender, red, patent-leather bag under her arm, when Richard Cooper said, "Hey, Yolande, you *jess* the girl we lookin for."

Fifty-six minutes later, she was dead.

5

She has done three-ways before, but this is what at first promises to be a four-way and then possibly a *five*-way if Richard puts in *his* two cents. She knows Richard from the hood, he deals good shit. In fact, he used to be in business together with Jamal for some time before they went their separate ways. She is not particularly eager for this to turn into a *five*-way with Richard in the equation, but as Jamal is fond of saying, "Business is business and never the twain shall meet."

At the same time, it's been a very busy night, thank God, and she's really very sleepy, and would like nothing better than to go back to the pad and present to Jamal the spoils of the night, so to speak, and then cuddle with him a little, he is very good at cuddling when you lay almost two thousand bucks on him. But Richard here is talking six hundred for the three preppies here, two hundred apiece for the next few hours, and giving her the nod to indicate he might wish to wet *his* wick a bit, too, in which case he will throw into the pot five jumbos.

What he is suggesting—and she is considering this seriously now, even though she is bone-tired and cold besides—is that they all go up to his place to do some crack and get down to *realities*, sistuh, you hear whut I'm sayin? She is thinking six hundred and the five jumbos, which at today's market price is fifteen for the red-topped vials, and wondering how she can escalate

96

this thing a bit higher, it being so late at night or so early in the morning, depending on where you're coming from. She wonders if they'll go for a big one and ten jumbos. She decides that's too far a reach. Instead, she tells Richard—and the three preppies who are nodding sympathetically while ripping off her clothes with their eyes—tells Richard she's been out since eleven last night and it's been a long one, bro, so maybe we ought to just pass unless we can sweeten the pot a little, hm? He asks her what she means by sweeten it, how sweet does she wish to sweeten it, and she decides to push the envelope, what the hell.

"If you'll be joining the party," she says, "I'll need ten jumbos . . ."

"No problem," Richard says at once.

Jesus! she thinks.

"And a grand from the college boys here."

The preppies are flattered that she thinks they're from Princeton or Yale instead of some shiny little boys' school in Vermont or wherever the fuck. But the thousand-dollar tab sticks in their craw, she can see that, so she says at once, "Though you're all so cute, I might do it for nine."

One of the preppies—she later learns they're all named Richard, this is going to be *some* kind of confusing gang bang—immediately says, "Make it eight," but she knows he's just trying to sound like his banker father in Michigan or wherever, so she says, "I can't do it for less than nine. Hey, you're all real cute, but . . ."

"How about eight-fifty?" one of the other Richards asks.

"It has to be nine or I'm out of here," she says.

She does not know, at that juncture in time, that if she walks right this minute, she will still be alive fifty-one minutes from now. She does not begin to realize she's in serious danger until it is almost too late, when things begin getting out of hand. This is much later. Right now, they are haggling over price, and if she walks she still has a shot at survival. The boys go into a kind of a football huddle—she later learns they're all stars on their school's football team—come clapping out of it, big financial meeting over, big white Ps on the back of their parkas, and one of them says, "Will you accept traveler's checks?" Richard busts out laughing. Laughing with him, Yolande says, "Done deal."

She has done three-ways before and in fact has enjoyed some of them, especially when it's two girls and a guy. With most of the girls you fake it, you know, you make a lot of lapping, slurping sounds, and you moan Oh yeah, honey, *do* it, while nobody's doing anything to anybody. But the john gets all excited thinking he's got two hot lezzies here really getting it off. With some girls in a three-way, though, you're *really* doing what the john *thinks* you're doing, and it can be quite enjoyable, really, all that tongue play, because another girl knows just where the target is, knows just which buttons to push, so yeah it can be really really good.

Two guys and a girl, you kind of lose control. It's that they get all macho on you, one of them fucking you from behind while you're blowing the other one, and they start saying, You *love* it, don't you, cunt?, all

98

that, it gets degrading when there are two guys flexing their muscles and trying to prove how big their cocks are. It's not that she thinks she's a *princess* or anything, she *knows* what she does for a living, she knows she's a fucking *whore*, I mean, she *knows* that. It's just that when there are two guys, she really begins to feel *used*, you know, she really begins to feel they have no respect at all for her, and she comes away with a dirty feeling afterward, no matter how much she tells herself she was detached the whole time. It's that they *used* her, is all. They flat out *used* her.

So now, here in Richard's pad—where she remembers coming to a party once with Jamal when the two of them were first starting out in business together, dealing pot to kindergarten kids, that's a joke, son, they never went *near* any of the schools, you think they're crazy? Can remember coming to a party here, but not *this* kind of party with three white preppies and a black guy has a shlong the size of a python. The only black guy she does it with is Jamal and that's because he takes care of her and she loves him. She knows how big black guys can be, and she gcts sorc cvcn aftcr shc docs it with Jamal, which is not too frequently because business is business and never the twain shall meet.

Anyway, what she shares with Jamal transcends mere sex, he was the one took her under his wing when she got off the bus from Cleveland, he's the one makes sure nobody hurts her. Anybody gets funny with her, she tells Jamal about it and he breaks the guy's legs. Besides, Jamal is regularly fuckin this other girl he takes care of, whose name is Carlyle, which Jamal gave her. Carlyle is black and very beautiful, Yolande can understand the attraction. Occasionally they do three-ways together. Jamal Stone and Carlyle Yancy (which he also gave her) and Marie St. Claire. Sometimes Yolande wonders how she ever got into all this stuff, boy. But listen, what the hell.

She is wondering now how she got into *this* stuff *tonight* when she's so goddamn bone-weary, but of course nine bills is nine bills, not to mention the ten jumbos, which are worth a cool hundred and fifty. *Plus*, the preppies are sharing *their* stash with her, everybody beaming up to the *Enterprise* on the boys' nickel, until they're all sitting stoned in their underwear and grinning at each other, Jesus what a shlong on Richard, the *black* Richard, which is when she discovers they're all *four* of them named Richard, how cute. Richard—the black Richard—is standing in front of her now and idly gliding the head of his long dick over her lips, while a preppie on either side of her is grabbing a tit and the third preppie is watching and jerking off in preparation.

So far, no one has called her cunt or bitch.

Or cocksucker is a favorite, too.

Later, she will wonder how this got so out of hand.

Nobody seemed to know where Jose Santiago was.

This was now six-forty in the morning, nobody knew where he was. His mother didn't know, his sister didn't know, none of his friends knew, the guy behind the counter at the local hangout hamburger joint didn't know, nobody knew, the whole neighborhood had suddenly gone deaf, dumb, and blind. In police work, you took this to mean that *everybody* knew where Santiago was, but you are The *Man*, man, and nobody is going to tell you, *señor*.

A faint hint of morngloam only seemed to touch the sky. It was still thirty-five minutes till dawn, the night refused to yield. The bleak January morning was still flat, dull and dark, but there was activity in the streets now. Even on a Sunday, there was work to be done in this city, and early risers were beginning to move sluggishly toward the subways and the bus stops, passing revelers and predators who were just now heading home to bed. The homeless, sensing dawn, anticipating the safety that would come with full light, were already crawling back into their cardboard boxes.

Outside a candy store on the corner of Santiago's block, a man was carrying in a tied bundle of newspapers. He was still wearing his overcoat and earmuffs. The scalloped edge of the furled green awning over the front of the store read: **HERNANDEZ VARIETY- NEWSPAPERS- LOTTERY-COFFEE.** They assumed he was Hernandez himself; there was a bustling air of ownership about him. The store lights beckoned warmly behind him. Coffee sounded pretty good just about now.

"Cops, right?" Hernandez asked the moment they stepped inside.

"Right," Hawes said.

"How did I know, right?"

Not a trace of an accent. Hawes figured him for a third-generation Puerto Rican, grandfather probably came over on the *Marine Tiger* with the first wave of immigrants from the island. Probably had kids in college.

"How *did* you know?" he asked.

Hernandez shrugged as if to indicate he couldn't waste valuable time answering such a ridiculous question. He had still not taken off the overcoat and earmuffs. The store was cold. The entire universe was cold this morning. Ignoring them, he busied himself cutting the cords around the newspaper bundles. The big headline on the morning tabloid read:

PIANIST
SLAIN

On the so-called quality paper, big headlines were reserved for acts of war or national disaster. But a smaller headline over a boxed article in the right-hand corner of the front page read:

VIRTUOSO MURDERED
SVETLANA DYALOVICH VICTIM OF
SHOOTING

Easy come, easy go.

"You serving coffee yet?" Carella asked.

"Should be ready in a few minutes."

"Know anybody named Jose Santiago?" Hawes asked.

What the hell, they'd already asked everyone else in the neighborhood. He looked to Carella for approval. Carella was watching the hot plate on a narrow shelf behind the counter. Brewing coffee dripped steadily into the pot. The aroma was almost too much to bear.

"Why, what'd he do?" Hernandez asked.

"Nothing. We just want to talk to him."

Hernandez shrugged again. The shrug said that this statement was also too ridiculous even to acknowledge.

"Do you know him?" Hawes persisted.

"He comes in here," Hernandez admitted offhandedly.

"Know where he is right now?"

"No, where?"

Little joke there. Hee hee hee.

"Do you or don't you?" Hawes asked.

They were smelling something besides coffee here.

"Why? What'd he do?"

"Nothing."

Hernandez looked at them.

"Really," Hawes said.

"Then try the roof of his building. He keeps pigeons."

Richard, the black Richard, has already come—all over her face, as a matter of fact, which she didn't quite appreciate, but he's the one set up the party, after all. He's sitting in a corner now, a blanket around him, watching television, so she knows for sure he's not the one who starts this thing going haywire. For once you can't blame the black guy, mister.

She doesn't think it's the Richard with the red hair, either, because he's sort of content to keep toying with her right tit, which she has to admit she has terrific knockers, even back in Cleveland they said so. The Richard with the dark hair is now sticking his fingers inside her, searching for her clit, good luck, mister, the condition you're in. He's very hard. She has his cock in her hand and she is stroking it pretty fiercely, hoping she can bring him off this way, get this thing over with, go home to bed. But he's spreading her legs now, and trying to climb into her, they're all so fuckin stoned nobody knows how to do diddly, except the preppie who's licking her nipple like it's his own mother's. *He* knows *just* what he's doing, and he seems to be having a nice time doing it, maybe he can come this way, she certainly hopes so, kill two birds with one stone here.

So it must be the blond Richard who pulls the plastic freezer bag over her head.

She knows at once that she is going to die.

She knows this is going to be her worst nightmare realized.

She is going to suffocate inside a plastic freezer bag, one of those sturdy things you stuff a leg of lamb in, not the kind of thin plastic that clings to your face, they warn you to keep away from children. No, she's not going to die with plastic clinging to her nostrils and her lips. Instead, she's going to exhaust all the oxygen inside the bag, she's going to die that way, there'll be no more oxygen left to breathe inside the bag, she is going to die . . .

"No, cunt," he says, and takes the bag from her head and sticks his cock in her mouth.

She is actually grateful for the cock. She will accept a cock any day of the week over a freezer bag on her head, accept the one in her mouth and the one in her hand and the one in her vagina—she always thinks of it as her vagina, it is her *vagina*, thank you, same as the vagina on a lady in London. So happy is she that the freezer bag isn't on her head anymore, she will even accept black Richard's big shlong again, if he would like to bring it over right this minute. But no, black

Richard seems content to be lying there in the corner all huddled up, watching television. She wonders if she should yell over to him that this preppie son of a bitch tried to scare her a minute ago by putting a freezer bag over her head.

"Cocksucker," the preppie says.

And pulls the bag over her head again.

Steaming cardboard containers of coffee in their hands, the detectives climbed the six stories to the roof of Santiago's building, opened the fire door, and stepped outside. The city almost caught them by surprise. They almost found it beautiful. They stood by the parapet, sipping their coffees, staring down at the lights spread below them like a nest of jewels. Darkness was fading fast. On the far side of the roof, they could hear the gentle cooing of Santiago's pigeons. They walked over to the coop.

The perching pigeons were hunkered down inside their grey and white overcoats.

The floor of the coop was covered with feathers and shit.

Santiago was nowhere in sight.

The time was 6:53.

In three minutes, Yolande would be dead.

The preppie whose cock was in her hand a minute ago now has her by the right wrist, and the one who was fucking her has hold of her left wrist, and now they all join in the fun, the three Richards, two of them keeping her pinned down, the third one making sure the bag is in place over her head and tight around her neck. She is going to die, she knows she is going to die. She knows that in a minute, in thirty seconds, in two seconds, she will run out of breath and . . .

"No, bitch."

And yanks off the bag, and sticks his cock in her mouth again.

This is a game for them, she thinks. She hopes. Only a game. Put the bag on, take the bag off. They have read someplace that depriving a person of oxygen heightens the sexual pleasure. She hopes. But then why are they calling her cunt and bitch and cocksucker and shitface, why is one of them pushing . . .

"No!" she screams, but it is too late, he has already shoved it inside her, what*ever* it is, hurting her, tearing her, no, please, and now the plastic bag is on her head again, and she hears over the ringing in her ears black Richard from across the room mumbling, "Hey, man, whut's . . . ?" and she screams inside the bag, *tries* to scream inside the bag, and she hears black Richard yelling, "The fuck you *doin*?" and she thinks *Help*! and she screams "Help!" inside the bag, and this time she *knows* she is going to die, this time the pain below is so overwhelming, why is he *doing* this to her, twisting something jagged and sharp inside her, she is going to *die*, please, she *wants* to die, she can't breathe, she can't bear it a moment . . .

"*No*, cunt!" he shouts, and yanks the bag from her head.

The rush of oxygen is so sweet.

She feels something sticky and wet on her lips.

She thinks this will be the end of it. They will leave her alone now. She hurts too badly. She is too torn and

106

ragged below, she knows she is hemorrhaging below. Please, she thinks. Just leave me alone now. Please. Enough.

"You guys crazy?"

Richard.

Good, she thinks. This is the end of it.

But the bag is over her head again.

And they are holding her down again.

They were back in the car maybe two or three minutes when they caught a 10-29 to proceed to 841 St. Sebastian Avenue. The dispatcher wouldn't call this a homicide for sure because all she had was a dead body in the alleyway there and nobody yet knew what the cause of death was. Could've been a heart attack there in the alley. So she told them the blues had a corpse there, and mentioned that she had also notified Homicide just in case, which is how Monoghan and Monroe got into the act for the second time that night.

The time was a quarter past seven, the sun was just coming up, sort of. This wasn't going to be any rosy-fingered dawn, that was for sure. This was just the end of another hard day's night, the shift almost having run its course, except that now they *did*, as it turned out, have another homicide on their hands. The freezer bag over the girl's head told them that.

The girl looked like a hooker, but nowadays it was difficult to separate the wheat from the chaff. You got Hollywood starlets showing up at the Academy Awards wearing dresses that made them look like streetwalkers, but you also got bona fide prosties standing on the corner looking like apple-cheeked college girls from Minnesota, so who was to say for sure?

"A hooker," Monoghan said.

"For sure," Monroe said.

"Prolly her pimp done her," Monoghan suggested.

"That's why her handbag's gone."

Which was keen deduction. Carella figured if he hung around long enough, he might learn something. He was wondering why, if this *had* been a pimp, the guy hadn't simply stabbed her. Or shot her. Why get fancy? Why a freezer bag over her head? It was obvious that someone, pimp or whoever, had dragged her into the alley. She was lying on her back in a sticky pool of coagulating blood, but bloody smears led to the curb, where the track seemed to have begun. Had someone driven her here, and then dragged her to where she now lay beside a bank of garbage cans and stacks of black-bagged garbage?

"She might have been pregnant," Monroe speculated. "All that blood."

"Nowadays, people kill you so they can tear the baby out of your belly," Monoghan said.

"It's ancient times all over again," Monroe said.

"There's no civilization anymore," Monoghan said.

"Fucking *savages* nowadays," Monroe said, with more feeling than Carella had ever thought he'd possessed.

In the dim light of a cold grey dawn, the girl's face under the plastic freezer bag was as white as the ice on the alley floor.

* * *

108

They had wrapped her in the sheet before carrying her down to black Richard's car, and then had driven a mile uptown on St. Sab's, where they'd dragged her into the alley still wrapped in it. But black Richard knew cops had ways of *tracing* sheets and shit, and he'd convinced the others to roll her out of it before they left her there by the garbage cans, rats big as cats running all over the alley, made him shiver all over again just to think of them.

Fuckin honkies wanted no part of him once they'd used his car to drop the bitch off, but he reminded them it wasn't him had suffocated her, wasn't *him* had torn her open, was three fuckin *rich* guys named *Richard*, from a school named *Pierce* Academy, which was stitched on the front of all they fuckin P parkas the fuckin football on the back, dig? So either they helped him clean up the car and the apartment and get rid of the bloody sheet, or whut *he* was gonna do, ole *black* Richard here, was run straight to the cop shop. They believed him. Maybe cause he also showed them a switchblade knife bigger than any of they dicks and tole them he was gonna circumscribe them real bad if they tried to split on him now.

Ended up they'd tidied up the apartment like four speed queens come to work from a cleaning service. Weren't no car washes open this time of night, day, whatever the fuck, and Richard didn't want to go to no garage, neither, blood all over the backseat that way, he never knew anybody could bleed that bad. He remembered a movie he'd seen one time, blood and shit all over a car from a shootin inside it, this wasn't like that, but there was plenty blood, anyway, and he didn't know any big-shot gangster he could call to come set it straight. All he knew was these honkies had better help him or they name was shit.

In movies and on television, blacks and whites were all pals and shit, that was all make-believe. In real life, you never saw blacks and whites together hardly at all. In that movie where the guy's brains were spattered all over the car, this black guy and this white guy were two contract hitters tighter'n Dick's hatband. But that was make-believe, callin each other "nigger" and all that, black guy callin the white guy "nigger," white guy callin the nigger "nigger" right back, break his fuckin *head* any white man called Richard "nigger," never mind that movie bullshit! Was a *white* man wrote that movie, the fuck he knew about black folk?

What was *real*, my friend, was equality never *did* come to pass here in this land of the free and home of the brave, wasn't no black man ever trusted a white man and vice versa, *never*. Richard didn't trust these three white bastards and they didn't trust him, either, but they *needed* each other right now cause a girl had been killed in his apartment and *they* were the ones killed her. The white guys, not him. But it was his apartment, don't forget that. Cops had a way of never forgettin little black mishaps like that, fuckin cops.

So this was what you might call strange bedfellows here, which was what it actually *was* called in a book Richard read one time. Oh, he was literate, man, don't kid your fuckin self. Read books, saw movies, even went to see a play downtown one time had all blacks in it about soldiers. His opinion blacks were the best actors in the world cause they knew what *sufferin* was

110

all about. That movie with the brains all over the car, was the *black* guy shoulda got the Cademy Award, never mind the white guy.

So here they were, the four of them, three white guys didn't know *shit* about anything, and one black guy teachin them all about survival here in the big bad city. Thing they didn't know was that soon as they cleaned up his car and got rid of the sheet they'd wrapped the bitch in, he was gonna stick it to them good.

The girl's name was Yolande Marie Marx. Her fingerprints told them that. She had a B-sheet not quite as long as her arm, but long enough for a kid who was only nineteen. Most of the arrests were for prostitution. But there were two for shoplifting and half a dozen for possession, all bullshit violations when she was underage that had got her off with a succession of slaps on the wrist from bleeding-heart judges. When she turned eighteen, she finally did three months at Hopeville, some name for a female correctional facility. She worked under the name Marie St. Claire, which alias was on the record. Her pimp's name was there, too.

The shift had changed without them.

At fifteen minutes to eight, give or take, the eight-man team of detectives on the day shift had relieved six of the detectives on the morning shift, but not Carella and Hawes, who were still out in the field. They were there, instead of home in bed, because maybe they had something to go on in the murder of Yolande Marie Marx. Her death might never make newspaper headlines; she was not Svetlana Dyalovich. Even if they caught whoever had brutally slain her, her murder would never result in anything more than brief media mention. But they had the name of her pimp. And the man had a substantial record, including an arrest for a New Orleans murder some ten years ago, for which he had done time at Louisiana's Angola State Penitentiary. He was now gracing *this* city with his presence; a policeman's lot was not a happy one.

Especially not at eight in the morning, when Carella and Hawes knocked on Jamal Stone's door and four bullets came crashing through the wood even before they announced themselves.

"Gun!" Hawes shouted, but Carella had already hit the deck, and Hawes came tumbling down immediately afterward. Both men lay side by side in the hallway outside the door now, breathing hard, sweating heavily despite the cold, heads close together, guns in their hands.

"Guy's a mind reader," Hawes whispered.

Carella was wondering when the next shots would come.

Hawes was wondering the same thing.

The door opened, surprising them.

They almost shot him.

"Who the fuck are *you*?" Jamal asked.

What it was—or so he explained in the second-floor interrogation room up at the old Eight-Seven—he was expecting someone else, was what it was. Instead, he got two policemen breaking down the door. Crack of dawn. Two cops.

112

"You always shoot at people who knock on your door?" Hawes asked.

"Only when I expect them to shoot *me*," Jamal said.

This was now beginning to get interesting. In fact, Bert Kling was almost happy they'd asked him and Meyer to sit in on the interrogation. It was still early enough on the shift to enjoy a cup of coffee with colleagues who'd been out in the freezing cold all night long. But aside from the camaraderie, and the bonhomie, and the promise of some entertainment from a man who'd been around the block once or twice and who felt completely at home in a police station, the doubling-up was a way of bringing them up to speed on one of the two squeals Carella and Hawes had caught during the night.

There used to be a sign on the squadroom wall (before Detective Andy Parker tore it down in a fit of pique) that read: IT'S YOUR CASE! STICK WITH IT! The Dyalovich murder and the Marx murder did indeed belong to Carella and Hawes as the detectives who'd caught them. But they would not be on duty again until 11:45 tonight and meanwhile there were two long eight-hour shifts between now and then. In police work, things could become fast-breaking in the wink of an eye; briefing the oncoming team was a ritual these men observed more often than not.

Jamal figured the two new cops for the brains here. The ones asking the questions were the ones almost got themselves shot, so how smart could they be? But the big bald-headed guy—his ID tag read DET/2ND GR MEYER MEYER, must've been a computer glitch—looked smart as could be. The tall blond guy

113

with the appearance of a farm boy, DET/3RD GR BERT KLING, was probably the one played Good Cop to the bald guy's Bad Cop when they were working some cheap thief. Right now, though, both of them were as still as coiled snakes, watching, listening.

"Who were you expecting to shoot you?" Carella asked.

This was all vamping till ready. They didn't actually *care* who wanted to shoot him, good riddance to bad rubbish, as Carella's mother was fond of saying. All they really wanted to know was whether Jamal was the one who'd put that freezer bag over Yolande's head. Toward that end, they would let him talk forever about all his real or imagined enemies out there, make him feel comfortable, ply him with cigarettes and coffee, wait for him to reveal through word or gesture that he already *knew* why he was here being questioned by a pair of detectives, which no one had yet told him, and which he hadn't yet asked about, either. Which might or might not have meant something. With experienced felons, it was difficult to tell.

Jamal puffed on his cigarette.

Meyer and Kling watched him.

Their presence was a bit unsettling. He was beginning to wonder if they were cops from headquarters or something. What kind of thing *was* this, two cops from headquarters here observing? But he knew better than to ask why he was up here. Too easy to step into shit that way. So he puffed on his cigarette and sipped at his coffee and told them all about this Colombian crack dealer who thought he'd stole some shit from him, which he hadn't, but who let the word out that he was looking for him and was going to kill him. So when he heard somebody banging on the door eight o'clock in the morning, the sun hardly up, he figured he'd better make the first move here because there might not *be* no second move. Which is why he'd pumped four through the door. Then, not hearing a sound out there, he figured he'd nailed whoever had done the knocking, and he opened the door expecting to find Manuel Diaz bleeding on the floor—

"That's his name, Manuel Diaz, I just gave you something."

As if they didn't already know the names of all the dealers in most of the precincts up here.

"But instead it was you two guys, who I almost shot, by the way, before you yelled 'Police.' " Jamal shrugged. "So here we are," he said.

"Here we are," Hawes agreed.

Jamal still knew better than to ask what this was all about. The big bald guy and the tall blond guy were both looking very stern now, as if he'd said something wrong a minute ago. He wondered what it could have been. Fuck em, he thought. I can wait this out as long as you can. He lit another cigarette. Meyer nodded. So did Kling. Jamal wondered why they were nodding. These two guys were making him very nervous. He felt relieved when Carella asked another question.

"Who was the girl with you?"

"Friend of mine," Jamal said.

Carlyle Yancy was one of the two girls he ran. Her real name was Sarah Rowland, which he'd changed for her the minute he put her on the street. Jamal wasn't about to discuss either her profession or his. "Friend of mine" covered a lot of territory.

"How old is she?" Hawes asked. This also covered a lot of territory. Cops always asked how old a girl was, figuring you'd wet your pants if she was underage.

"Twenty," Jamal said. "No cigar."

"What's she do?"

"What do you mean, what's she do?"

"Is she a prostitute?"

"Hey, come on. What kind of question is that?"

"Well, Jamal, considering your record . . ."

So that's how they'd got to him. But why? And calling a man by his first name was an old cop trick Jamal knew quite well, thank you.

"I haven't been in that line of work for a long time," he said.

Meyer raised an eyebrow. He was wondering how being a pimp qualified as work. So was Kling. *And* Carella. *And* Hawes. Jamal read their faces and figured them for a bunch of cynics.

"How about murder?" Carella asked. "Have you been in *that* line of work recently?"

"I paid my debt to society," Jamal said with dignity.

"So we understand. Released last April, is that right?"

"That's right. The slate is clean."

Still with dignity.

"What have you been doing since?"

"Different kinds of work."

"Different from pimping?" Hawes asked.

"Different from murder?" Carella asked.

"Just different jobs here and there."

"Here and *where*?"

"Here in the city."

"Lucky us," Hawes said.

"What *kind* of different jobs?" Carella asked.

They were harassing him now. Trying to put him on edge. He knew it and they knew it. He remained unruffled. He'd been involved with cops ever since he was twelve. Wasn't a cop in the world could rattle him now.

"Drove a taxi, drove a delivery truck, worked as a waiter," he said. "Odd jobs like that."

"By the way," Hawes said, "we have another B-sheet here," and turned it so Jamal could see the name typed across the top of it. MARX, YOLANDE MARIE, and below that, in parentheses, alias MARIE ST. CLAIRE.

"Know her?" Carella asked.

If they had her B-sheet, they knew he was pimping for her. Was she in some kind of trouble again? The last time she'd shoplifted, he told her he'd break both her legs she ever brought down heat again. Whatever this was, he figured it was time to play it straight.

"I know her," he said.

"You're her pimp, right?"

"I know her."

"How about the pimp part?"

Jamal nodded, shrugged, wagged his head, waggled his fingers, all intended to convey uncertainty, they guessed. They looked at him silently, waiting for elaboration. He was wondering what Yolande had done *this* time. Why had they punched up her B-sheet? He said nothing. Wait them out, he thought. Play the game.

"When did you see her last?" Hawes asked.

"Why?" Jamal said.

"Can you tell us?"

"Sure, I can tell you. But why?"

"Just tell us, okay?"

"I drove her down by the bridge around ten o'clock."

"Put her on the street at ten?"

"Well . . . yeah."

"Which bridge?"

"The Majesta Bridge."

"What was she wearing?"

"Little black skirt, fake-fur jacket, black stockings, red boots, red handbag."

"See her after that?"

"No. Is she in jail?"

The detectives looked at each other. As Yogi Berra once said, "When you come to a crossroads, take it." They took it.

"She's dead," Carella said, and tossed a photograph onto the desk. The photo had been taken in the alley on St. Sebastian Avenue. It was a black-and-white picture with the address of the crime scene camera-lettered in white at the bottom of the picture, the date and time in the right-hand corner. Jamal looked at the picture. So that was it. Dead hooker, you go to her pimp.

"So?" Hawes said.

"So, I'm sorry. She was a good kid. I liked her."

"Is that why you put her on the street in her underwear last night? Twelve fuckin degrees out there, you *liked* her, huh?"

"Oh, did she *freeze* to death?" Jamal asked.

"Don't get smart," Hawes warned.

"Nobody twisted her arm," Jamal said. "What was it? An overdose?"

"You tell us."

"You think *I* did her? What for?"

"Where were you around seven this morning?"

"Home in bed."

"Alone?"

"No, I was with my friend. You saw her. That's who I was with."

"Carlyle Yancy, is that her name?"

"That's what she told you, isn't it?"

"Is that her real name?"

"She's never been busted, forget it."

"What's her real name?"

"Sarah Rowland."

"We'll check, you know."

"Check. She's clean."

"From what time to what time?" Carella asked.

"What do you mean?"

"Was she with you."

"She got home around three-thirty. I was with her from then till you came busting down my door. We were waiting for Yolande, in fact."

"We'll check that, too, you know."

"She'll tell you."

Meyer turned to Carella.

"You looking for a bullshit gun bust?" he asked.

"I'm looking for a murderer," Carella said.

"Then go home, there's nothing but a 265.01 here." He turned to Jamal.

"You, too," he said. "We'll keep the piece, thanks."

6

When you pull the boneyard shift, you quit work at eight, nine in the morning, sometimes later if a corpse turns up in your soup. Say you're lucky and you get home at nine, nine-thirty, depending on rush-hour traffic. You kiss the wife and kiddies, have a glass of milk and a piece of toast, and then tumble into bed by ten, ten-thirty. After a few days, when you've adjusted to the day-for-night schedule, you can actually sleep through a full eight hours and wake up feeling refreshed. This would put you on your feet again at six, six-thirty in the evening. That's when you have your lunch or dinner or whatever you might choose to call it at that hour. You're then free till around eleven P.M. At that time of night, it shouldn't take more than half an hour, forty-five minutes to get to the precinct.

While you're asleep or spending some time with your family or friends, the precinct is awake and bustling. A police station is in operation twenty-four hours a day, seven days a week, every day of the year. That accounts for its worn and shoddy apple-green look. Criminals never rest; neither does a police station. So while Carella and Hawes slept, the day shift worked from 7:45 in the morning to 3:45 in the afternoon, when the night shift took over. And while Carella was having dinner with Teddy and the twins, and Hawes was making love with Annie Rawles, the night shift learned some things and investigated some things but only some of these had to do with their two homicide cases.

During the hours of nine-fifteen that Sunday morning, when Carella and Hawes left the squadroom, and eleven forty-five that night, when they reported back to work again, things were happening out there.

They would learn about some of these things later.

Some of these things, they would never learn about.

At nine-thirty that Sunday morning, two of the Richards were in the empty lot across the street from the abandoned produce market, waiting for the other two Richards to come back with fresh pails of water. They had done a good job of cleaning the trunk of the black Richard's car, but now they wanted to make sure there weren't any bloodstains anyplace else. The other two had gone for fresh water and fresh rags at a car wash some three blocks away, under the expressway. This part of Riverhead was virtually forlorn at nine-thirty on a Sunday morning. Hardly a car passed by on the overhead expressway. Empty window frames with broken shards of glass in them stared like eyeless sockets from abandoned buildings. The sun was shining brightly now, but there was a feel of snow in the air. Richard the Lion-Hearted knew when snow was coming. It was a sense he'd developed as a kid. He hoped snow wouldn't screw up what he had in mind. He was telling Richard the Second how he saw this thing.

"The girl dying was an accident," he said. "We were merely playing a game."

"Merely," Richard the Second said.

121

"She should've let us know if she was having difficulty breathing."

"That would've been the sensible thing to do."

"But she didn't. So how were we to know?"

"We couldn't have known."

"In a sense, it was her own fault."

"Did you come?" Richard the Second asked.

"Yes, I did."

"I didn't."

"I'm sorry, Richard."

"Three hundred bucks, it would've been nice to come."

"I think *he* took the money, you know."

Who?"

"Richard. Took her money *and* the jumbos he'd given her earlier. Nine hundred bucks and ten jumbos. You didn't see her bag anywhere around, did you? When we carried her down to the car?"

"No, I didn't, come to think of it."

"I'm sure he stole her bag with the money and the jumbos in it. Which is how we're going to tie him to this thing."

"Tie him to what thing?"

"The girl's accident. Yvonne. Whatever her name was."

"Claire, I think her name was. I wish I could've come before she passed out."

"Well, that was her fault."

"Even so."

"We have to find that bag, Richard."

"Which bag is that?"

"It's not in the car, I looked. It has to be in his apartment."

"Which bag, Richard?"

"The one with the money and the jumbos in it. Once we find it, we can link him to the accident."

"How?"

"If he stole the bag, his fingerprints'll be on it."

"He might've wiped them off."

"They only do that in the movies. Besides, he wouldn't have had time. We were all of us together, don't you remember? Wrapping her in the sheet, getting her downstairs into the trunk? He wouldn't have had time."

"She was heavy."

"She was."

"She looked so small. But she was heavy."

"Deceptive, yes."

"I still don't understand about the bag."

"What don't you understand?"

"How will it link him to the accident?"

"Well, his *prints* are on it."

"Yes, but . . ."

"The prints will *link* him to it."

"But if we go to the police with her bag . . ."

"No, no, no, we can't do that."

"Then what?"

"We leave it alongside the body."

"You think it's still there? She's probably in the morgue by now, don't you think?"

"I'm not talking about *her* body, Richard."

* * *

Paul Blaney was trying to determine which had come first, the chicken or the egg. Had the white female corpse on his autopsy table suffocated to death, or had her death been caused by severe hemorrhaging from the genital area? He had already determined that there was a sizable amount of cocaine derivative in the girl's bloodstream. The girl had not died of an overdose, that was certain, but the detectives nonetheless would want to know about the presence of the drug, which could mean that the murder was drug-related—so what else was new? He wasn't confident that the detectives would care a whit whether she was so badly injured below that she had bled to death or whether the bag over her head had caused her to suffocate. But it was Blaney's job to determine cause of death and to establish a postmortem interval.

He was not paid to speculate. He was paid to examine the remains and to gather the facts that led to a scientific conclusion. Suffocation in his lexicon was described as "traumatic asphyxia resulting when obstructed air passages prevent the entrance of air into the lungs." But if the girl had suffocated, then where were all the telltale signs? Where was the cyanosis of the face, the blue coloration he always found somewhat frightening, even after all these years of performing autopsies? Where were the small circular ecchymoses on the scalp, those tiny bruises indicative of strangulation, smothering, or choking? Where were the minute blood spots in the whites of the eyes? Lacking any of these certain indications, Blaney cut open the girl's chest.

* * *

What black Richard was thinking as he lugged the water back from the car wash was he would go to the police and tell them these four rich kids from a prep school in Massachusetts someplace, Connecticut, wherever, a school named Pierce Academy—stitched right there on the front of their parkas—these three rich white football players had come to him to see did he have any dope to sell, which of course he did, you all *know* I deal a little dope every now and then, who's kidding who here? I'm not here to lie to you, gents, I'm here to help you.

Cops lookin at him like Sure, the nigger's here to help us. Started as a mere clocker in the hood, and now he's dealing five, six bills a day, he's here to help us. Get lost, nigger.

Hey, no. I seen these boys do a *murder*.

Ah?

Ears perkin up now.

"What're you smiling at?" Richard the Third asked. Hulking along in his blue parka with the big white P on the back, little football right under the P, carrying two pails of water, same as black Richard himself. Both of them with clean rags from the car wash stuffed in they pockets. Shagging along under the expressway. If it was nighttime stead of mornin right now, they could both get killed, this neighborhood.

"Whut I'm thinking," Richard said, "is soon as we finish here, you go your way, I go mine."

And never the twain shall meet, he thought.

"It was a shame what happened to the girl," the other Richard said.

"Mm."

"But it wasn't our fault."

"Sure as shit wasn't *my* fault, Richard thought. *You* were the ones holdin her down, doin her with the bag. Which is why I'll feel safe goin to the police. By then, my car be all spic-and-span, my apartment clean as a whistle, my bedsheets burned to ashes along with all the rags we used. Get *that* little bonfire started soon as we finish with the car. Watch it all go up in smoke. Then kiss the boys goodbye and go straight to the cops.

"Still," the other Richard said, "I feel sort of sorry for her."

Oh, man, you don't *know* how sorry you gonna feel, Richard thought. Cause what I'm goan do is *sell* you to the police. I'm going to trade you ass for money, white boy, whatever the traffic will bear. Cause this is going to be a *big* bust, three rich white kids from a fancy prep school suffocating a white *hooker*? Oh, this is a *dream* bust, cops up here in the asshole of the universe would *kill* for a bust like this one, never mind just layin out three, four large from a slush fund they keep handy for hot information like this. Might be worth even *five* grand, information like this, three rich white kids? I can see the motherfuckin cops salivatin.

Just got to keep clear of it, is all.

Keep myself out of it.

Make it plain I had nothin to do with it.

I only *seen* them do it.

Which, anyway, is the truth.

"I wish you'd stop smiling that way," Richard said. "You look like a hyena."

Oh yes, Richard thought.

* * *

126

There was something that kept troubling Jamal about the picture the cops had shown him. Well, sure, Yolande being *dead* and all, that was very troubling. Laying on her back there in the alley, skirt hiked up over all that blood on the inside of her legs, plastic bag over her head, that was troubling. To see her that way. Beautiful young girl, dead that way. Man, you never knew.

But there was something *else* troubling him about that picture and he didn't realize what it was until he was back in the apartment again, telling Carlyle all about his encounter with The Law.

"Thing they do," he said, "they tries to wait me out, like I don't know they got some *reason* to have me up the *prec*inc, like I'm some dumb nigger fum Alabama visitin Granma the big city. They finey gets aroun to Yolande . . ."

"Are you telling me she's dead?" Carlyle asked.

Sitting at the kitchen table eating one of the croissants he'd brought back from the All Right Bakery on the Stem. Sipping coffee the color of her skin. Café au lait was what you could call Carlyle Yancy, who was Sarah Rowland when he first met her fresh and sassy at nineteen. Twenty years old now, a fire-cracker pussy and a dedicated crack addict, thank you, Jamal Stone.

"Yes, she is dead," Jamal said, affecting a pious tone and a mournful look. Carlyle kept eating her buttered croissant. She appeared thoughtful for a moment, bad failing for a hooker. You never wanted them to start thinking about the perils of the occupation. But then she gave a slight shrug and took another bite of the croissant. Jamal went back to his tale of Derring-Do in the Face of Imminent Arrest and Incarceration.

"They had these two big dudes from headquarters there, I knew this was something big even before they brung up Yolande's name. Then they lays her B-sheet on me, and asts when I seed her last and whut she was wearin an all that shit, and they thows a disgustin pitcher of her dead in a alley on St. Sab's, bleedin from her snatch."

"Urgh," Carlyle said, and bit into the croissant again.

"Yeah," Jamal said, "with a plastic bag over her fuckin head."

Carlyle got up and went to the stove. She was wearing just this little silk wrapper he'd got her from Victoria's Secret, floral design on it, all lavender looking, and high-heeled bedroom slippers, she looked as delicious as any of the croissants on the table. Man, he loved this girl. Yolande had been a good money-maker, but this one he loved. Even if she never again made a dime for him, he'd keep her and take care of her. Well, maybe. He watched her as she poured more coffee into her cup. Watched her tight little ass, actually. Wouldn't care if she never brought home a *nickel*, this one.

Which was when he realized what was wrong with the picture the cops had shown him.

"The bag," he said.

Carlyle turned from the stove, puzzled.

"Yolande's bag. That red bag she has."

"The patent leather," Carlyle said, nodding.

"She was carryin it last night."

Carlyle sipped at her coffee.

"But it wasn't in the pitcher."

"What picture?"

"The one they showed me. Ain't them crime scene pitchers spose to show *jus* how everything was?"

"I don't know."

"They can't touch nothin before they take they pitchers, can they?"

"I don't know."

"So where was the bag?"

"Whoever done her must've taken it," Carlyle said.

"Yeah, with *my* fuckin money in it," Jamal said.

He started making his calls at ten minutes past ten.

"Hello," the recorded voice said, "welcome to the Mayor's Action Center, the front door to city government. If you are calling from a touch-tone phone and you want to continue in English, press One."

He had dialed 300-9600, and now he pressed One.

"We aim to guide you if you don't know where to go, to listen thoughtfully to your opinions, and to help you if you have a problem. We can't promise to always solve what's wrong, but we can promise to do our best. By pressing selected buttons on your phone, this twenty-four-hour-a-day service can answer many of your questions without your speaking to an operator. It also allows you to leave your opinion of city policies. To speak directly to one of our representatives between the hours of nine and five, press Zero at any time. However, if you choose this option, please understand that you may need to hold for a while."

He chose the option.

He pressed Zero.

"You will experience a slight delay on the transfer. Please do not hang up."

He did not hang up.

"Hello, you have reached the Mayor's Action Center. All service representatives are currently serving clients. Your call will be handled by the next available representative. Please make sure that you have all the materials relevant to your request available. Please provide as much detail as possible so that we can serve you promptly."

He waited for exactly thirty seconds.

"All service representatives are still busy. Please continue to hold for the next available representative."

He waited another thirty seconds.

The same announcement repeated itself.

He waited again.

Five minutes of utter silence. Then:

"Mayor's Action Center. How may I help you?"

"Hello, my name is Randolph Hurd? To whom do I speak about noise pollution?"

"What kind of noise pollution?"

"The honking of horns in the vicinity of the Hamilton Bridge. Which I believe is against the law *anywhere* in the city."

"The honking of *what*?"

"Horns. Car horns, taxicab horns, truck horns . . ."

"You want Environmental Protection. Let me give you the number there."

She gave him the number.

337-4357.

He dialed it.

"This is the Department of Environmental Protection. If you are calling about a water or sewer problem, air or noise pollution . . ."

Good, he thought.

". . . asbestos or hazardous materials, please hold. Our customer service agents handle calls in the order they come in, twenty-four hours a day. We will get to your call as quickly as possible. Thank you for waiting."

He waited for a minute or so.

"All of our agents are still busy," the recorded voice said. "would you please continue to hold?"

The announcement repeated itself a moment later.

And then there was silence for two or three minutes.

"Environmental Protection," a man's voice said.

"Hello," Hurd said, "I'd like some information about noise pollution?"

"What type of noise pollution?"

"The honking of automobile horns? Taxis, trucks, cars? In the vicinity of the Hamilton Bridge?"

A silence. Then:

"*What* type of noise is that again?"

"Horns. Taxicab horns, truck . . ."

"You want the Taxi and Limousine Commission," the man said. "That's 307-8294."

He dialed the number.

"This is the Taxi and Limousine Commission," a recorded voice said. "If you are calling from a touch-tone phone, press One for further information."

He pressed One.

"If you are calling to report a complaint, press One. If you are calling regarding property left in a taxi, press Two. All other inquiries, press Three."

He had a complaint.

He pressed One.

"All complaints must be made in writing," a recorded voice advised him, and then went on to give him an address to which he could write.

"To return to the main menu," the recorded voice said, "press Eight."

He pressed Eight.

He listened to the options again. "All other inquiries" suddenly sounded very good. He pressed Three. A recorded voice said, "If you are calling for licensing or owner information, press One. If you have a question about a hearing, summons, or appeal, press Two. If you have an inquiry regarding driver medallion renewal . . ."

He thought it over for a moment, figured that what he most certainly wanted was a hearing of *any* kind, and pressed Two. There were yet more recorded options. Did he want to reschedule a hearing? Did he want to check his subpoena status? Did he . . . ?

"If you are calling regarding an appeal," the recorded voice said, "press Four."

He pressed Four.

"Please remain on the line. There will be a brief moment of silence."

He felt as if he were standing at the Tomb of the Unknown Solider.

He waited.

The brief moment of silence passed.

"Appeals," a voice said.

"Are you a recording?" he asked.

"No, sir, I am a person."

"God bless you," he said, and eagerly told her that he wasn't calling regarding an actual *appeal* as such, but that he just wanted to talk to a human being who might be able to give him some information about motor vehicles blowing horns in the vicinity of the . . .

"You want Public Affairs," she said. "That's 307-4738."

"Is that still the Taxi and Limousine Commission?"

"Yes, sir, it is."

"Thank you," he said, and dialed the number.

"Public Affairs," a man's actual voice said.

He was on a roll.

"Sir," he said, "is it against the law for taxicabs to blow their horns?"

"Except in an emergency, yes, sir," the man said. "It's part of the Vehicle and Traffic Law."

"Are taxi drivers *told* it's against the law?"

"They're supposed to know it, yes, sir."

"But who informs them? Is the information in a booklet or something?"

"They're supposed to familiarize themselves with the law, yes, sir."

"How?"

"They're supposed to know it, sir."

"Well, they don't seem to be too familiar with it."

"Do you have a complaint about a taxi driver blowing his horn, sir?"

"I have a complaint about ten *thousand* of them blowing their horns!"

"11,787, sir," the man corrected. "But if you have a *specific* taxi in mind, you can call 307-TAXI with your complaint."

"I don't have a specific taxi in mind."

"Then you should call DEP-HELP. They'll be able to take a nonspecific complaint."

He hung up, and immediately dialed DEP-HELP, realizing an instant too late that this was in reality 337-4357 . . .

This is the Department of Environmental Protection. If you are calling about a water or sewer problem, air or noise pollution, asbestos or hazardous materials, please . . ."

He waited through two more announcements telling him that everyone was busy, and finally he got a live customer service agent. He explained that he wanted to make a nonspecific complaint about the honking of horns in the vicinity of the Hamilton Bridge between the hours of . . ."

"The honking of *what*?"

"Horns. Car horns, taxi horns, truck horns."

"And you say you wish to make *what* kind of a complaint?"

"Nonspecific. I've just been informed it's against the law, and that you would take my complaint."

"I don't know if it's against the law or not. If you want a copy of the Noise Pollution Rules, you can send four dollars and seventy-five cents to this address, have you got a pencil?"

"I don't want a copy of the rules. The Taxi and Limousine Commission just told me the honking of horns is against the Vehicle and Traffic Law."

"Then you want Traffic," the agent said. "Let me give you a number."

She gave him a number and he dialed it. The line was busy for four minutes. Then a voice said, "Customer Service."

"Hello," he said, "I'm calling to complain about the honking of horns . . ."

"You want Traffic," the woman said.

"Isn't *this* traffic?"

"No, this is Transit."

"Well, have you got a number for Traffic?"

She gave him a number for traffic. He dialed it.

"Hello," he said, "I'm calling to complain about the honking of horns in the vi—"

"We only take complaints for traffic lights and streetlights."

"Well, to whom do I talk about . . . ?"

"Let me give you Traffic."

"I thought this *was* traffic."

"No, I'll switch you."

He waited.

"Department of Transportation."

"I'm calling to complain about the honking of horns in the vicinity of. . ."

"What you want is the DEP."

"I want the what?"

"Department of Environmental Protection. Hold on, I'll give you the number."

"I have the number, thanks."

He called Environmental Protection again. All agents were busy again. After a wait of some six minutes, he got someone on the phone and told her

135

about his problem all over again. She listened very patiently.

Then she said, "We don't take auto horns."

"Are you telling me that the Department of Environmental Protection can't do anything about *noise* pollution?"

"I'm not saying there's *no* one here can do anything about it," she said. "All I'm saying is *we* don't take auto horns."

"Well, isn't the honking of auto horns considered noise pollution?"

"Not in this department. Day construction, night construction, all that kind of stuff is what we call noise pollution."

"But not horn honking?"

"Not horn honking."

"Even though it's against the law?"

"I don't know if it's against the law or not. You can check that with your local precinct."

"Thank you," he said.

He looked up the number for the precinct closest to the Hamilton Bridge. The 87th Precinct. 41 Grover Avenue. 387-8024. He dialed it.

A recorded voice said, "If this is an emergency, hang up and dial 911. If this is not an emergency, hang on and someone will be with your shortly."

He hung on.

"Eighty-seventh Precinct, Sergeant Murchison."

He went straight for the jugular.

"The honking of automobile horns is against the law," he said. "Isn't that true?"

"Except in an emergency situation, yes, sir, that very definitely is true."

Good, he thought.

"But it's a law that's extremely difficult to enforce," Sergeant Murchison said. "Because, sir, we can't pinpoint who's *doing* the actual honking, do you see, sir? Where the honk is *coming* from, do you see? If we could find out who was actually *leaning* on his horn, why, we'd give him a summons, do you see?"

He did not mention that standing on the corner of Silvermine and Sixteenth, listening to the infernal, incessant cacophony of horns, he could without fail and with tremendous ease pinpoint *exactly* which cabdriver, truck driver or motorist was doing the honking, sometimes for minutes on end.

"What if he gets a summons?" he asked.

"He goes to court. And gets a fine if he's found guilty."

"How much is the fine?"

"Well, I would have to look that up, sir."

"Could you do that, please?"

"You mean right now?"

"Yes."

"No, I can't do that right now, sir. We're very busy here right now."

"Thank you," he said, and hung up.

He sat with his hand on the telephone receiver for a very long time, his head bent. Outside, the noise was merciless. He rose at last, and went to the window, and threw it wide open to the wintry blast and the assault of the horns.

"Shut up," he whispered to the traffic below. "Shut up, shut up, shut up, shut up, shut up, shut up, shut *up*!" he shouted.

Ten minutes later, he shot and killed a cabdriver who was blowing his horn on the approach ramp to the Hamilton Bridge.

The car looked as if it had just come out of the showroom. Black Richard had never seen it looking so good. He told the three rich white fucks they should go into the car wash business together. They all laughed.

In an open bodega not far from the car wash, they bought a can of starter fluid and then found a soot-stained oil drum that had already been used for fires a hundred times before. This neighborhood, when it got cold the homeless gathered around these big old cans, started these roaring fires, sometimes roasted potatoes on a grate over them, but mostly used them just to keep warm. It was warmer in the shelters, maybe, but in a shelter the chances were better of getting mugged or raped. Out here, standing around an oil drum fire, toasting your hands and your ass, you felt like a fuckin cowboy on the Great Plains.

They started the fire with scraps of wood they picked up in the lot, old newspapers, picture frames without glass, wooden chairs with broken legs, a dresser missing all of its drawers, curled and yellowing telephone directories, broomstick handles, whatever they could find that was flammable. On many of the streets and roadways in this city, in most of the empty lots, the discarded debris resembled a trail left by war refugees. When the fire was roaring and crackling, they threw in the bloody sheets and rags, and then stirred them into the flames with a broomstick, Richard the First intoning, "Double, double toil and trouble," Richard the Second chiming in with "Fire burn and cauldron bubble," which black Richard thought was some kind of fraternity chant.

They stayed around the oil drum till everything in it had burned down to ashes. Well, not everything. Still some wood in there, turning to charcoal, beginning to smolder. But anything they were worried about was now history. No more bloody sheets, no more bloody rags. Poof. Gone.

"Time to celebrate," Richard the First said.

The man sitting at Meyer Meyer's desk was named Randolph Hurd. He was a short slender man, almost as bald as Meyer himself, wearing a brown three-piece suit and a muted matching tie, brown shoes, brown socks. An altogether drab man who had killed a cabdriver in cold blood and been apprehended by a traffic cop before he'd taken six steps from the taxi. The tagged and bagged murder weapon was on Meyer's desk. Hurd had just told Meyer about all the phone calls he'd made this morning. Brown eyes wet, he now asked, "Isn't horn-blowing against the law?"

There were, in fact, *two* statutes against the blowing of horns, and Meyer was familiar with both of them. The first was in Title 34 of the Rules of the City, which rules were authorized by the City Charter. Title 34 governed the Department of Transportation. Chapter 4 of Title 34 defined the traffic rules. Chapter 4, Subsection 12(i) read:

Horn for danger only. No person shall sound the horn of a vehicle except when necessary to warn a person or animal of danger.

The penalty for violating this rule was a $45 fine.

The second statute was in the City's Administrative Code. Title 24 was called Environmental Protection and Utilities. Section 221 fell within Chapter 2, which was called Noise Control, within Subchapter 4, which was called Prohibited Noise and Unnecessary Noise Standards. It read:

Sound signal devices. No person shall operate or use or cause to be operated or used any sound signal device so as to create an unnecessary noise except as a sound signal of imminent danger.

The fines imposed for violating this statute ranged from a minimum of $265 to a maximum of $875.

"Yes, sir," Meyer said. "Horn-blowing is against the law. But, Mr. Hurd, no one has the right to take . . ."

"It's the cabbies and the truck drivers," Hurd said. "They're the worst offenders. All of them in such a desperate hurry to drop off a fare or a precious cargo. Other motorists follow suit, it's contagious, you know. Like a fever. Or a plague. Everyone hitting his horn. You can't imagine the din, Detective Meyer. It's ear-splitting. And this flagrant breaking of the law is carried on within feet of traffic officers waving their hands or policemen sitting in parked patrol cars. Something should be done about it."

"I agree," Meyer said. "But Mr. Hurd . . ."

"*I* did something about it," Hurd said.

Meyer figured it was justifiable homicide.

* * *

Priscilla Stetson thought she was keeping Georgie Agnello and Tony Frascati as sex toys. Georgie and Tony thought they were taking advantage of a beautiful blonde who liked to tie them up and blindfold them while she blew them.

It was a good arrangement all around.

Anybody came near her, they would break his head. She was theirs. On the other hand, they were hers. She could call them whenever she needed them, send them home whenever she tired of them. It was an arrangement none of them ever discussed for fear of jinxing it. Like a baseball pitcher with a natural fast-breaking curve. Or a writer with a knack for good dialogue.

At eleven o'clock that Sunday morning, they were all having breakfast in bed together when Priscilla mentioned her grandmother.

Georgie and Tony hated eating breakfast in bed. You got crumbs all over everything, you spilled coffee all over yourself, they hated it. Priscilla was between them, naked, enjoying herself, drinking coffee and eating a cheese Danish. The boys, as she called them, had each and separately eaten her not twenty minutes ago, and they were waiting now for her to reciprocate in some small way, which she showed no sign of doing just yet. She did this to show the boys who was boss here. On the other hand, they occasionally beat the shit out of her, though they never hurt her hands or her face. Which she sometimes enjoyed, depending on her mood. But not very often.

It was all part of their arrangement.

142

Like the suite the hotel provided on the nights she played. That was another arrangement. It wasn't the presidential suite, but it went for four-fifty a night, which wasn't litchi nuts. They were in the suite now, which had been named the Richard Moore Suite after the noted Alpine skier who had stayed here back in the days when he was winning gold medals hither and yon, the Richard Moore Suite at the Hotel Powell, Priscilla naked between them, drinking coffee and munching on her cheese Danish, Georgie and Tony wearing nothing but black silk pajama tops and erections, trying not to spill coffee or crumbs on themselves. After breakfast, and after she had taken care of them, *if* she decided to take care of them, they might do a few lines of coke, who could say? Priscilla had connections. Georgie and Tony liked being kept in this state of heightened anticipation, so to speak. Priscilla liked keeping them there. She might decide to send them home as soon as she finished the second pot of coffee room service had brought up, who could say? Out, boys. I have things to do, Sunday is my day off. Or maybe not. It depended on how she felt ten minutes from now.

"I *know* she had money," she said out loud.

The boys turned to look at her. Bookends in black silk. The sheet lowered to their waists, Priscilla sitting there naked, breasts exposed. The boys made sly eye contact across her.

"Your grandmother, you mean?" Georgie asked.

Priscilla nodded. "Otherwise, why'd she keep saying I'd be taken care of?"

143

"How about taking care of *this* a little?" Tony asked, and glanced down at the sheet.

"She the one lived in the rat hole on Lincoln Street?" Georgie asked.

"Take care of *this* a little," Tony said, impressed by his earlier witty remark.

"She meant when she *died*," Priscilla said. "I'd be taken care of when she *died*."

"How?" Georgie said. "She didn't have a pot to piss in."

"I don't *know* how. But she said she'd take care of me."

"Take care of *this* a little," Tony said again.

"Maybe she had a bank account," Priscilla suggested.

"Maybe she left a will," Georgie said.

"Who knows?"

"Maybe she left you millions."

"Who knows?"

Tony was thinking these two had just escalated an old lady's empty pisspot into a fortune. "There are two old people in a nursing home," he said. "The man's ninety-two, the woman's ninety. They start a relationship. What they do, he goes into her room, and gets in bed with her, and they watch television together with his penis in her hand. That's the extent of the relationship. She holds his penis in her hand while they watch television."

"Don't you ever think of anything else?" Priscilla asked.

"No, wait, this is a good one. The woman is passing her girlfriend's room one night—she's ninety years old, too, the girlfriend—and lo and behold, what does she see? Her man is in bed with the girlfriend. They're watching television, she's holding his penis in her hand. The woman is outraged. 'How can you do this to me?' she wants to know. 'Is she prettier than I am? Is she smarter than I am? What has she got that I haven't got?' The guy answers, 'Parkinson's.'"

"That's sick," Priscilla said, laughing.

"But funny," Tony said, laughing with her.

"I don't get it," Georgie said.

"Parkinson's," Tony explained.

"Yeah, Parkinson's, Parkinson's, I *still* don't get it."

"You shake," Priscilla said.

"What?"

"When you have Parkinson's."

"She's jacking him off, "Tony explained.

"So what was the *other* one doing?"

"Just holding him in her hand."

"I thought *she* was jacking him off, too."

"No, she was just holding him in her hand," Tony said, and looked across at Priscilla. "Which is little enough to ask," he suggested pointedly.

"I'll bet all that money is still in her apartment," Priscilla said.

At that moment, a knock sounded on the door to the suite.

Jamal knew something the cops didn't know and that was where Yolande had been at what time. She had called him around five-thirty in the morning, told him she was just leaving the Stardust and would be home soon as she caught a cab. He'd asked her what the take was and she said close to two large, and he told her to hurry on home, baby, Carlyle's already here, we'll wait up for you. So from the Stardust to the alley on St. Sab's and First would've taken five, ten minutes at most, which would've put her uptown at twenty to six, a quarter to six, depending on how long it took her to find a taxi. Never mind the time in the corner of the picture: 07:22:03. All Jamal knew was that Yolande had been there almost an hour and a half *before* that. But who'd been there with her?

Jamal knew the nighttime city.

He knew the people who frequented the night.

He kissed Carlyle goodbye and went out into the glare of a cold winter morning.

He didn't have to go very far.

Richard the First had bought six bottles of Dom Pérignon, and he and all the other Richards had already consumed three of them by eleven-ten that morning. Or at least that's what black Richard thought. What he didn't know was that the other three Richards weren't drinking at all, but were instead laughing it up while one or the other of them took a walk to the bathroom, back and forth, emptying glass after glass of champagne behind his back, dumping down the toilet bubbly that had cost $107.99 a fifth.

The idea was to get Richard drunk.

The idea was to drown him.

What the bellhop delivered to Priscilla's suite was a plain white envelope with her name written on the front of it. She recognized her grandmother's frail

146

handwriting at once, tipped the bellhop a dollar, and immediately tore open the flap of the envelope.

A key was inside the envelope.

The accompanying notes in her grandmother's hand, read:

My darling Priscilla,

Go to locker number 136 at the Rendell Road

Bus Terminal.

your loving grandmother,

Svetlana.

Priscilla went to the phone, picked up the receiver, and dialed the front desk.

"This is Priscilla Stetson" she told an assistant manager. "A letter was just delivered to me?"

"Yes, Miss Stetson?"

"Can you tell me who left it at the desk?"

"A tall blond man."

"Did he give you his name?"

"No, he just said to be certain it was sent up to your suite. Sort of."

"What do you mean sort of."

"Well, he had a very heavy accent."

"What kind of accent?"

"I have no idea."

"Thank you," Priscilla said, and hung up.

"What the hell is this?" she asked aloud. "A spy movie?"

The white man who approached Jamal the moment he came out of his building was named Curly Joe Simms,

147

and he ran book up here in Diamondback. Jamal knew him because every now and then he would exchange a girl for a horse, so to speak, asking Curly Joe to lay two bills on a nag as an even swap for an hour with one of his girls. Jamal never ran more than two girls at any time. And nobody underage, thanks. He knew the law escalated from a class-A mis to a class-D felony if a person promoted "prostitution activity by two or more prostitutes" or "profited from prostitution of a person less than nineteen years old." He figured a judge might go easier on him if he didn't have say, five, six girls in his stable, ha ha. Anyway, even two girls were a handful, and to tell the truth, he got tired of them pretty soon and was always on the lookout for fresh talent.

Curly Joe was bald, of course, and he was wearing earmuffs on this frighteningly cold morning, his hands in the pockets of a brown woolen coat buttoned over a green muffler, his eyes watery, his nose red. He had not been waiting for Jamal, but when he spotted him coming out of his building, he walked right over.

"Jahm," he said. "It's me."

Jamal recognized him at once, and figured he was looking for a piece of ass.

"How you doin, man?" he said.

"Good, how you been?"

"I'm survivin," Jamal said.

"Cold as a fuckin witch's tit, ain't it?"

"Cold," Jamal agreed.

"Was that your girl last night?" Curly Joe asked. "Got herself juked on St. Sab's?"

"Yeah," Jamal said cautiously.

"I thought I recognized her from that time."

"Yeah."

"What a shame, huh?"

"Yeah."

"How'd she get all the way down there?"

Jamal looked at him.

"What do you mean?" he asked.

"Cause I seen her up here not long before," Curly Joe said.

"What do you mean?" Jamal asked again.

"Musta been six or so in the morning. I was in the diner havin a coffee. She got out of a taxi."

Jamal waited.

"You know Richie Cooper?"

"I know him," Jamal said.

"She went off with him and three young kids were pissing in the gutter. I seen them from the diner."

He had finally passed out, and they were dragging him into the bathroom where they had filled the tub with water. Not passed out entirely cold, but so sklonked he couldn't walk or even stand, didn't know what the hell was happening to him, just kept waving one arm in the air like a symphony conductor except that he was singing "I Want to Hold Your Hand" as they dragged him across the floor by the ankles. Something fell out of his pocket, the switchblade knife he'd threatened them with earlier tonight. Richard the First stooped to pick it up, jammed it in the pocket of his own jacket. He was sweating heavily. They were about to kill someone, but this had to be done. The girl had been an accident, but this was murder, but it had to be done. They all knew that. The three Richards were now *one*

149

Richard acting in concert, dragging yet another Richard into the bathroom where the tub full of water waited.

The water looked brownish, this city.

Richard the Third was the strongest of them, he grabbed black Richard under the arms, while the other two each grabbed a leg. "One . . . two . . . three," he said, and they hoisted him off the floor and swung him into the tub.

"Hey!" he yelled.

Too late.

Jamal knew Richard as a dope dealer pulled down what, five, six bills a day, maybe a thou when business was good and the cotton was high. Used to be in trade together many a moon back, before Jamal tipped to the fact that dealing was a hazardous occupation whereas living off the sweat and toil of the female persuasion was less strenuous and nowhere near as dangerous.

What puzzled Jamal now was what Yolande had been doing with Richard and three white dudes at six this morning, *directly* after she'd phoned to say she was on the way home. Had Richard decided to do a little freelance pimping on his own? In which case he had to be taught about territorial imperative and not stepping on a fellow entrepreneur's toes. Or had Yolande and Richard decided to share an early morning breakfast with the three honkies? In which case, what had happened to the red patent-leather handbag containing—by Yolande's own admission on the phone—close to two thousand dollars?

Teaching Richard a lesson was no longer necessary now that Yolande was dead.

Recovering that handbag with the money in it was of prime importance, however, and it was memory of that bag and anticipation of what was in that bag that propelled Jamal up the steps two at a time to Richard's third-floor apartment.

The time was three minutes to noon.

He started fighting the minute they threw him in the tub. He didn't know how to swim and the first thing that entered his mind was that he had somehow fallen into a swimming pool and was going to drown.

Only the second half of this supposition was true.

Jamal was thinking if Richard didn't hand that bag over the minute he asked for it, he was going to beat him senseless.

No cyanosis.

No bruises on the galea of the scalp.

No punctate hemorrhages in the conjunctivae.

And now no dark red fluid blood in the heart, or excess serous fluid in the lungs.

Ergo, no suffocation.

Considering the way she had bled, Blaney wondered if the girl had died from a botched abortion.

If the Pro-Lifers—a hypocritical designation if ever he'd heard one, and don't send me letters, he thought—had scared her away from seeking help at any of the city's legal clinics, perhaps she'd found a back-alley butcher to do the job or, worse yet, maybe

151

she'd tried to do it herself. Too many desperate women attempted tearing the fetal membrane to release the amniotic fluid, thereby causing uterine contractions and expulsion of the fetus. They used whatever long thin object they could find, not just the coat hanger depicted in the Pro-Choice propaganda— and don't *you* write to me, either, he thought—but also umbrella ribs and knitting needles.

Blaney was a doctor.

He felt the best and only place to perform a gynecological procedure was in a hospital.

Period.

By a trained physician.

Period.

But here in the silence of the morgue, there were no moral or religious judgments to be made, no political agendas to be met.

There was only search and discovery.

How had the girl died?

Period.

Blaney found no fetus, nor any fetal parts, in the girl's genital tract or peritoneal cavity. Moreover, after he had measured the thickness, length and width of the uterus, the density of the uterine wall, the length of the uterine cavity, the circumference of both the internal and external vaginal openings, and the length of the lower part of the uterus, he found no indication that the girl had been pregnant before her death. Nor was there any indication that the vaginal vault had been accidentally punctured while she'd been seeking to abort herself, unsurprising in that there had been nothing to abort.

What he found instead was a massive assault on the uterus by a sharp instrument with a saw-toothed edge. The instrument had passed through the cervix, wreaking havoc in its relentless wake, and had ripped through the abdominal cavity where it caused hugely significant damage; Blaney found eighteen inches of the small intestine severed and hanging in the uterus. The pain would have been excruciating. Hemorrhaging would have been profuse. The girl could have died within minutes.

Which might have been a blessing, he guessed.

Only one of the three Richards knew he had just for the fun of it inserted a bread knife with a serrated blade into the girl's vagina. The other two didn't know such a thing had happened although later they saw a lot of blood running down the inside of her legs and figured it was the black guy with his big shlong had hurt her somehow. Even the one who'd experimented with the knife didn't realize this was what had killed her. He figured the bag over her head had done it, the girl's stupidity in not informing them that the game had gone too far. She should have told them. No one had wanted her dead.

Every one of them wanted black Richard dead.

Black Richard was their link to the dead girl, who had died by accident, after all, and for whom they most certainly were not about to ruin their lives, all three of them accepted at *Harvard*? Hey.

So as Richard thrashed around in the tub, trying to keep his head above water, the three other Richards kept forcing him back under again, time after time, avoiding his pummeling fists, trying not to get themselves all wet, trying just to for Christ's sake *drown* him.

They were succeeding in doing just that, Richard finally succumbing to their overpowering insistence, subsiding below the surface of the water, hands unclenching at last, a final thin bubble of air escaping his mouth and rising, rising, when a voice behind them yelled, "The fuck you *doin*?"

They were each and separately, all three Richards, overwhelmed by a powerful feeling of déjà vu all over again, a black man standing there with outraged surprise on his face, only this time Richard the First had a knife, and he snapped the blade open at once because the last thing on earth they needed was yet another *asshole* linking them to a murder.

Jamal remembered too late what his sacred mother had taught him about the streets of this here city, and that was Mind yo own business, son, an stay out of harm's way. But this wasn't a city street, this was the bathroom of a onetime business associate and sometime friend, and he was being drowned in a bathtub by three fuckin college boys, or whatever they were, and one of them had a knife in his fist and he was coming at Jamal with a tiny little smile on his face. It was then that Jamal knew this was serious. Man with a big mother knife in his hand and a smile on his face was dangerous. But, of course, all of this was too late, the memory of his mother's admonition, the memory of smiles he had seen on the faces of other would-be assassins, of whom there were far too many in this part of the city in this part of the world.

Smiling, Richard the First slashed Jamal's jugular with a single swipe of the blade, and then dropped the knife as if it were on fire.

The other two Richards went pale.

And now it became the tale of a handbag.

The door to Svetlana Dyalovich's apartment was padlocked and a printed CRIME SCENE notice was tacked to it. But Meyer and Kling had obtained a key from the Property Clerk's Office, and they marched right in.

"What a dump," Meyer said.

"Smells, too," Kling said.

"Cat piss," Meyer agreed.

A pair of uniformed cops had already delivered the old lady's dead cat to the Humane Society for cremation, but Meyer and Kling didn't know that, and besides the apartment still stank. They *did* know that Carella and Hawes, and presumably the technicians from the Mobile Crime Unit, had conducted a thorough search of the apartment. But this morning Carella had suggested that they might have missed something—namely a hundred and twenty-five thousand dollars in cash—and another run-through might be a good idea.

They both thought about that kind of money for a moment.

A hundred and twenty-five thousand was about a third more than their combined annual salaries.

It was a sobering thought.

They began looking.

* * *

There was a dead man in the bathtub and another dead man on the bathroom floor. One of them had been drowned, and the other's throat had been slit. This almost had comic possibilities. Too bad the one bleeding all over the tile floor wasn't named Richard, too. Then there would have been *five* Richards in the apartment instead of just four, three of whom were running around looking for a red patent-leather bag. The fourth one wasn't doing any running at all. The fourth one would never do any running ever again. Nor swimming, either, which he'd never learned to do, anyway. None of the live Richards knew who the other dead man was, and they were squeamish about going through his pockets for identification. Slitting a man's throat was one thing. Frisking him was quite another.

Richard the First knew the girl's handbag had to be in this apartment someplace. It didn't have *legs*, did it? She herself had carried it up here, and they themselves had carried her out of here without it. So where the hell was it? He was eager to find that bag because it contained traveler's checks with their signatures on them, and these could all too easily link them to the dead girl, and by extension the man they'd drowned and the one whose throat they'd slit.

In his mind, the three Richards had acted and were still acting in concert. No longer was it he alone who'd slit the second black man's throat. Now it was they who'd done it. Just as it was *they* who were now looking for the patent-leather bag that would irrevocably tie them to the girl who'd died by accident because she'd been too reticent to tell them she was having difficulty breathing. An asthmatic shouldn't have been in her profession, anyway, the things unfeeling men asked her to do with her mouth.

Neither of the other two Richards quite shared the first Richard's feelings about the second murder. The *first* murder, of course, was drowning black Richard in the tub, a necessity. The girl had not been murdered; you couldn't count her as a murder victim. All of them firmly believed the girl had died by accident. However, both the second Richard and the third Richard knew damn well that neither of them had slit the black stranger's throat, whoever he may have been and no longer was. Richard the First was solely responsible for *that* little bit of mayhem. So whereas they dutifully turned that apartment upside down, trying to find that elusive handbag, they did so only because they didn't want the dead girl to come back to haunt them. And though neither of them would dare speak such a blasphemy aloud, if push ever came to shove they were quite willing to throw old Lion-Heart here to the lions.

At the end of a half hour's search, they still had not found the bag.

It was now twenty minutes to two.

"Where would *you* be if you were a red patent-leather handbag?" Richard the First asked.

"Where indeed?" Richard the Second asked.

Richard the Third stood in the center of the room, scratching his ass and thinking. "Let's reconstruct it minute by minute," he said. "From when we first met her on the street to when we carried her out of here."

"Oh yes, *let's* do that," Richard the Second said sarcastically. "Two dead *Negroes* in the bathroom,

157

with more of their friends possibly coming to visit, we have *all* the time in the world."

Richard the First hadn't heard anyone using the word "Negroes" in a very long time.

"She definitely had that bag in her hand when she stepped out of the taxi," he said.

"She had it here in this apartment, too," Richard the Third said. "She put the traveler's checks and the jumbos in it. I saw her do that with my own eyes."

"Okay, so where did she put it when we started making love?"

Richard the Second's use of this euphemism startled the other two. He saw their surprised looks and shrugged.

"Does anyone remember?"

No one remembered.

So they started searching the apartment yet another time.

Meyer and Kling were experienced at searching apartments. They knew where people hid money and jewelry. Lots of old people, they didn't trust banks. Suppose you fell down in the bathtub and hurt yourself and nobody found you till you starved to death and were all skin and bones, how could you go to the bank to take your money out? You couldn't, was the answer. Also, if you were an old person and you were squirreling away the bucks to give to your grandchildren, you didn't want a bank account because then there was a record, and Uncle Sam would come in and take almost all of it in inheritance taxes. So what lots of old people did, they kept their money or their jewelry in various hiding places.

Ice cube trays were a favorite. Everybody figured no thief would ever dream of looking for gems in a tray of frozen ice cubes. Except that some cheap writer of detective stories had written a book some time back in which a cheap thief froze diamonds inside ice cubes and now everybody in the world knew about it, including *other* cheap thieves. Meyer and Kling were not thieves, cheap or otherwise, but they did know about the ice cube ploy. So hiding your diamonds in an ice cube tray was a ridiculous thing to do since this was where most burglars looked first thing. Open the fridge door, check out the freezer compartment, *there* you are, you little darlings!

Another favorite hiding place was inside the bottom rail of a Venetian blind, which was weighted, and which had caps on either end of it. You could remove these end caps and slide wristwatches or folded bills into the hollow rail. This worked very nicely, except that every thief in the world knew about it. They also knew that people hid jewelry or money inside the bag on a vacuum cleaner, or at the bottom of a toilet tank, or inside the globe of a ceiling light fixture from which the bulbs had been removed so if anybody threw the switch you wouldn't see the outline of a necklace up there under the glass.

Meyer and Kling tried all of these favorite hiding places.

And found nothing.

So they looked under the mattress.

There was nothing there, either.

* * *

The envelope looked as if it had been through the Crimean War. Perhaps Georgie and Tony shouldn't have opened the envelope, but then again they had been entrusted with the key to locker number 136 at the Wendell Road Bus Terminal, and if Priscilla hadn't wanted them to examine whatever they found in that locker, she should have specifically said so. Besides, the envelope hadn't been sealed. It was just a thick yellowing envelope with the word *Priscilla* written across the front of it, a bulging envelope with a rubber band around it, holding the flap closed.

There was money in the envelope.

Hundred-dollar bills.

Exactly a thousand of them.

Georgie and Tony knew because they took the envelope into the men's room to count the bills.

A thousand hundred-dollar bills.

Which on their block came to a hundred thousand dollars in cold hard cash.

There was also a letter in the envelope.

This didn't interest them as much as the money did, but they read it, anyway, though not in the men's room.

It was Richard the Third who found the bag.

"Bingo!" he yelled.

Where he found the bag was under black Richard's mattress, the dope. Did he think they were so dumb they wouldn't look under the *mattress*, where for Christ's sake everybody in the entire *world* hid things? What he must have done, they figured, was slide it in between the mattress and the bedsprings while they were ripping off the sheets to wrap her in.

Nobody had yet touched the bag.

Richard the Third was still standing beside the bed with his parka on because it was freezing cold in this part of the city unless you turned on a kerosene heater or a coal stove, grinning from ear to freckle-faced ear, holding up the corner of the mattress to reveal the red patent-leather bag nestled there all shiny and flat.

Richard the Second took a pair of gloves from the pocket of his parka and pulled them on with all the aplomb of a surgeon about to perform brain surgery. Gingerly, he lifted the bag from where it rested on the bedsprings. He unsnapped the flap, opened the bag, and reached into it.

There was nineteen hundred dollars in cash in the bag.

Plus the ten jumbo vials black Richard had paid the girl for his piece of the action.

Plus nine hundred dollars in traveler's checks respectively signed Richard Hopper, Richard Weinstock, and Richard O'Connor. They each and separately pocketed the checks at once, and then debated whether or not to leave all the money and crack in the bag, or to take some of it for all the trouble they'd gone through. It was Richard the First who suggested that a good way to extricate themselves *entirely* was to link the dead girl to the two dead men. If they left her handbag in the bathroom, the presence of such a large amount of cash, not to mention the sizable stash of crack, would lend credibility to the police theory that the hooker had been killed in a robbery. Or what he *hoped* would be the police theory.

All three of them went into the bathroom.

Jamal, whose name they didn't yet know, was still lying on his back on the floor with his throat slit. He had stopped bleeding. Black Richard was lying on the bottom of the tub. Richard the Second suggested that they leave the bag open on the floor, with a lot of hundred-dollar bills and a few jumbo vials spread on the tiles, as if the two of them had been fighting over it before they killed each other.

Richard the Third looked puzzled.

"What is it?" Richard the First asked.

"What's the scenario here?"

"Scenario?"

"Yes, how did this *happen*?"

"I see his point," Richard the Second said.

"What point? They were fighting over the bag. They killed each other."

"How can a person stab another person while that person is drowning him?"

"That's *not* how it happened."

"Then how *did* it happen?"

Richard the First thought this over for a moment.

"They were fighting over the bag," he said again.

The other two waited.

"Richard stabbed him, whoever he is."

They still waited.

"Then he got in the tub so he could wash off the blood."

"With his clothes on?"

"He was drunk," Richard the First said. "That's why he got in the tub with all his clothes on. In fact, that's how he *drowned*. He was trying to wash himself, but he fell in the tub. He was *drunk*!"

He looked at the other two expectantly.

"Sounds good to me," Richard the Second said.

"Just might fly," Richard the Third said.

Grinning, Richard the First winked at himself in the mirror over the bathroom sink.

It was snowing when they left the apartment for the bus terminal.

The time was ten minutes past two.

8

Detective/First Grade Oliver Weeks—known far and wide, but particularly wide, as *Fat* Ollie Weeks, though never to his face—got into the act because the two dead bodies were found in an apartment in the Eighty-eighth Precinct, which happened to be his bailiwick.

The discovery was made by a woman who lived on Richard Cooper's floor, who happened to be passing by his door when she saw it standing wide open. She called in to him, and then stepped inside the apartment and saw a mess there, clothes thrown all over every which way, drawers pulled out, and figured somebody's been in there and ripped him off, so she went downstairs to tell the super. This was at seventeen minutes past five, about a half hour after Ollie and his team had relieved the day watch. The super went upstairs with her and found the two bodies in the bathroom and ran right down again to dial Nine-One-One. The responding blues radioed the precinct with a double DOA and Ollie and an Eight-Eight detective named Wilbur Sloat, who sounded black but who was actually a tall, thin blond man with a scraggly blond mustache, rode over there to Ainsley and North Eleventh. They got there at a quarter to six.

Since Ollie was a bigot in the truest sense of the word—that is to say, he hated *everyone*—he was naturally tickled to death to see two of the precinct's more contemptible black specimens dead by their own hands. For such was what it appeared to be at first glance.

"Make either one of them?" Sloat asked.

He was a new detective, and he affected mannerisms and speech he heard on cop television shows. Ollie would have liked it better if Sloat had stayed back in the squadroom, answering telephones and picking his nose. Ollie was a loner. He preferred being a loner. That way, you didn't have to deal with assholes all the time.

The one with his throat slit, he recognized at once as a small-time pimp named Jamal "The Jackal" Stone, formerly known as Jackson Stone before he picked himself a name he thought sounded African. Jamal, my ass. Ollie had recently read in *Newsweek* magazine that forty-four percent of all persons of color in America preferred being called "black," whereas only twenty-eight percent liked to be called "African-American." So why did all these niggers (Ollie's own choice of appellation by a personal margin of one hundred percent) give themselves African names and run around celebrating African holidays and wearing fezzes and robes, what the hell was it?

The way Ollie looked at it, a simple fact of American life was that one out of every three black males was currently enmeshed in the criminal justice system. That meant that thirty-three and a third percent of the black male population was either in jail, on parole, or awaiting trial. So, yeah, if a white guy crossed the street when he saw three black men approaching him, it was because one of them might be

Johnnie Cochran, sure, and another might be Chris Darden, okay, but the third one might be O.J. Simpson.

So here were two dead black men in a bathroom.

Big surprise.

The way Ollie saw it, there were two institutions that should be reinstated all over the world. One of them was dictatorship and the other was slavery.

He told Sloat who the one on the floor was.

"Got himself juked real good," Sloat said.

Juked, Ollie thought. Jesus.

The one in the tub he didn't recognize under all that water, which distorted his good looks. But when the M.E. had him pulled out of the tub so he could examine him, Ollie pegged him at once, an ugly two-bit drug dealer named Richard Cooper, who once broke both a man's legs for calling him Richie. The M.E. wouldn't even *speculate* that the cause of death was drowning, having been burned on a similar call years ago where it turned out a man had been shot before someone shoved his head facedown in a toilet bowl. The one on the floor had definitely been slashed, though, so the M.E. had no trouble determining that the cause of death was severance of the carotid artery.

The two Homicide detectives working the night shift were called Flaherty and Flanagan. Ollie told them he knew both of the victims, one of them by his ugly face, the other by his ugly reputation. Sloat suggested that perhaps they'd got into a fight over the handbag there on the floor, one thing leading to another, and so on and so forth, the same old story.

Same old story, Ollie thought. Fuckin dope's been a detective hardly three months, he's talkin about the same old story.

"A clutch," Flaherty said.

"Well, I don't know whether they were grabbing each other or not," Sloat said. "I'm only suggesting they may have done each other."

Done each other, Ollie thought.

"The bag, I mean," Flaherty said. "A clutch."

"It's called a clutch," Flanagan said.

"The type of bag," Flaherty said.

"A clutch bag."

"A handbag without handles."

"What's that got to do with the price of fish?" Ollie asked impatiently.

"For the sake of accuracy," Flaherty said. "In your report. You should call it a clutch bag."

"A red patent-leather clutch handbag," Flanagan said.

Most Homicide Division detectives favored wearing black, the color of mourning, the color of death. But black suited these two more than it did many of their colleagues. Tall and thin, with pale features and slender waxen hands, the two resembled vampires who had wandered in out of the snowy cold, the shoulders of their black coats damp, their eyes a watery blue, their lips bloodless, their shoes a sodden black. They were both wearing white woolen mufflers, a limp sartorial touch.

"How much money is that on the floor?" Flanagan asked.

"Five C-notes," Sloat said.

C-notes, Ollie thought.

"Don't forget the three jumbo vials," Flaherty said.

"Hey, you!" Ollie yelled to one of the technicians. "Okay to look in this bag now? This clutch bag? This red patent-leather clutch handbag?"

The technician turned off his vacuum cleaner, walked over to where they were standing, and began dusting the bag for latents. The detectives wandered around the apartment, waiting for him to finish.

"No sheets on the bed, you notice that?" Flaherty said.

"What do these people know about sheets?" Ollie said. "You think they have sheets in Africa? In Africa they sleep in huts with mud floors, they have flies in their fuckin eyes day and night, they drink goat's milk with blood in it, what the fuck do they know about sheets?"

"This ain't Africa," Flanagan said.

"And there *still* ain't no sheets on the bed," Flaherty said.

"Looks like somebody really tossed the place," Flanagan said, observing the clothes strewn everywhere, the open dresser drawers and kitchen cabinets, the overturned trash basket.

"Maybe it was an interrupted crib job," Sloat suggested.

"Jamal's a fuckin pimp," Ollie said. "What does he know about burglaries?"

"Which one is Jamal?"

"The one with his tonsils showing."

"Maybe he was the one being burglarized. Maybe he walked in and found the other guy . . ."

"No, the mailbox says Cooper. Who don't like to be called Richie. You gonna take all day with that fuckin *clutch* bag?" Ollie yelled to the technician.

"You can have it now," the technician said, handing it to him.

"What'd you get?"

"Some good ones. Patent's a good surface."

"What do they look like?"

"Smaller ones may be female. The others, who knows?"

"When can I have something?"

"Later today?"

"How much later? I go home at midnight."

"A *quarter* to midnight," Sloat amended.

"Soon as we process them," the technician said.

"Run them through Records at the same time, okay?" Ollie said. "See if we come up roses."

"Sure."

"So what time?"

"What's the rush? *They're* not going anywhere," he said, and glanced toward the open bathroom door, where the police photographer was taking his Polaroids.

"I'm just wonderin what really happened here, is all," Ollie said. "Send me what you get the minute you get it, okay? The Eight-Eight. Oliver Weeks."

"Sure," the technician said, and shrugged and went back to his vacuuming.

"I think what happened here is what the kid *says* happened here," Flaherty said.

Sloat looked flattered.

"They killed each other, right?" Ollie said. He was already beginning to go through the bag the technician had handed him. The *clutch* bag, excuse me all to hell. Looked like some more hundred-dollar bills in here...

"Dude's about to take a bath," Sloat suggested, "he hears somebody coming in the apartment, he immediately grabs for a knife . . ."

"I think the kid's got it," Flaherty said, and beamed approval again.

Fuckin Homicide jackass, Ollie thought. Fourteen hundred in the bag, plus the five on the floor, came to nineteen. Money like that spelled dope or prostitution. More red tops on the bottom of the bag, looked more like a dope thing every minute. He fished out a driver's license with a photo ID on it.

"What've you got?" Flanagan asked.

"Ohio driver's license," Ollie said.

"Out-of-towner," Sloat surmised.

"Probably mugged her, one or the other of them, then got into a fight over the bag."

"When was this?" Ollie asked. "Before he turned the apartment upside down or after?"

"What?"

"Whoever got killed first. Give me the sequence, Wilbur."

He made the name sound like a dirty word.

"Start with the muggin," Flanagan said.

"Cooper mugged her, brought the bag back to his apartment," Sloat said.

"Who's Cooper?" Flaherty asked.

"The one who drowned."

170

From the door, where he was putting on his hat, the M.E. called, "I didn't say he drowned."

"*If* he drowned," Sloat said.

"For all I know, he was poisoned."

Yeah, bullshit, Ollie thought.

"Good night, gentlemen," the M.E. said, and headed downstairs to the snow and the wind.

Ollie looked at his watch.

A quarter to seven.

"So let's hear it, Wilbur," he said.

"I've got an even *better* idea," Sloat said.

"Even better than your *first* one?" Ollie said, sounding surprised.

"They *both* mugged her."

"That's very good," Flaherty said appreciatively.

"Came back here to celebrate. All these empty champagne bottles? They were drinking champagne."

"Got drunk, got wild, started throwing around clothes and stuff," Flanagan suggested.

"I like it," Flaherty said.

"A drunken party," Sloat said. "Cooper goes in the bathroom to run a tub. Jamal comes in after him, and they start arguing about how to split the money."

"Better all the time," Flaherty said.

"Cooper pulls a knife, slashes Jamal. Jamal shoves out at him as he goes down. Cooper falls in the tub and drowns."

"Case closed," Flaherty said, grinning.

Assholes, Ollie thought.

"Hey, you!" he yelled to the technician.

The technician turned off his vacuum cleaner again.

"I want the knife and the champagne bottles dusted. I want every fuckin surface in this dump dusted. I want comparison prints lifted from both those two black shits in the bathroom. I want comparison hairs from their heads, and comparison fibers from their clothes, and I want them checked against whatever you pick up with that fuckin noisy vacuum of yours. Where'd you buy that vacuum, anyway? From a pushcart in Majesta?"

"It's standard departmental issue," the technician said, offended.

"Stand on *this* awhile," Ollie said, and clutched his own genitals with his right hand and then released them at once. "I want to know was there anybody *else* in this dump besides those two ugly bastards in the bathroom. Cause there's nothing I'd like better than to nail *another* son of a bitch up here in Diamondback. You got that?"

The technician was glaring at him.

"I go off at a quarter to twelve," Ollie said. "I want to know before then."

The technician was still glaring at him.

"You got it?" Ollie said, glaring back.

"I've got it," the technician snapped. "You fat tub of shit," he muttered, which he was lucky Ollie didn't hear.

Along about then, Steve Carella was just waking up.

Georgie and Tony had a serious problem on their hands.

"The thing is," Georgie said, "the old lady probably didn't even *remember* putting that money in the locker."

172

"An old lady, *how* old?" Tony asked. "How *could* she remember?"

"You see the envelope it's in?"

The envelope was in the inside pocket on the right-hand side of his jacket. It bulged out the jacket as if he was packing, which he was not. Georgie only carried a gun when he was at the club protecting Priscilla. Carrying a gun was too dangerous otherwise. People would think you were an armed robber or something. Georgie preferred subtler ways of beating the System. Beating thc System was what it was all about. But now, Priss Stetson had in some strange mysterious way *become* the System.

"Even the envelope looks ancient," Georgie said, lowering his voice.

The men were in the bus terminal rcstaurant, eating an early dinner and trying to figure out what to do about this large sum of money that had come their way. The place wasn't too crowded at a little past seven. Maybe a dozen people in all. Black guy and what looked like his mother sitting at a nearby table. Three kids in blue parkas, looked like college boys, sitting at another table across the room. Old guy in his sixties holding hands with a young blonde maybe thirty or forty, she was either his daughter or a bimbo. Two guys hunched over racing forms, trying to dope out tomorrow's ponies.

It had been snowing since two this afternoon. Beyond the restaurant's high windows, sharp tiny flakes, the kind that stuck, swirled dizzily on the air, caught in the light of the streetlamps. There had to be six inches on the ground already, and the snow showed

173

no sign of letting up. Inside the restaurant, there was the snug, cozy feel of people hunched over good food in a safe, warm place. Outside, buses came and went. The hundred thou in the yellowing envelope was burning a hole in Georgie's pocket.

"The question here," he said, "is what is our obligation?"

"Our *moral* obligation," Tony said, nodding.

"*If* the old lady forgot the money was there."

"My grandmother forgets things all the time."

"Mine, too."

"She says it, too. I mean, she *knows* it, Georgie. She says if her head wasn't on her shoulders she'd forget where she put it."

"They forget things. They get old, they forget things."

"You know the story about the old guy in the nursing home?"

"Yeah, you told us."

"No, not that one."

"Parkinson's? You told us."

"No, this is another one. This old guy is in a nursing home, the doctor comes in his room, he says, 'I've got bad news for you.' The old guy says, 'What is it?' The doctor says, 'First, you've got cancer, and second, you've got Alzheimer's.' The old guy goes, 'Phew, thank God I don't have cancer.' "

Georgie looked at him.

"I don't get it," he said.

"The old guy already forgot," Tony explained.

"Forgot what?"

"That he has cancer."

"How can a person forget he has cancer?"

"Cause he has Alzheimer's."

"Then how come he didn't forget he has Alzheimer's?"

"Forget it," Tony said.

"No, you raised the question. If he can forget he has one disease, how come he doesn't forget he's got the *other* disease?"

"Cause then it wouldn't be a joke."

"It isn't a joke, anyway."

"A lot of people think it's a joke."

"If it isn't funny, how can it be a joke?"

"A lot of people think it's funny."

"A lot of people are pretty fuckin *weird*, too," Georgie said, and nodded in dismissal.

Both men sipped at their coffee.

"So what do you want to do here?" Tony asked.

"About the envelope?" Georgie asked, lowering his voice.

"Yeah."

Both of them whispering now.

"Let's say the old lady put it there ten years ago, forgot it was there."

"Then why did she send Priss the key?"

"Who knows why old ladies do things? Maybe she had an apparition she was about to get knocked off."

"Uh-huh."

"Anyway, it doesn't matter either way. The old lady's *dead*, how can she tell Priss what was in that locker?"

"Her note didn't say anything about what was in the locker. All it said was go to the locker, that's all."

"What it said *exactly* was go to locker number one thirty-six at the Rendell Road Bus Terminal."

"Exactly."

"What I'm saying," Georgie said, "is if Priss knew there was a hundred large in that locker, you think she'd have trusted us to come for it?"

"Us? She'd have to be out of her mind."

"Exactly the point."

"What you're saying is she *didn't* know."

"What I'm saying is she *doesn't* know."

Silence. The clink of silverware against coffee cups and saucers. The trill of the black woman's laughter at the nearby table. The buzz of conversation from the college boys on the other side of the room. Other voices. And the loudspeaker announcing the arrival of a bus from Philadelphia at gate number seven. At the center of all this, the core of Tony's and Georgie's thoughtful silence.

"*We're* the only ones who know," Tony said at last.

"So why should we turn it over to her?" Georgie asked.

Tony merely smiled.

The next bus back to school wouldn't be leaving for an hour yet. This gave them plenty of time to work out what in the film industry was called a back story.

What seemed perfectly apparent to them was that the only people with whom they'd had any contact after the bouncer tossed them out of the Jammer were all now dead. This was definitely in their favor. If they hadn't even *talked* to anyone after telling the bouncer to go fuck himself, then there wasn't anyone alive who could say they were uptown in Diamondback getting involved with three people who would later cause trouble for each other, the girl by refusing to mention she was suffocating, the two black drunks getting into a fight over her money and her stash, one of them ending up drowned, the other stabbed, boy.

"What about the cabdriver?" Richard the Second asked.

"Uh-oh, the cabbie," Richard the Third said.

"What about him?" Richard the First said. "He picked us up downtown, he dropped us off uptown. So what?"

Two guys who looked like gangsters in a Martin Scorsese movie were walking past the table, on their way out of the restaurant. The boys lowered their voices, averted their eyes. In this city, it was best to be circumspect. Witness what had happened uptown when they'd got too chummily careless with three people who'd turned out to be unwholesome types.

"See that bulge under his coat?" Richard the Third whispered as soon as the men pushed through the door into the terminal proper. Outside, despite the snow, buses kept coming and going. The two men disappeared in the swirling flakes.

"How'd you like to meet one of *those* guys in a dark alley?" Richard the Second said.

None of the Richards seemed to realize that they themselves were now prime candidates for guys you would not care to meet in a dark alley. Or anywhere else, for that matter. They had killed three people. They qualified. But the odd thing about what had happened was that it now seemed to be something they'd read about or watched on television or seen on a stage or in a movie theater. It simply did not seem to have happened to *them*.

So as they discussed whether or not the cabdriver who'd driven them to Diamondback posed any kind of a threat, they dismissed from their reasoning the *reason* for their concern. They had been sitting in the back of a dark cab, he could not have seen their faces clearly. There had been a thick plastic partition between them and the driver's seat, further obscuring vision. They had placed the fare and a reasonable tip into the little plastic holder that flipped out toward them. The only words that passed between them and the cabbie was when Richard the First told him their destination. Ainsley and North Eleventh, he'd said. The driver hadn't even muttered acknowledgment.

The way Richard the First figured it, and he told this to the other two Richards now, the camel jockeys in this city were involved solely with calculating how many more months they'd have to work here before they saved enough to go back home. This was why they never spoke to anyone. Never even nodded to indicate they'd heard you. Never said thank you, God forbid. They were too busy reckoning the nickels and dimes they'd need to build their shining palaces in the sand.

"He won't be a problem," Richard the First said.

But none of them acknowledged the events that had *followed* that fateful ride uptown. None of them even whispered the possibility that they may have been *seen* by someone as they entered black Richard's building in the company of that unfortunate girl who'd later been too timid or stupid to mention or even indicate

178

that she was having trouble breathing. Acknowledging the *cause* of their concern would concede implication.

No.

The boys were clean.

Their bus would leave in forty-five minutes.

They would be back at school in an hour and forty-five minutes.

Everything there would be white and still and clean.

"Nothing happened," Richard the First said aloud.

"Nothing happened," the other two Richards said.

"Swear," Richard the First said, and placed his clenched fist on the tabletop.

"I swear," Richard the Second said, and covered the fist with his hand.

"I swear," Richard the Third said, and likewise covered the fist.

The loudspeaker announced final boarding of the seven-thirty-two bus to Poughkeepsie.

The boys ordered another round of milk shakes.

Two pieces of significant information came into the squadroom in the final hour of the night shift. Detective Hal Willis, sitting in his shirtsleeves in the overheated room, watching the snowflakes swirling outside, took both calls. The first came at a quarter past eleven. It was from a detective named Frank Schulz who asked to speak to either Carella or Hawes, and then settled for Willis when he said he'd give them the information.

Schulz was one of the technicians who'd examined the Cadillac registered to Rodney Pratt. He informed Willis, by the way, that the limo had already been

179

returned to the owner, receipt in Schulz's possession, did Willis want it faxed over or could Schulz drop it in the mail, the receipt? Willis told him to mail it.

"What we got was a lot of feathers" Schulz said. "Now, I don't know if you're familiar with the difference between down and contour feathers . . ."

"No, I'm not," Willis said.

"Then I won't bother you with an explanation because we're both busy men," Schulz said, and then went on to give a long, erudite dissertation on feather sacks and quills and shafts and barbs and barbules and hooklets and knots, all of which differed in various orders of birds, did Willis happen to see the movie Alfred Hitchcock wrote?

Willis didn't think Hitchcock had written it.

"The determination of which feathers came from what order of bird is important in many investigations," Schulz said.

Like this one, Willis thought.

"I don't know whether the Caddy was being used for any illegal activity, but that's not my domain, anyway."

Domain, Willis thought.

"Suffice it to say," Schulz said, "that the feathers we recovered from the backseat of the car were chicken feathers. The shit is anybody's guess."

"Chicken feathers," Willis said.

"Pass it on," Schulz said.

"I will."

"I know you're busy," Schulz said, and hung up.

The second call came from Captain Sam Grossman some ten minutes later. He told Willis that he'd examined the clothing of the murder victim Svetlana Dyalovich and had come up with nothing of any real significance except for what he'd found on the mink.

Willis hoped he was not about to hear a dissertation on the pelts of slender-bodied, semiaquatic, carnivorous mammals of the genus *Mustela*. Instead, Grossman wanted to talk about fish. Willis braced himself. But Grossman got directly to the point.

"There were fish stains on the coat. Which in itself is not unusual. People get all sorts of stains on their garments. What's peculiar about *these* stains is their location."

"Where were they?" Willis asked.

"High up on the coat. At the back, inside and outside, near the collar. From the location of the stains, it would appear that someone had held the coat in both hands, one at either side of the collar, thumbs outside, fingers inside."

"I can't visualize it" Willis said, shaking his head.

"Have you got a book handy?"

"How about the Code of Criminal Procedure?"

"Fine. Pick it up with both hands, palms over the spine, fingers on the front cover, thumbs on the back."

"Let me put down the phone."

He put down the phone. Picked up the book. Nodded. Put down the book and picked up the phone again.

"Are you saying there are fingerprints on the coat?"

"No such luck," Grossman said. "But the stains at the back are smaller, which might've been where the thumbs gripped it near the collar. And the larger ones inside the coat could have been left by the fingers of each hand."

"So what you're saying . . ."

"I'm saying someone with fish oil on his or her hands held the coat in the manner I just described. Talk to you," he said, and hung up.

Fish oil, Willis thought. And chicken feathers.

He was glad this wasn't his case.

9

"Anything happen while we were gone?" Carella asked.

"Same old shit," Willis said. "How are the roads?"

"Lousy."

The clock on the squadroom wall read eleven-forty P.M. It was twenty minutes to midnight. Cotton Hawes was just coming through the gate in the slatted rail divider that separated the squadroom from the corridor outside. Beyond the steel mesh on the high squadroom windows, it was still snowing. This meant they could add a half hour, maybe forty minutes to any outside visits they made.

"Frozen tundra out there," Hawes said, and took off his coat. Carella was leafing through the messages on his desk.

"Chicken feathers, huh?" he asked Willis.

"Is what the man said," Willis answered.

"And fish stains on the mink."

"Yeah."

"What kind of fish, did Grossman say?"

"I didn't ask."

"You should have. Just for the halibut."

Willis winced.

"Meyer and Kling tossed the piano player's apartment again," he said. "Zilch."

"That means a hundred and twenty-five K is still kicking around someplace."

"For what it's worth, Kling thinks the burglar theory's the one to go with."

"That's why we're looking for whoever stole that gun," Hawes said.

"*If* somebody stole it," Carella said.

"Otherwise, Pratt's our man."

"Alibi a mile long."

"Sure, his wife."

"Gee, detective work is so exciting," Willis said, and put on his hat and walked out.

"Chicken feathers," Carella said.

"What did he say about the shit?"

"Anybody's guess."

"We can dismiss illegal hunting . . ."

"Nobody hunts chickens."

"So that leaves theft from a chicken market."

"Not too many chicken markets around these days."

"Lots of them in Riverhead and Majesta. Some of the ethnics like their chickens fresh-killed. Hangover from the old country."

"Don't Orthodox Jews kill their chickens fresh?"

"You think it was a *dead* chicken in the Caddy?"

"Or chickens. Plural."

"Then how come no bloodstains?"

"Good point. So it was a *live* chicken."

"Or chickens."

"You know how to make Hungarian chicken soup?"

"How?"

"First you steal a chicken."

"Okay, let's say somebody stole a chicken."

"Took it for a ride in the backseat of Pratt's Caddy."

"Would you make that movie?"

"I wouldn't even go *see* that movie."

"But, okay, just for the halibut, let's say somebody was hungry enough or desperate enough to steal a chicken from a chicken market . . ."

"Do pet shops sell chickens?"

"Chicks."

"In January?"

"Around Easter."

"Anyway, a chick ain't a chicken."

"No, this had to be a chicken market."

"How about a petting zoo? Where they have goats and cows and chickens and ducks . . ."

"Do people pet chickens?"

"They *cook* chickens."

"So, okay, first you steal a chicken."

"They also *sacrifice* chickens."

"Voodoo."

"Mm."

Both men fell silent.

It was midnight.

Blue Monday.

And still snowing.

"Let's ask around," Hawes said.

The technician who had thought vile thoughts about Fat Ollie Weeks nonetheless got back to him just as he was leaving the squadroom at a few minutes past midnight. Except for the names on desktop plaques and bulletin-board duty rosters, the squadroom here at the Eight-Eight was an almost exact duplicate of the one at the Eight-Seven, or, for that matter, any other police station in the city. Even the newly constructed

185

buildings began to look shoddy and decrepit with time, an apple-green pallor overtaking them seemingly at once. Ollie looked at the speckled face of the wall clock, remembering that he'd told the tech he wanted the stuff by a quarter to, and thinking he was lucky Ollie was still here, otherwise it would have been his ass. He ripped open the manila envelope and yanked out the report.

No latents at all on the champagne bottles and the knife used to slit the estimable Jamal's throat. No latents on any of the bathroom fixtures or any of the doorknobs in the apartment, either. Meaning that if there had been any other person or persons in the room, then he, she, or they had seen a lot of movies and knew enough to wipe up after themselves. So the only thing they could compare against the corpses' fingerprints—which the tech had dutifully lifted from the two stiffs in the bathroom, copies of which were included in the packet—was the prints on the red patent-leather clutch. The smaller prints on the bag matched the prints of the woman named Yolande Marie Marx, whose Ohio driver's license Ollie had found in the red patent-leather clutch. Apparently, Yolande was now lying in the morgue at Buenavista Hospital; the fingerprints the tech had lifted from her bag identified her as a white, nineteen-year-old shoplifter and prostitute with an arrest record that went back several years. The other prints on the bag matched the late Richie Cooper's. According to the report, Jamal Stone hadn't touched the bag.

Ollie kept reading.

Of hairs, there had been many, and only some of them matched those plucked from the heads of the poor unfortunate victims. Some of the hairs were blond, and they matched samples taken from the head of the dead girl. Fibers vacuumed in the apartment matched fibers from the short black skirt and red fake-fur jacket she'd been wearing at the time of her death.

There were other fibers and other hairs.

There were a significant number of dark blue wool fibers. They did not match any fibers from the clothing of the two victims.

There were red hairs.

And black hairs.

And blond hairs.

Some of them were head hairs.

Some of them were genital hairs.

All of them were hairs from white human beings.

All of them were male hairs.

Three white males, two dead black dudes, and a dead white hooker, Ollie thought, and farted.

El Castillo de Palacios would have been ungrammatical in Spanish if the *Palacios* hadn't been a person's name, which in this case it happened to be. *Palacio* meant "palace" in Spanish, and *palacios* meant "palaces," and when you had a plural noun, the article and noun were supposed to correspond, unlike English where everything was so sloppily put together, thank God. *El Castillo de* los *Palacios* would have been the proper Spanish for "The Castle of the Palaces," but since Francisco Palacios was a person, *El Castillo* de *Palacios* was, in fact, correct even

187

though it translated as "Palacios's Castle," a play on words however you sliced it, English *or* Spanish. And worth repeating, by the way, as were many things in this friendly universe the good Lord created.

Francisco Palacios was a good-looking man with clean-living habits, now that he'd served three years upstate on a burglary rap. He owned and operated a pleasant little store that sold medicinal herbs, dream books, religious statues, numbers books, tarot cards and the like. His silent partners were named Gaucho Palacios and Cowboy Palacios, and they ran a store *behind* the other store, and *this* one offered for sale such medically approved "marital aids" as dildos, French ticklers, open-crotch panties (*bragas sin entrepierna*), plastic vibrators (eight-inch and ten-inch in the white, twelve-inch in the black), leather executioner's masks, chastity belts, whips with leather thongs, leather anklets studded with chrome, penis extenders, aphrodisiacs, inflatable life-sized female dolls, condoms every color of the rainbow including vermilion, books on how to hypnotize and otherwise overcome reluctant women, ben-wa balls in both plastic and gold plate, and a highly popular mechanical device guaranteed to bring satisfaction and imaginatively called Suc-u-lator, in case you missed all this while you were out in the fragrant cloisters reading your vespers.

Selling these things in this city was not illegal; the Gaucho and the Cowboy were breaking no laws. This was not why they ran their store *behind* the store owned and operated by Francisco. Rather, they did so out of a sense of responsibility to the Puerto Rican community of which they were a part. They did not, for example, want a little old lady in a black shawl to wander into the backstore shop and faint dead away at the sight of playing cards featuring men, women, police dogs and midgets in fifty-two marital-aid positions, fifty-four if you counted the jokers. Both the Gaucho and the Cowboy had community pride to match that of Francisco himself. Francisco, the Gaucho, and the Cowboy were, in fact, all one and the same person, and they were collectively a police informer, a stoolie, a snitch, or even in some quarters a rat.

El Castillo de Palacios was in a ratty quarter of the Eight-Seven known as El Infierno, which until the recent influx of Jamaicans, Koreans, Haitians, Vietnamese and Martians had been almost exclusively Puerto Rican, or—if you preferred—"of Spanish origin," which was both clumsy and cumbersome but favored over the completely phony "Latino." On the politically correct highway, both of these categorizing expressions fell far behind the ever-popular (by fifty-eight percent) simple descriptive term "Hispanic." Ten percent of the Hispanics queried didn't care *what* they were called, so long as it wasn't "spic" or late for dinner.

El Infierno meant guess what?

The Inferno.

It was.

Palacios was just closing up when they got there at about twenty past midnight after a snowy fifteen-minute ride crosstown which under ordinary circumstances would have taken five minutes. Palacios wore his black hair in a high pompadour, the way kids used to wear it back in the fifties. Dark brown eyes. Matinee-idol teeth. It was rumored in the Inferno that Palacios had three wives, which—like the tax-fraud violation the police held dangling over his head—was against the law. All of which Hawes and Carella and every other cop in the precinct (and every other human being in the *world*) already knew, but so what? Nobody was counting, and nobody was sending anyone to jail just yet—provided the information was good.

It was.

Symbiosis, Hawes thought.

A nice word and a cozy arrangement.

Hawes sometimes felt the entire world ran on cozy arrangements.

"Ai, *maricones*," Palacios said, "*qué pasa?*"

He knew the cops could send him up anytime they felt like. Meanwhile, he could be friendly with them, no? Besides, *maricon* meant "homosexual," and *maricones* was the plural of that, which he didn't think they knew. They *did* know, but they also knew it was a friendly form of greeting among Hispanic men, God knew why, and God protect any non-Hispanic if *he* used it in greeting.

They got straight to the point.

"Voodoo."

"Mm, voodoo," Palacios said, nodding.

"Anything go down this past Friday night?"

"Like what?"

"Any Papa Legbas sitting on the gate?"

"Any Maîtresse Ezilis tossing their hips?"

"Any Damballahs?"

"Any Baron Samedis?"

"Any chickens getting their throats slit?"

"You know some voodoo, huh?"

"*Un poquito*," Hawes said.

"No, no, *mu*chi*simo*," Palacios said, praising him as extravagantly as if he'd just translated Cervantes.

"So," Carella said, cutting through the bullshit, "anything at all this past Friday?"

"Talk to Clotilde Prouteau," Palacios said. "She's a *mamaloi* . . ."

"A what?"

"A priestess. Well, sometimes. She also conjures. I sell her War Water and Four Thieves Vinegar, Guinea Paradise and Guinea Pepper, Three Jacks and a King, Lucky Dog, jasmine and narcisse, white rose and essence of van van—whatever she needs to conjure. Tell her Francois sent you. *Le Cowboy Espagnol*, tell her."

The three of them were sitting at a table somewhat removed from the piano and the bar, Priscilla trying to control her anger while simultaneously venting it, Georgie and Tony trying to catch her whispered words. This was Sunday night—well, Monday morning already—and Priscilla's night off, but the bar was open and the drinks were free and this was a good quiet place to talk on a Sunday, especially when it was snowing like mad outside and the place was almost empty.

Priscilla was steamed, no doubt about it.

She had been steamed since eight P.M. when the boys finally got back to the hotel with an envelope they'd retrieved from the pay locker at the Rendell

Road Terminal. The envelope had contained a letter that read:

My dearest Priscilla:

In the event of my death, you will have been directed to this locker where you will find a great deal of cash.

I have been saving this money for you all these years, never touching it, living only on my welfare checks and whatever small amounts still come in on record company royalties.

It is my wish that the cash will enable you to further your career as a concert pianist.

I have always loved you.

Your grandmother,

Svetlana

In the envelope, there was five thousand dollars in hundred-dollar bills.

"Five *thousand*?" Priscilla had yelled. "This is a great deal of cash?"

"It ain't peanuts," Georgie suggested.

"This is supposed to take *care* of me?"

"Five grand is actually a lot of money," Georgie said.

Which it was.

Though not as much as the ninety-five they'd stolen from the locker.

"Five thousand is supposed to buy a career as a fucking *concert* pianist?"

She still couldn't get over it.

Sitting here at ten minutes to one in the morning, drinking the twenty-year-old Scotch the bartender had brought to her table, courtesy of the house, Priscilla kept shaking her head over and over again. The boys sympathized with her. Priscilla looked at her watch.

"You know what *I* think?" she asked.

Georgie was afraid to hear what she was thinking. He didn't want her to be thinking that they'd opened that envelope and stolen ninety-five thousand dollars from it. Priscilla didn't notice, but his knuckles went white around his whiskey glass.

He waited breathlessly.

"I think whoever delivered that key went to the locker *first*," she said.

"I'll bet," Georgie said at once.

"And cleaned it out," she said.

"Left just enough to make it look good," Tony said, nodding.

"Exactly," Georgie said.

"Made it look like the old lady was senile or something," Tony said. "Leaving you five grand as if it's a fortune."

"*Just* what he did," Priscilla said.

"Well, it *is* sort of a fortune," Georgie said.

Priscilla was getting angrier by the minute. The very *thought* of some blond thief who couldn't even speak English cleaning out the locker before delivering the

193

key to her! Tony kept fueling the anger. Georgie kept listening to him in stunned amazement.

"Who *knows* how much cash could've been in that locker?" he said.

"Well, after all, five grand is quite a lot," Georgie said, and shot Tony a look.

"Could've been *twenty* thousand in that locker," Tony suggested.

"More," Priscilla said. "She told me I'd be taken *care* of when she died."

"Could've been even *fifty* thousand in that locker," Tony amended.

"There *was* five, don't forget," Georgie said.

"Even a *hundred*, there could've been," Tony said, which Georgie thought was getting a little too close for comfort.

Priscilla looked at her watch again.

"Let's go find the son of a bitch," she said, and rose graciously. Flashing a dazzling smile at the seven or eight people sitting in the room, she strode elegantly into the lobby, the boys following her.

They found Clotilde Prouteau at one A.M. that Monday, sitting at the bar of a little French bistro, smoking. Nobody understood the city's Administrative Code prohibiting smoking in public places, but it was generally agreed that you could smoke in a restaurant with fewer than thirty-five patrons. Le Canard Bleu met this criterion. Moreover, even in restaurants larger than this, smoking was permitted at any bar counter serviced by a bartender. There was no bartender on duty at the moment, but Clotilde was covered by the size limitation, and so she was smoking her brains out. Besides, they weren't here to bust her for smoking in public. Nor for practicing voodoo, either.

A fifty-two-year-old Haitian woman with a marked French accent and a complexion the color of oak, she sat with a red cigarette holder in her right hand, courteously blowing smoke away from the detectives. Her eyes were a pale greenish-grey, accentuated with blue liner and thick mascara. Her truly voluptuous mouth was painted an outrageously bright red. She wore a patterned silk caftan that flowed liquidly over ample hips, buttocks and breasts. Enameled red earrings dangled from her ears. An enameled red pendant necklace hung at her throat. Outside a snowstorm was raging and the temperature was eight degrees Fahrenheit. But here in this small smoky bistro a CD player oozed plaintive Piaf, and Clotilde Prouteau looked exotically tropical and flagrantly French.

"Voodoo is not illegal, you know that, eh?" she asked.

"We know it."

"It is a religion," she said.

"We know."

"And here in America, we can still practice whatever religion we choose, eh?"

The Four Freedoms speech, Carella thought, and wondered if she had a green card.

"Francisco Palacios tells us you sometimes do the ceremony."

"*Pardon*? Do the *ceremony*?"

"*Conduct* the ceremony. Whatever."

195

"What ceremony do you mean?"

"Come on, Miss Prouteau. We're talking voodoo here, and we're talking the lady who implores Papa Legba to open the gate, and who sacrifices . . ."

"Sacrifices? *Vraiment, messieurs . . .*"

"We know you sacrifice chickens, goats . . ."

"No, no, this is against the law."

"But nobody cares," Carella said.

She looked at them.

The specific law Clotilde had referred to was Article 26, Section 353 of the Agriculture and Markets Law, which specifically prohibited overdriving, overloading, torturing, cruelly beating, unjustifiably injuring, maiming, mutilating, or killing any animal, whether wild or tame. The offence was a misdemeanor, punishable by imprisonment for not more than a year, or a fine of a thousand dollars, or both.

Like most laws in this city, this one was designed to protect a civilization evolved over centuries. But cops rarely ever invoked the law to prevent animal sacrifice in religious ceremonies, lest all the civil rights advocates demanded their shields and their guns. Clotilde was now weighing whether these two were about to get tough with her for doing something that was done routinely all over the city, especially in Haitian neighborhoods. Why bother with me? she was wondering. You have nothing better to do, *messieurs*? You have no *trafiquants* to arrest? No *terroristes*? And how had they learned about Friday night, anyway?

"What is it you are looking for precisely?" she asked.

"We're trying to locate a person who may have driven a live chicken to a voodoo ceremony," Hawes said, and felt suddenly foolish.

"I am sorry, but I did not drive a chicken anywhere," Clotilde said. "Live or otherwise. A *chicken*, did you say?"

Hawes felt even more foolish.

"We're trying to find a person who may have stolen a gun from a borrowed Cadillac," Carella said.

This didn't sound any better.

"I did not steal a gun, either," Clotilde said.

"But *did* you conduct a voodoo ceremony this past Friday night?"

"Voodoo is not against the law."

"Then you have nothing to worry about. Did you?"

"I did."

"Tell us about it."

"What is there to tell?"

"What time did it start?"

"Nine o'clock?"

An indifferent shrug. Another drag on the cigarette in its red holder that matched the earrings, the necklace and the pouty painted lips. A cloud of smoke blown away from the two detectives.

"Who was there?"

"Worshipers. Supplicants. Believers. Call them whatever you choose. As I have told you, it is a religion."

"Yes, we've got that, thanks," Hawes said.

"*Pardon*?"

"Can you tell us what happened?"

"Happened? Nothing unusual happened. What is it you think happened?"

We think someone delivered a chicken for sacrifice and stole a gun from the car while he was at it. Is what we think happened, Hawes thought, but did not say.

"Did anyone arrive with a chicken?" Carella asked.

"No. For what?"

"For sacrifice."

"We do not sacrifice."

"What *do* you do?" Hawes insisted.

Clotilde sighed heavily.

"We meet in an old stone building that was once a Catholic church," she said. "But, as you know, there are many elements of Catholicism in voodoo, although our divinities constitute a pantheon larger than the holy trinity. It is my role as *mamaloi* to call upon Papa Legba . . ."

"Guardian of the gates," Carella said.

"God of the crossroads," Hawes said.

"Yes," Clotilde whispered reverently. "As you mentioned earlier, I implore him to open the gate . . ."

". . .*Papa Legba, ouvrez vos barrières pour moi. Papa Legba, où sont vos petits enfants?*"

The gathered faithful in the old stone church close their eyes and chant in response, "*Papa Legba, nous violà! Papa Legba, ouvrez vos barrières pour le laisser passer!*"

"Papa Legba," Clotilde pleads, "open the gate . . ."

"Open the gate," the faithful intone.

"Papa Legba, open the gate . . ."

"So that we may pass through."

Call and response.

Africa.

"When we will have passed . . ."

"We will thank Legba."

"Legba who sits on the gate . . ."

"Give us the right to pass."

The strong African elements in the religion.

And now a girl of six or seven glides toward the altar. She is dressed entirely in white and she holds in either hand a lighted white candle. In a thin, high, liltingly haunting voice, she begins to sing.

"The wild goat has escaped.

"And must find its way home.

"I wonder what's the matter.

"In Guinea, everyone is ill.

"I am not ill.

"But I will die.

"I wonder what's the matter."

Clotilde fell silent. The detectives waited. She drew on the cigarette again, exhaled. Piaf was still singing of unrequited love. "Guinea is Africa," Clotilde explained. She fell silent again, as if drifting back to Haiti and beyond that to Africa itself, to the Guinea in the child's plaintive song, to the Grain Coast and the Ivory Coast and the Gold Coast and the Slave Coast, to the empires of the Fula and the Mandingo and the Ashanti and Kangasi, the Hausa and the Congo. Still the detectives waited. Clotilde drew on the cigarette again, exhaled a billow of smoke, and began speaking in a low, hoarse voice. From the rising smoke of the cigarette and the hypnotic smoke-seared rasp of her voice, the old stone church seemed to materialize again, a young girl in white standing before Clotilde, the priestess sprinkling her hair with wine and oil and water, whitening her eye-lids with flour.

Clotilde blows out the candles.

The faithful are chanting again.

"Mistress Ezili, *come* to guide us!

"If you *want* a chicken,

"We will *give* one to you!

"If you *want* a goat,

"It is *here* for you!

"If you *want* a bull,

"We will *give* one to you!

"But a goat without horns,

"Oh, *where* will we find one . .

"*Where* will we find one . . .

"*Where* will we find one?"

The bar went silent.

Clotilde exhaled another cloud of smoke, blowing it over her shoulder, away from the detectives.

"That is essentially how the ceremony goes," she said. "The faithful call to Ezili until she appears. Usually this takes the form of a woman being mounted. . ."

"Mounted?"

"Possessed, you would say. Ezili possesses her. The goddess Ezili. I left out some things, but essentially. . ."

"You left out the sacrifice," Carella said.

"Well, yes, in Haiti a goat or a chicken or a bull may be sacrificed. And perhaps, centuries ago in Africa, the sacrifice may have been human, I truly don't know. I suppose that's what the goat without horns is all about. But here in America? No."

"Here in America, yes," Carella said.

Clotilde looked at him.

"No," she said.

"Yes," Carella said. "After the oil and the water . . ."

"No."

". . . and the wine and the flour, someone slits the throat of a chicken or a goat . . ."

"Not here in America."

"Please, Madame Proteau. This is where the priestess dips her finger into the blood and makes a cross on the girl's forehead. This is where the sacrifice is placed on the altar and the drumming begins. The sacrifice is what finally convinces Ezili to appear. The sacrifice . . ."

"I am telling you there are no blood sacrifices in our ceremonies."

"We're not looking for a cheap three-fifty-three bust," Hawes said.

"Good," Clotilde said, and nodded in dismissal.

"We're working a homicide," Carella said. "Any help you can give us . . ."

"*Mais, qu'est-ce que je peux faire?*" she said, and shrugged. "If there was no chicken, there was no chicken." She ejected the cigarette stub from the holder, and inserted a new one into its end. Piaf was singing "Je Ne Regrette Rien." Taking a lighter from her purse, Clotilde handed it to Hawes. He lighted the cigarette for her. She blew smoke away from him and said, "There are cockfights all over the city on Friday nights, did you know that?"

The interesting thing about Jamal Stone's yellow sheet was that it listed the names of several hookers in his on-again off-again stables. Among these, and apparently current until her recent demise, was one Yolande Marie Marx, alias Marie St. Claire, who had left behind in the apartment of the dead Richard Cooper her handbag and samples of hair and fibers. Ah, yes, Ollie thought, doing his world-famous W. C. Fields imitation even within the confines of his own mind, a small world indeed, ah, yes. Another one of Stone's current racehorses was a girl named Sarah Rowland, alias Carlyle Yancy, whose address was listed as the very same domicile Stone had inhabited while among the living, ah, yes.

Ollie didn't expect to find a working girl home at this hour of the night. But even the good Lord rested on Sunday (although it was already Monday), so he drove downtown through the snow and into 87th Precinct territory, getting to Stone's block at about a quarter past one, and stopping for a cup of coffee in the open diner before going into Stone's building—smell of piss in the hallway—and then upstairs to the third floor to knock on his door. Lo and behold, and would wonders never, a girl's voice answered his knock.

"Yes, who is it?"

"Police," Ollie said, "sorry to be bothering you so late at night, would you mind opening the door, please?" All in a rush in the hope that she'd just open the goddamn door before she began thinking about a search warrant, and police brutality, and invasion of privacy, and civil rights, and all the bullshit these people up here thought about day and night.

"Just a minute," she said.

Footsteps inside, approaching the door.

He waited.

The door opened a crack, pulled up short by a night chain. Part of a face appeared in the wedge. High-yeller girl looked about nineteen, twenty years old. Suspicious brown eye peering out at him.

"What is it?"

"Miss Rowland?"

"Yes."

"Detective Weeks, Eighty-eighth Squad," he said, and held his shield up to the wedge. "Okay to come in a minute?"

"Why?" she asked.

He wondered if she knew her pimp was dead. News traveled fast in the black community, but maybe it hadn't reached her yet.

"I'm investigating the murder of Jamal Stone," he said, flat out. "I'd like to ask you a few questions."

She knew. He could see that on her face. Still, she hesitated. White cop banging on a black girl's door one o'clock in the morning. Did he think nobody watched television?

"What do you say, miss? I'm trying to help here," he said.

He saw the faint nod. The night chain came off. The door opened wide. She was wearing a short silk robe with some kind of flower pattern on it, black with pink petals, sashed at the waist, black silk pajama bottoms under it, black bedroom slippers with pink pom-poms. She looked very young and very fresh, but he knew in her line of work this wouldn't last long. Not that he gave a shit.

"Thanks," he said, and stepped into the apartment.

She closed the door behind him, locked it, put on the chain again. The apartment was cold.

"Police been here already?" he asked.

"Not about Jamal."

"Oh? Then who?"

"Yolande."

"Oh? When was this?"

"Yesterday. Two detectives from the Eight-Seven."

"Uh-huh. Well, this is about Jamal."

"Do you think they're related?"

"The murders, do you mean?"

"Yes."

"Well, I don't know. You tell me."

"Richie was killed, too," she said. "Isn't that right?"

"He didn't like to be called Richie."

"I didn't know that."

"Yeah. He liked to be called Richard."

The scumbag, he thought.

"Do you think somebody was after all three of them?" she asked.

"Well, I don't know. You tell me."

Ollie often found this effective. Get them speculating, they told you all kinds of things. Sometimes, they speculated themselves right into a Murder One rap. Cause they all thought they were so fuckin smart. Far as he knew, this sweet, innocent-looking doll here had torn open the other hooker and drowned Richard the scumbag and then slashed her own pimp, who the hell knew? These people? Who could tell? So they ask do you think they're related, and do you think somebody was after all three of them, which could all be a pose, the one person you could never trust was anybody.

"All I know is the last time I saw Jamal, he was going out to look for her bag."

"Her bag, huh?"

"This red clutch bag she was wearing when she left here."

"Which was when?"

"Saturday night. Jamal drove her down the bridge."

"Which bridge?"

"The Majesta."

"What time was this?"

"They left here around a quarter to ten."

"What time did Stone get back?"

"Around eleven. He came to pick me up, take me to this party he arranged with some businessmen from Texas."

"How many?"

"The Texans? Three of them."

"Remember their names?"

"Just their first names. Charlie, Joe, and Lou."

"Where was this?"

"The Brill. They had a suite there."

"On Fawcett?"

"Yeah."

"What time did you get there?"

"Jamal dropped me at midnight. I took a cab home."

"When?"

"Three."

"What kind of car did he drive? Stone."

"A Lexus."

"Know where he kept it?"

"A garage around the corner. On Ainsley. Why?"

"Might be something in it, who knows?"

He was thinking dope. There might be dope in the car. Jumbos on the bathroom floor and in the girl's handbag, this might've been a dope thing, who the hell knew, these people.

"You know the license plate number?" he asked.

"No."

"Did they know him at the garage?"

"Oh, sure."

"On Ainsley, you said?"

"Yeah."

"You know the name?"

"No, but it's right around the corner from here."

"Okay. So you say you got back here around three. Was Yolande home yet?"

"No. Just Jamal."

"What time did Yolande get home?"

"She didn't. Next thing we know, two cops are banging down the door."

"When was this?"

"Eight o'clock Sunday morning. Jamal thought it was this crazy Colombian crack dealer who said Jamal stole some bottles from him and he was gonna kill him for it, which Jamal didn't, by the way."

"Didn't steal no crack from him, you mean."

"Right. Still, Jamal popped four caps through the door, thinking it was this crazy buck Diaz, but it was two cops instead."

"Shot at two cops, huh?"

"Yeah."

"Not a good idea."

"Tell me about it."

"Who were they, do you remember?"

"Two guys from the Eight-Seven. One of them had red hair."

"Hawes, was that his name?"

"I don't know."

"What's Diaz's first name? The crack dealer."

"Manny. Manuel, actually. You think he killed them?"

"Well, I don't know. You tell me."

"I think he *coulda* killed Jamal, cause he's crazy, you know, and he thinks Jamal stole some shit from him, which he didn't. But I don't see how that ties in with Yolande or Richie."

"Richard. You know him?"

"Just to say hello."

"He deals, too, you know."

"Yeah."

"You think he might've known this Diaz guy?"

"I don't know."

"So Jamal pops four through the door. . ."

"Yeah."

". . . so naturally they arrest him."

"Yeah."

"Then what?"

"Dragged him out of here."

"How come he was on the street again? How come they didn't lock him up?"

"I guess they figured they didn't have nothing on him."

"How about the gun? He shot at two fuckin cops, they didn't lock him up?"

"He thought it was Diaz."

"Did he have a license for the gun?"

"I think so."

"Guy with a record, they gave him a license?"

"Then maybe not."

"So why'd they let him go?"

"I got no idea."

Ollie was thinking that sometimes a bull shit class-A misdemeanor wasn't even worth taking downtown. This included violations of 265.01, where criminal possession of a firearm could get you a year in prison, which wasn't insignificant even if you behaved yourself and got back on the street in three and a third months.

But this Jamal jerk had popped four at a pair of cops, which should have irked them considerably and caused them to haul his ass downtown toot sweet. Unless they were thinking he'd be more valuable to them outside, lead them to whoever had torn out that dead hooker's insides, who the hell knew? Take a shot at Ollie, first thing you'd be picking up all your teeth, and next thing you'd be downtown waiting for arraignment with your shoes falling off and your pants falling down cause they took away your belt and your shoelaces and your brand-new stolen Rolex.

Or—and this was a possibility—maybe they figured with a murder on their hands and the shift changing, they didn't want to bother with booking and mugging and printing and court appearances on an A-mis where the guy might even walk if he pulled a bleeding-heart black judge. Better to let the shithead walk now, especially since he'd been trying to chill *another* shithead, which maybe next time he'd succeed, and more power to him. There are more things in police work, Horatio, than are dreamt of in your potato patch.

Still, Ollie would ask.

Next time he was up the Eight-Seven, he would ask why they let a nigger in criminal possession of a weapon stroll right out of that li'l ole squadroom, ah, yes, m'dear boys, yes, indeed.

"So Yolande, and Jamal left here about a quarter to ten. . ."

"Yeah."

"And Jamal got back around eleven. . ."

"Yeah."

"And drove you to the Brill."

"That's right."

"And he was here when you got home around three..."

"Three-thirty, it must've been."

"He was home."

"Yes."

"But Yolande never made it."

"No. Which is funny."

"Funny how?" Ollie asked.

"Cause she called to say she was on her way."

"Oh? When was this?"

"Around five-thirty in the morning."

"Called here?"

"Yeah. Told Jamal she was just leaving the Stardust . . ."

"The Stardust? Down on Coombes?"

"Yeah."

"And said she was coming home?"

"Soon as she could catch a cab," Carlyle said.

Bingo, Ollie thought.

10

The uniformed radio motor patrol cops who pulled the taxi to the curb didn't think it was a stolen vehicle or anything because a 10-69 was specifically a noncrime incident. But then why had the dispatcher radioed *all* cars and asked them to stop and detain the taxi bearing this particular license plate? Stop, detain, and report back. That was the message.

So they pulled the cab over and asked the driver for his license and while one of the cops looked it over as if he were intercepting a huge dope shipment from Colombia, the other one radioed home to say they had the perp and what should they do now? The dispatcher asked where they were and told them to sit tight till a Detective Oliver Weeks from the Eight-Eight arrived on the scene. Meanwhile, Max Liebowitz was sitting behind the wheel, wetting his pants.

This was a bleak area of Calm's Point. Liebowitz had just dropped off two suspicious-looking black guys who, it turned out, were stockbrokers getting home late from a party celebrating a multimillion-dollar merger. He didn't like being in this part of the city at a quarter to two in the morning, and he didn't like being pulled over by cops, either—both of *them* black, by the way—especially when they wouldn't tell him what the violation was, and especially since he was losing money sitting here by the side of the road. Eventually a battered Chevy sedan pulled up in front of the cops' car, and a fat guy wearing a lightweight trench coat open over his beer barrel belly got out. Under the trench coat Liebowitz could see a plaid sports jacket, also unbuttoned, and a loud tie that looked like it had on it every meal the guy had eaten for the past week. He waddled over to where the two black cops were sitting in their car flashing lights like it was still Christmas, and rapped on the driver's side window, and held up a badge. Liebowitz caught a flash of gold. A detective. The guy behind the wheel rolled down the window but didn't get out of the car. The fat guy seemed impervious to the cold. Had to be three above zero out there, still snowing, and he was leaning on the window with his coat wide open like a flasher, chatting up the two black cops. Finally he said something like "I've got it," or "I'll take it," and thanked the two of them, and waved them off into the night, their car trailing white exhaust fumes.

Ollie walked over to the taxi.

"Mr. Liebowitz?" he asked.

"Yeah, what's the trouble?" Liebowitz said.

"No trouble, Mr. Liebowitz. I'm Detective Weeks, there's a few questions I need to ask you."

"I'm losing money here," Liebowitz said.

"I'm sorry about that, but this is a homicide, you see."

Liebowitz went pale.

"Okay to come sit inside?" Ollie asked.

"Sure," Liebowitz said. "What do you mean, a homicide?"

"Three of them, actually," Ollie said cheerfully, and came around to the passenger side and opened the door to the front seat. He climbed in and made himself comfortable behind the meter hanging above the dash. Reading from the card, he said, "Max R. Liebowitz, huh? What's the R for?"

"Reuven," Liebowitz said.

"I'll bet that's Jewish, right?" Ollie said, and grinned.

Something in the grin told Liebowitz everything he had to know about Fat Ollie Weeks. Not for nothing had he lost half his family to the ovens at Auschwitz.

"That's right, Jewish," he said.

"Nice," Ollie said, still grinning. "So tell me, Max, did you pick up a young lady outside the Stardust Club yesterday morning around five-thirty?"

"How should I remember who I picked up yesterday morning at five-thirty?"

"The Hack Bureau tells me your call sheet lists a five-thirty pickup outside the club, is that right, Max?"

"I really can't remember."

He was thinking this was a vice cop.

He could already see the headlines.

"Could you turn down your heater a little?" Ollie said. "It's very hot in here. Don't you find it hot in here?"

Max was freezing to death.

He turned down the heater.

"This would've been a blond girl," Ollie said, "nineteen years old, wearing a short black skirt and a fake-fur jacket, red. Carrying a shiny red handbag. A clutch, they call it. Do you remember such a girl, Max?"

"I think I do, yeah. Now that you mention it."

"She's dead, Max."

"I'm sorry to hear that."

"So are two other people she may or may not have known. Dead, I mean. Not sorry like you. Well, maybe sorry, too, considering they're dead. Two black guys, Max. Were there any black guys with her when you picked her up?"

"No, she was alone."

"You remember now, huh?"

"Yeah."

"This was five-thirty?"

"Around then."

"Your call sheet said five-thirty."

"Then that's what it must've been. Cause we have to write it down, you know."

"I know. Max, did you drop her off on Ainsley and North Eleventh, like your call sheet says?"

"Yes, I did."

"At what time, Max?"

"It must've been six o'clock."

"Took you half an hour to drive three miles from the Stardust to Ainsley and North Eleventh?"

"Yeah."

"How come, Max? That time of day, it should've taken no more than ten, fifteen minutes."

"Must've been traffic," Liebowitz said, and shrugged.

"Five-thirty on a Sunday morning?"

"Well, sometimes there's traffic."

"So you're saying there was traffic, huh?"

He was leaning in close to Liebowitz now. The front seat of the cab seemed suddenly very crowded. The man had terrible body odor; Liebowitz was thinking it

213

wouldn't hurt he should take a bath every now and then. Some people, they claimed it wasn't the person, it was the *clothes* that smelled, clothes that hadn't been dry-cleaned in a while. But how could clothes start to smell unless the person wearing them smelled? Liebowitz was willing to bet this guy hadn't bathed since Rosh Hashanah, which last year had fallen on September 24. Also, his breath stank of garlic and onions. Besides, what the hell did he want here, while the meter wasn't ticking?

"I don't remember whether there was traffic or not," he said. "I know it took whatever time it took to go from wherever to wherever."

"Half an hour, you said."

"If that's what it took, that's what it took," Liebowitz said. "Now listen, Detective, I'm a working man, I got a living to earn. You want to know something about this girl, ask me. Otherwise, let me get back to work."

"Sure," Ollie said. "Did you know she was a prostitute?"

"No, I didn't know that," Liebowitz said, lying. "She told me she was a topless singer and dancer."

"What I'm trying to find out, Max, is whether you might have dropped the girl off at St. Sab's and First . . ."

"No, I . . ."

". . . instead of Ainsley and Eleventh. You didn't see her going in an alley on St. Sab's and First, did you?"

"No."

"Because that's where she was found dead, in an alley there, you see. We're wondering did these two black shits *really* rob her and kill her, or was it some *other* shits? This is a serious thing here, Max."

"I know it is."

"So if you dropped her someplace different from what it says on your call sheet . . ."

"No."

"Or if she stopped someplace to score . . ."

"No, no."

"Cause she was in possession of ten jumbo bottles, you see."

"I don't know what that is, jumbo bottles."

"Crack, Max. Big vials of crack. Red tops."

"I didn't take her anyplace but Ainsley and Eleventh."

"Not even for a minute."

"Not even for ten seconds."

"So what took you so long to go three miles uptown, Max?"

The taxi went silent.

"Max, are you lying to me?"

"Why would I lie to you?"

"Well, I don't know. You tell me, Max."

Outside on the street, an ambulance siren wailed to the night. Liebowitz was silent. Ollie waited. The sound of the ambulance melted into the city's constant nighttime song, a murmur that rose and fell, rose and fell, the pulse beat of a giant metropolis. Still Ollie waited.

"Max," he said.

"Okay," Liebowitz said, "the young lady and I had relations, okay?"

"You and the young lady are *related*?" Ollie asked, being deliberately dense.

215

Liebowitz cleared his throat.

"No, we *had* relations."

"Ah," Ollie said. "Your mutual relatives are dead?"

"We had sex," Liebowitz whispered.

"Sex?"

"Yes."

"You mean you had *intercourse* with her, Max?"

"No, no."

"Then what *do* you mean, Max?"

"She performed . . . uh . . . fellatio on me."

"Ah."

"That's why it took so long to get uptown."

"Ah."

"I'm not a young man anymore, you see."

"I see."

"It takes a while."

"I see. Max, you could've got arrested, do you know that, Max?"

"I know."

"You did a foolish thing, Max. You could contract AIDS, Max, do you know that?"

"Please. Don't even mention such a thing."

"Very dangerous, what you did, Max."

"I know, I know."

"Anyway, that explains it."

"Yes."

"A half hour to drive only three miles uptown."

"Yes."

"But you *did* drop her off at Ainsley and Eleventh, is that right?"

"Oh yes."

"No stops along the way."

"Well, yes. I pulled over to the curb while she . . . uh . . . did . . ."

"Where?"

"I don't remember. A dark street. I picked a spot that looked dark."

"And then went directly to Ainsley and Eleventh afterward, is that right?"

"Yes. Dropped her right at the curb."

"Where'd she go then, did you happen to notice?"

"Well, no. I guess she went off with these people who were waiting for her."

"What?" Ollie said.

"Some people were waiting for her."

"Who? What people?"

"Three white kids and a black guy," Liebowitz said.

"Tell me what they looked like," Ollie said.

The night manager at the Hotel Powell had given Priscilla the addresses and phone numbers of both the manager and doorman who'd been on duty when the tall blond man delivered the envelope containing the key to the pay locker. The letter had been delivered at a little past eleven on Sunday morning and this was now a little before two on *Monday* morning, but Priscilla felt it wouldn't be *tomorrow* until she went to bed and woke up again.

This was not a view shared by James Logan, who was asleep at one-fifteen A.M. when Priscilla telephoned him to say she was coming over, and who was still asleep at one fifty-eight A.M. when she rang his doorbell. Swearing mildly, Logan got out of bed in his pajamas, pulled on a robe, and went mutteringly to the front door. He would have told anyone else exactly where to go at this hour of the night, but Miss Stetson was a performer who brought mucho bucks into the hotel's café. Putting on a false smile, he opened the door and welcomed her as if she were Princess Di, whom she slightly resembled, to tell the truth.

Logan was gay.

He would have combed his hair had he known she was bringing two men along, one of whom wasn't at all bad looking. As it was, he stood there in the doorway wearing his ratty robe, his wrinkled striped pajamas, his worn bedroom slippers, and his unconvincing smile, and asked them all to please come in, wouldn't they? They all went in. Logan offered them a drink. The good-looking one—Georgie, was that his name?—said he wouldn't mind a little Scotch if Logan had some, thanks a lot. Rough trade if Logan was any judge. He poured the Scotch. The other one, Tony, said he'd thought it over, and he wouldn't mind a little Scotch, too, please. Logan poured another glass. With a splash of soda, please, Tony said. Logan went to fetch a bottle of club soda from the refrigerator. This was turning into a regular little tea party at two o'clock in the morning. With a black kid named Daryll in the bedroom.

"I want to know whatever you can tell me about the man who delivered that letter to me this morning," Priscilla said.

"*Yesterday* morning," Logan corrected, since he himself had already gone to bed and awakened again. *Been* awakened, more accurately.

"Did he give you his name?" Priscilla asked.

"You asked me that yesterday morning," Logan said. "No, he didn't give me his name."

"What did he say exactly?"

"He said to be sure the envelope was delivered to your suite."

"He said *suite*?"

"Yes."

"Not *room*?"

"He specifically said suite."

"So he knows I have a suite there," Priscilla said to Georgie. Georgie nodded wisely and sipped at his Scotch. His job here was to make sure she *never* found this tall blond guy, whoever he was, because then he would tell her the envelope was very fat when he'd left it in the locker. Then it would become a matter of believing some tall blond stranger or two Italian guys looked like they just got off the boat from Napoli, albeit in Armani threads. In Georgie's experience, blond broads always trusted blond men over swarthy wops. So next thing you knew, she'd be asking them how come the envelope was now so *skinny*, and before you could say Giuseppe Umberto Mangiacavallo, she'd actually be accusing them of having *stolen* the fuckin ninety-five K—all because they were Italian. Boy.

"Tell me what he looked like," Priscilla said.

"Tall blond man."

"How tall?"

"Six-two."

"Would you say a blond blond or a dirty blond?"

"More like a dirty blond."

"Like Robert Redford?"

"Not as blond. Redford tints, I'll bet."

219

"But a dirty blond, right?"

"Muddy, I'd say. Actually, he looked like Redford."

"Robert Redford delivered the envelope?" Tony said, astonished.

"No, no. But he *resembled* Redford. Except for the accent."

"What accent?"

"I told you. Some kind of heavy accent."

"Russian?"

"I really couldn't say. There are so *many* accents in this city."

"What was he wearing?"

"A dark blue overcoat."

"Hat?"

"No hat."

"A scarf?"

"Yes. A red muffler."

"Gloves?"

"No."

"What color shoes?"

"I couldn't see them from behind the desk."

"Beard? Mustache?"

"Clean-shaven."

Priscilla didn't know that the cops had asked virtually these same questions on the night of her grandmother's murder. Nor did she realize, of course, that the man who lived down the hall from her had given them this exact description.

"Anything else you remember about him?"

Sounding more and more like a cop.

Maybe she'd missed her calling.

"Well . . . this will sound funny, I know," Logan said.

"Yes?"

"He smelled of fish."

"What do you mean?"

"When he handed the envelope across the desk, there was a faint whiff of fish rising from his hands."

"Fish?"

"Mm."

"James?" a voice from the bedroom called.

"Yes, Daryll?"

"Man, you goan be out there all night?"

"I think we're about finished," Logan called. In explanation, he added, "My cousin. From Seattle."

Georgie raised his eyebrows.

They called on Danny Gimp because they couldn't find The Cowboy again, and they didn't particularly like to deal with Fats Donner, the third man in their triumvirate of reliable informers. Danny, unlike most good informers, was not indebted to the police. They had nothing on him that could send him away. Or, if they did, they'd forgotten what the hell it was. Danny was a businessman, plain and simple, a superior purveyor of information who enjoyed the trust of the criminal community because they knew he was an ex-con, which was true. What was not true was that he'd been wounded during a big gang shoot-out, hence the limp. Danny limped because he'd had polio as a child, something nobody had to worry about anymore. But pretending he'd once been shot gave him a certain cachet he considered essential to the business of informing. Even Carella, who'd been shot once or twice himself, thanks, had forgotten that Danny's story about getting shot was a lie.

"You ever notice that most of the cases we work together, it's wintertime?" Danny asked.

"Seems that way."

"I wonder why," Danny said. "Maybe it's cause I hate winter. Don't you hate winter?"

"It's not my favorite season," Carella said.

He was behind the wheel of the police sedan, driving Danny and Hawes to an all-night deli on the Stem. The snow had stopped and they were in a hurry to get *going* on this damn thing, but Danny was something of a prima donna who didn't like to be treated like some cheap snitch who transferred information in back alleys or police cars. Hawes was sitting in back. Danny didn't ask Hawes what *his* favorite season was because he didn't particularly like the man. He didn't know why. Maybe it was the white streak in his hair. Made him look like the fuckin bride of Frankenstein. Or maybe it was the faint trace of Boston dialect that made him sound like one of the fuckin Kennedys. Whatever, he directed most of his conversation to Carella.

There were maybe three, four other people in the diner when they walked in, but Danny looked the place over like a spy about to trade atomic secrets. Satisfied he would not be seen talking to cops, he chose a booth at the back, and sat facing the door. Gray and grizzled, and looking stouter than he actually was because of the layers of clothing he was wearing, Danny picked up his coffee cup in both hands and

222

sipped at it as if a Saint Bernard had carried it through a blizzard. His leg hurt. He told Carella it hurt whenever it snowed. Or rained. Or even when the sun was shining, for that matter. Fuckin leg hurt *all* the time.

Carella told him what they were looking for.

"Well, there ain't no cockfights on Sunday nights," Danny said.

He hadn't been to bed yet, either; to him, it was still Sunday night.

"You get them on Saturday nights, different parts of the city," he said, "mostly your Spanish neighborhoods, but you don't get them on Sunday nights."

"How about Friday nights?"

"Sometimes, when there's heat on, you know, they change the night and the location. But usually, it's Saturday night."

"We're looking at Friday."

"This past Friday?"

"Yes."

"There might've been one, I'll have to make some calls."

"Good, make them."

"You mean now? It's two in the morning!"

"We're working a homicide," Carella said.

"What are those, the magic words?" Danny said. "Let me finish my coffee. I hate to wake people up, the middle of the night."

Carella shrugged as if to say you want to do business or you want to lead a life of indulgence and indolence?

Danny took his time finishing the coffee. Then he slid out of the booth and limped over to the pay phone on the wall near the men's room. They watched him as he dialed.

"He doesn't like me," Hawes said.

"Naw, he likes you," Carella said.

"I'm telling you he doesn't."

"He came to the hospital when I got shot," Carella said.

"Maybe *I* ought to get shot, huh?"

"Bite your tongue."

They sipped at their coffees. Two Sanitation Department men came in and took stools at the bar. Outside the deli, their orange snowplows sat at the curb. The night was starless. Everything was black outside, except for the orange plows. Danny had reached his party. He was leaning in close to the mouthpiece, talking, nodding, even gesticulating. He limped back to the table some five minutes later.

"It'll cost you," he said.

"How much?" Hawes asked.

"Two bills for me, three for the guy you'll be talking to."

"Who's that?"

"Guy who had a bird fighting in Riverhead on Friday night. There was also supposed to be a fight in Bethtown, but it got canceled. Big Asian community there, this ain't only a Spanish thing, you know."

"Where in Riverhead?" Hawes asked."

"The bread, please," Danny said, and rolled his thumb against his forefinger.

Hawes looked at Carella. Carella nodded. Hawes took out his wallet and pulled two hundred-dollar bills from it. Danny accepted the money.

"*Gracias*," he said. "I'll take you up there, introduce you to Luis. Actually, I'm surprised you don't know about this already."

"How come?" Carella asked.

"The place got busted Friday night. That's the only reason he's willing to talk to you."

Ramon Moreno was the doorman who'd been on duty outside the hotel on Sunday morning, when the tall blond man delivered the envelope. They had telephoned him at the Club Durango, down in the Quarter, and he was just packing up to go home when they got there at a quarter past two. Ramon was a musician. He worked days at the hotel to pay the bills, but his love was the B-flat tenor saxophone, and he played whatever gig came his way whenever. He told Priscilla—who he knew was a fellow musician—that he'd played the Durango three nights running so far, and he was hoping it would turn into a steady gig. The club was Mexican, and they played all the old standby stuff like "El Jarabe de la Botella" and "La Chachalaca" and the ever-popular and corny "Cielito Lindo," but occasionally they got a hip crowd in and could cut loose on some real jazz with a Hispanic tint. When he wasn't playing the Durango, he did weddings and anniversary parties and birthday parties . . .

"A girl's fifteenth birthday is a big thing in the Spanish culture . . ."

. . . and whatever else might come along. He even played a bar mitzvah a couple of weeks ago.

All of which is very fucking interesting, Georgie thought.

The way he got to be a tenor player was very strange, Ramon said. He *used* to play the alto, an instrument better suited to his size in that he was only five feet six inches tall. At the time, he was playing in a band with a four-piece sax section, and one of the guys playing tenor was this big tall guy, six-three, six-four, which was appropriate because the tenor is a fairly large instrument, not as big as your baritone sax, but a good-sized horn, you understand? Then one day, during rehearsal, they switched instruments just for fun, and discovered they were better suited to the horns they'd borrowed, the short guy, Ramon himself, blowing this tenor sax almost bigger than he is, and the tall guy, Julius, playing the smaller alto, which looked almost like a toy saxophone in his hands.

All of which is even *more* interesting, Georgie thought.

"About yesterday morning," Priscilla said, cutting to the chase.

"Yeah," Ramon said, sounding a bit offended. "What did you want to know?"

"Tall blond man wearing a dark blue coat and a red scarf. Walked in around eleven, walked out a few minutes later. Did you see him?"

"Not when he walked in," Ramon said.

He still sounded miffed, Georgie thought. Probably wondering why his dumb story about a tall guy playing a small sax and a short guy playing a big sax wasn't quite wowing the crowds here in the big bad city. Hell with you, Georgie thought. Just don't tell her anything'll lead her to the blond guy.

"But you did see him," Patricia said.

"Yeah, when he came out. Cause he asked me to get him a cab."

"What'd he sound like?"

"Sound like?"

"His accent."

"Oh. Yeah. That's right."

"Was it a Spanish accent?"

"No. Definitely not."

"He didn't speak Spanish to you, did he?"

"No. It was English. But with an accent. Like you say."

"Russian?"

"Italian, maybe. I'm not sure."

"*Did* you get him a cab?"

"Yeah."

"Do you know where he was going?"

"As it happens, yes," Ramon said.

They waited breathlessly.

Master of suspense, Georgie thought.

"The doormen at the Powell are trained to ask our guests their destinations, and to relay this information to the cabdriver," Ramon said, as if reciting from the hotel's brochure. "Many of our guests are foreigners," he said. "They will have an address scribbled on a piece of paper, and will have no idea where that address might be. Japanese people, for example. Arabs. Germans. We try to help them out. As a courtesy," he said. "These people who can barely speak English."

But the blond guy *did* speak English, Georgie thought.

"So where *was* he going?" Priscilla asked impatiently.

Georgie hoped he wouldn't remember.

"I remember because I played there once," Ramon said.

"Where?" Priscilla insisted.

"A place called The Juice Bar," Ramon said. "It's an after-hours club on Harris Avenue. In Riverhead. Near the Alhambra Theater."

At two-thirty that morning, Luis Villada was waiting outside the Alhambra Theater when Danny Gimp arrived with the two detectives. Danny introduced them all around, told them he was sure they had no further use for his services, hailed a cab and headed downtown without so much as a backward glance. Hawes was ever more certain that the man simply didn't like him.

Luis looked the two detectives over.

He was not afraid of telling them anything they wanted to know about Friday night because every cop in the city already *knew* what had gone down. Or at least every cop in Emergency Service and every cop in the Four-Eight Precinct and every cop on the Riverhead Task Force, not to mention twenty agents from the ASPCA, which not very many Japanese, German, or Arabian tourists knew stood for the American Society for the Prevention of Cruelty to Animals. As if cockfighting was being cruel to animals. Besides, they couldn't charge him with anything more than they already had. As a spectator, he'd been arrested for one misdemeanor count of cruelty to animals and another misdemeanor count for participating in animal fights.

"They kept us in the theater overnight," he said, "writing tickets."

Not a trace of an accent. Carella figured him for another third-generation Puerto Rican.

"They let us go after they gave us dates for court appearances," he said. "I have to go downtown on February twenty-eighth."

He looked the cops dead in the eye.

"Danny says you have something for me," he said.

Hawes handed him an envelope.

Luis didn't bother to open it or to count what was inside it. Hey, if you couldn't trust cops, who *could* you trust? Ho ho ho. He pocketed the envelope and began walking them down a long dark alley smelling of piss, toward the back wall of the theater, where he said there was a door the police had broken down Friday night and couldn't padlock afterward. The door was in splinters, small wonder. Nailed to the lintel was a printed CRIME SCENE notice, which should have detained anyone from seeking entry, door or no door. But Luis believed that printed notices from the police were to be ignored, and so he stepped over the surviving bottom panel of the door and into a blackness deeper than the one outside. The detectives followed him in. Hawes turned on a penlight.

"*Mejor*," Luis said.

Hawes flashed the light around.

They moved deeper into the theater.

Luis began talking.

He seemed to think he'd been given a four-million-dollar publishing advance to cover a major sporting event, rather than a mere three hundred bucks for information about whatever he'd seen and heard this past Friday night. Like an eyewitness about to describe a major disaster like an earthquake, an avalanche, or a plane crash, he began setting the scene by describing the excitement of the night, the sheer joy of being there on this special occasion. Taking a penlight Carella offered him, he led them through the abandoned movie theater that had served as the arena. Where once there had been upholstered seats, there were now bleachers surrounding a carpeted ring. Dried blood stained the carpet.

"The walls are on rollers," Luis explained. "If the police come, the promoters slide them back to make it look like a prizefight is going on. They have two guys in boxing trunks and gloves in the back office. The lookout sounds the alarm, the walls move out, the boxers are in the ring hitting each other, everything's nice and legal. Cockfighting shouldn't be against the law, anyway. It's legal in some states, you know. Louisiana, Oklahoma, I forget the other two. It's legal in four states altogether. So why should it be against the law here? Farmers in the South get to see cockfights, but here in a sophisticated city like this one, it's against the law. *Shit*, man! I go to a cockfight to enjoy myself, and all of a sudden I'm charged with two misdemeanors, I can go to jail for a year on each. What for? What crime did I commit? This was a social gathering here."

The social gathering, as he tells it to them, began at nine o'clock on Friday night, when the spectators, some two hundred and fifty of them, began gathering at this theater on Harris Avenue in the Harrisville section of Riverhead, both avenue and neighborhood named for a long-ago councilman named Albert J. Harris. The fight was supposed to take place on Saturday night, at another venue, but someone leaked it to the police and so the date and the place were changed— although, as it turned out, someone leaked *this* to the police as well.

This is an important event tonight because it's the first big fight of the season, which begins in January and runs through July. Roosters don't molt during these months. When they're molting, blood flows into their quills, causing them to become vulnerable and incapable of fighting . . .

"Did you see that movie *The Birds*?" Luis asked. "There was a line in it where the girl says that birds get a hangdog expression when they're molting. That was a very funny line Hitchcock wrote. Because how can birds get hangdog expressions?"

Carella shook his head in wonder.

"Anyway, there was only one other event after the holidays, and then came this one on Friday night, which was supposed to be the next night, but the promoters sold a lot of tickets in advance, and it was just a matter of letting people know the date had been changed and instead of the athletic club on Dover Plains, it was now the Alhambra here on Harris. The tickets cost . . ."

. . . twenty dollars each, which is practically giving the seats away. The promoters don't expect to make a lot of money on the gate. What's twenty times two-fifty? Five K? So what's that? Where they make the real money is selling food and alcohol. And, of course, the betting. Thousands of dollars are wagered on each of the fights. During a typical three-hour night, there can be anywhere from twenty to thirty matches, depending on the ferocity and duration of each contest. The average match will run fifteen minutes, but some will end in five and others—the more popular ones with the crowd—can last as long as half an hour or even forty minutes, the birds literally tearing themselves apart in frenzy.

There is a huge indoor parking garage across the street from the Alhambra, and it is here that the paying customers park their cars, hidden from the eyes of prying police officers—though on this Friday night, informers have already been paid, and a massive raid is in preparation even before the first of the cars arrives. Inside, there is joviality and conviviality, an atmosphere reminiscent of the old days on the island, where cockfighting is still a gentleman's sport. Luis can remember attending his first fight when he was seven years old. His father was a breeder of fighting birds, and he recalls feeding them special diets of raw meat and eggs supplemented with vitamins to fortify their stamina and strength. Now, here in this city, the owners of fighting birds sometimes pay three, four hundred dollars a month to hide their roosters on clandestine farms in neighboring states. These are expensive birds. Some of them are worth five, ten thousand dollars.

"It's a gentleman's sport," he says again.

Drinking rum at the bar, eating *cuchifritos*, speaking their native tongue, the customers—mostly men, but here and there one will see a pretty, dark-haired, dark-eyed woman dressed elegantly for the occasion—relax in an ambiance of total acceptance and fond recall. There could easily be tropical breezes blowing through this converted theater, the swish of palm fronds outside, the rush of the sea against a white sand beach. For a moment, there is respite for these transplanted people who more often than not are made to feel foreign in this city.

The fights are furious and deadly.

This is a blood sport in every sense.

The roosters are crossbred with pheasants to fortify their most aggressive traits. Nurtured on steroids that increase muscle tissue, dosed with angel dust to numb pain, they are equipped with fighting spurs and then are moved into the carpeted cockpit to kill or be killed. In India, where the sport enjoys wide popularity, the birds fight "bare-heeled," using only their own claws to shred and destroy. In Puerto Rico, the trainers attach to the birds' heels a long plastic apparatus that resembles a darning needle. Here in this city, the chosen device is called a slasher. It is a piece of steel honed to razor-sharp precision. These spurs are fastened to both claws. They are twin weapons of mutilation and destruction.

Luis himself can't bear to watch the final moments of a fight, when the roosters, doped up with PCP, rip and tear at each other with their metal talons, blood and feathers flying, the crowd screaming for a kill. More often than not, *both* birds are killed.

"It's a sad thing," Luis says. "No one likes to see animals hurt. This is a gentleman's sport."

The police who raided the theater at eleven twenty-seven P.M. last Friday apparently disagreed with his premise. Captain Arthur Forsythe, Jr., who led the team of E.S. officers who spearheaded the operation, later told the press that the forced combat of these birds was nothing less than barbaric, a criminal act that had to be abolished if this city were ever to call itself civilized. His men had taken out the two lookouts posted at the entrance, handcuffing them and putting them down on the sidewalk before they could sound an alarm. They then went in wearing bulletproof vests and carrying machine guns, followed by teams from the Four-Eight, the Task Force, and the ASPCA.

"There's cameras and guard dogs," Luis said. "I don't know how they got in so quick and easy."

Even so, by the time the raiders broke into the actual ring area upstairs, some of the false walls had already been moved back and the event's organizers were fleeing over rooftops and through tunnels, one leading out to Harris Avenue, another running underground to a beauty parlor adjacent to the parking garage. The police caught only one of the promoters, a man named Anibal Fuentes, who was charged with two felony counts.

"This shouldn't be allowed to happen," Luis said, shaking his head. "Kings and emperors used to have cockfights, did you know that? Even American *presidents*! Thomas Jefferson! George Washington! The father of the nation, am I right? He liked to watch cockfights. This is a sin, what they're doing. Persecuting people who enjoy an honest-to-God sport!"

In his report to the Police Commissioner, Captain Forsythe noted that on the street behind the theater his men had found twenty-five bloodied roosters, all fitted with metal talons, twenty of them dead, the rest still alive and twitching in agony. In rooms behind the false walls, officers from the Four-Eight found another forty birds in cages, pillowcases over their heads to keep them calm in the dark before they were tossed into the ring.

"They came from all over," Luis said. "Florida and Pennsylvania, Connecticut and Washington, D.C. Some trainers brought their birds all the way from San Juan and Ponce! This was a big event, man! There were birds coming to the ring from all over! Like toreadors arriving!"

"You didn't happen to notice a black limo, did you?" Carella asked.

What the hell, he thought, *toreadors* arriving!

"Oh sure," Luis said.

"What *kind* of limo?" Carella asked at once.

"A Caddy."

"Where'd you see it?"

"Back of the theater. When I was walking over from the garage. The door we came in before. Where the trainers take the birds in, you know? The stage door, I guess they call it. The one that's busted now."

235

"You saw a trainer taking a chicken out of a black Caddy limousine, is that right?"

"Not a chicken. A *rooster*. A fighting *cock*!"

"Trainer drove him up in a Caddy, is that right?"

"That's right. Took him out of the backseat."

"In a cage, or what?"

"No cage. Just a pillowcase over his head. Just his legs showing."

"You wouldn't *know* this trainer, would you?"

"Not personally."

"Then how?"

"I looked up his name."

"I'm sorry, you did what?"

"On the card."

"The card."

"Yeah, the owners' names are on the card. I recognized him when he was carrying the bird in the ring. Remembered him driving up in the Caddy. Figured he was a big shot, you know? I mean, a fuckin movie star bird in a limo, am I right? So I looked up his name on the card."

"And what *was* his name?" Carella asked, and held his breath.

"Jose Santiago," Luis said.

11

Priscilla and the boys could not find the club.

Their taxi drove up and down Harris Avenue forever, passing the darkened marquee of the Alhambra theater more times than they cared to count. On their last swing past it, two men in heavy overcoats, both of them bareheaded, one of them a red-head, were climbing into an automobile. Priscilla thought they looked familiar, but as she craned her neck for a better look through the fogged rear window, the car doors slammed shut behind them. A third man, smaller, slighter, and wearing a short green barn coat that looked as if it had come from L. L. Bean or Lands' End, stood on the sidewalk, watching the car as it pulled away.

"Back up," Priscilla told the cabdriver.

"I'm not gonna spend all night here looking for this club," the cabbie said.

"Just back up, would you please?" she said. "Before *he* disappears, too."

The cabbie threw the car into reverse and started backing slowly toward where Luis Villada, his hands in his coat pockets, was walking away from the Alhambra. At this hour of the morning, in this neighborhood, Luis would have run like hell if this was anything but a taxi. Even so, he was wary until he saw the blond woman sitting on the backseat, lowering the window on the curbside.

"Excuse me," she called.

He stood where he was on the curb, not moving any closer to the taxi because now he saw that the blonde was with two *men*, both of them wearing hats. He didn't trust men who wore hats.

"Yeah?" he said.

"Are you familiar with a club called The Juice Bar?"

"Yeah?" he said.

"Do you know where it is?"

"Yeah?"

"Could you help us find it, please?"

"There's no sign," he said.

"We can't even find the address," she said.

"Half the addresses up here, the numbers are gone."

"It's supposed to be 1712 Harris."

"Yeah, that's up the block," he said, taking his right hand from his pocket and pointing. "Between the dry cleaners and the *carnicería*. They probably don't have numbers, either."

"Thank you very much."

"It's a blue door," Luis said. "You have to ring."

"Thank you."

"*De nada*," he said, and put his hand back in his pocket, and began walking home.

He was mugged on the next corner.

His hatless assailant stole his watch, his wallet, and the envelope containing the three hundred dollars the detectives had paid him for his time and his information.

In this city, you could legally serve alcoholic beverages till four in the morning, but the underground clubs operated till a bit before sunrise, when all the vampires had to be back in their coffins. The Juice Bar offered booze, beer, wine and the occasional fruit drink right up to the legal closing limit, and then—to the accompaniment of a three-piece jazz band—began serving anything that turned you on. At six, the club offered breakfast while a lone piano player filled the air with dawnlike medleys.

It was close to three o'clock when Priscilla rang the bell button set in the jamb to the right of the blue door.

"The fuck *is* this?" Georgie wanted to know. "Joe sent us?"

They waited.

A flap in the door opened.

Fuckin speakeasy here, Georgie thought.

Priscilla held up her card.

"I'm here to listen to the band," she said.

"Okay," the man behind the flap said at once, and opened the door. Fact of it was he hadn't even glanced at her card. Until four A.M. the club would be operating legally and he'd have admitted even a trio of Barbary pirates carrying swords and wearing black eye patches.

The club was constructed like a crescent moon, with the bandstand at the apogee of its arc, farthest from the entrance door. The entrance and the cloakroom were side by side on the curving flank of the arc's left horn. The bar was on the right horn, a dozen stools ranked in front of it. Priscilla and the boys left their coats with a hatcheck girl who flashed a welcoming smile as she handed Georgie the three claim checks. She was wearing a black mini and a white scoop-necked blouse, and Georgie looked her up and down as if auditioning her for a part in a movie. The equivalent of a *maître d'*—that is to say, he was wearing a jacket—offered to seat them at a table, but Priscilla said she preferred sitting at the bar, closer to the band. In any club, it was always the bartender who noticed who came in when and did what where. It was always the bartender who had information.

The band was playing "Midnight Sun."

The tune almost brought tears to Priscilla's eyes, possibly because she realized she could never hope to play it as well as the piano player here in this Riverhead dive, possibly because her grandmother's pathetic note had expressed a hope abandoned long ago. Priscilla knew she would never become a concert pianist. The thought that Svetlana had still considered this a viable ambition was heartbreaking, more so when one considered the meager sum of money she'd left for the achievement of such an impossible goal. Or had there been more in the envelope? Which, after all, was why she was here looking for the tall blond man who'd delivered it. But even so, even if there'd been a *million* dollars in that shabby yellow packet, Priscilla knew she didn't have, would never have the stuff. How could she even begin to *approach* a beast like the *presto agitato* movement of the Moonlight Sonata when she hadn't yet truly mastered the chart to "Midnight Sun"? She dabbed at her eyes and ordered a Grand Marnier on the rocks. The boys ordered Scotch again.

The bartender looked like an actor.

Every would-be actor in this city was either a bartender or a waiter.

Long black hair pulled into a ponytail. Soulful brown eyes. Delicate, long-fingered hands. Great profile.

His name was Marvin.

Change it, Priscilla thought.

"I'll tell you why we're here, Marvin," she said.

Marvin. Jesus.

He was looking at her card, impressed. He figured the two goons were bodyguards. Lady played piano at the Powell, she needed bodyguards. He hoped that one day, when he was a matinee idol, or a movie star, or both, he would have bodyguards of his own. Meanwhile he was honored that she was here in their midst. Shitty little dump like this, hey.

"The man we're looking for, Marvin . . ."

Jesus.

". . . is someone who would've been here yesterday morning around eleven-thirty, maybe a bit later."

She was figuring half an hour or so to get uptown by cab, on a Sunday morning, when the traffic would've been light. The blond man had left the hotel at a little past eleven. Placing him on Harris Avenue at eleven-thirty was reasonable.

"Yeah, it's possible," Marvin said. "We start serving breakfast at six."

"Are you still serving at eleven-thirty?"

"On Sundays, yeah. We get a big brunch crowd, serve till two-thirty, three o'clock, then open again at nine. We're open all weekend, closed on Mondays and Tuesdays, dead nights here in the city."

"Were you working this past Saturday night?"

"I come on at four *every* night. That's when we go underground and the shift changes. Well, not Tuesdays or Wednesdays."

"Did you come on at four this past Saturday night?"

"Yeah. Well, Sunday *morning* it was, actually."

"Four A.M., right?"

"Yeah."

"Were you here at eleven-thirty, twelve o'clock?"

"Yeah, I work through till we close. Sunday's a long day. I put in almost twelve hours. Rest of the week, we close at nine in the morning. It's like a courtesy breakfast we serve. For the all-night crowd."

Georgie was wondering how come, if Marvin came on at *four* every morning but Tuesday and Wednesday, how come he was here, now, at *three*, three-fifteen, whatever the hell it was on a *Monday* morning? He looked at his watch. Twenty after. So how come, Marvin?

Marvin was a mind reader.

"Jerry called me to come in early," he explained.

Who's Jerry? Georgie wondered.

"Cause Frank started throwing up."

Who's Frank? Georgie wondered.

"Must've been one of those flu bugs," Marvin explained.

"So today you came in early, is that what you're saying?" Tony asked.

"Yeah, I got here about an hour ago."

"How about yesterday?" Priscilla asked.

"I got here the usual time."

"Four A.M."

"Right."

"The man we're looking for would've been blond," Priscilla said.

"You're a cop, right?" Marvin said.

"No, I'm an entertainer. You saw my card."

"How about your two friends here? Are they cops?"

"Do they look like cops?" Priscilla asked.

They didn't look like cops to Marvin.

"Tall blond man wearing a blue coat and a red scarf," Priscilla said.

Marvin was already shaking his head.

"See anyone like that?" Georgie asked.

He was pleased that Marvin was shaking his head. What he wanted to do now was get out of here fast, before Marvin the mind reader changed his mind.

"I don't remember anyone who looked like that," Marvin said.

Good, Tony thought. Let's get the hell out of here.

"But why don't you ask Anna?" Marvin said. "She's the one would've taken his coat."

They finally found Jose Santiago at 3:25 A.M. that Monday. They figured that a man who kept pigeons, and also drove a fighting rooster around in the backseat of a borrowed limo, had to be a bird fancier of sorts. So they checked out the roof of his building again, and sure enough, there he was, sitting with his back against the side wall of his pigeon coop. Last time they were here, dawn was fast approaching on a cold Sunday morning. Now, on an even colder Monday morning, sunrise was still approximately four hours away, and they were no closer to learning who had killed Svetlana Dyalovich on Saturday night. Nor did it appear that Santiago was going to offer any assistance in that direction. Santiago was weeping. He was also very, very drunk.

"Jose Santiago?" Hawes asked.

"That is me," Santiago said.

"Detective Cotton Hawes, Eighty-seventh Squad."

"*Mi gusto*," Santiago said.

"My partner, Detective Carella."

"*Igualmente*," Santiago said, and tilted a bottle of Don Quixote rum to his lips and took a long swallow. It was perhaps two degrees below zero out here, but he was wearing only blue jeans, a white shirt, and a pink V-necked cotton sweater. He was a slender man in his early thirties, Carella guessed, with curly black hair, a pale complexion, and delicate features. His dark brown eyes seemed out of focus, moist at the moment because he was still weeping. Immediately after the detectives introduced themselves, he seemed to forget their presence. As if alone here on the roof, he began shaking his head over and over again, weeping more bitterly, clutching the rum to his narrow chest, his knuckles white around the neck of the bottle. In the bitter cold, his breath plumed onto the night.

"What's the matter, Jose?" Hawes asked gently.

"I killed him," Santiago said.

"Here in the dead of night, the pigeons still and silent behind Santiago, both detectives felt their backs stiffen. But the man who'd just confessed to murder seemed completely harmless, sitting there sobbing, clutching the bottle to his chest, hot tears rolling down his face and freezing at once.

"Who'd you kill?" Hawes asked.

244

Voice still gentle. The night black around them. Carella standing beside him, looking down at the sobbing man in the pink cotton sweater, ridiculous for this time of year, sitting with his knees bent, his back to the dark silent pigeon coop.

"Tell us who you killed, Jose."

"Diablo."

"Who's Diablo?"

"*Mi hermano de sangue.*"

"My blood brother."

"Is that his street name? Diablo?"

Santiago shook his head.

"It's his real name?"

Santiago nodded.

"Diablo *what*?"

Santiago tilted the bottle again, swallowed more rum, began coughing and sobbing and choking. The detectives waited.

"What's his last name, Jose?"

Hawes again. Carella stayed out of it. Just stood there with his right hand resting inside the overlapping flap of his coat, where three buttons were unbuttoned at the waist. He may have looked a bit like Napoleon with his hand inside his coat that way, but his holster and the butt of a .38 Detective Special were only inches away from his fingertips. Santiago said nothing. Hawes tried another tack.

"When did you kill this person, Jose?"

Still no answer.

"Jose? Can you tell us when this happened?"

Santiago nodded.

"Then when?"

"Friday night."

"This past Friday night?"

Santiago nodded again.

"Where? Can you tell us where, Jose? Can you tell us what happened?"

And now, in the piercing cold of the night, Santiago began a rambling recitation in English and in Spanish, telling them it was all his fault, it wouldn't have happened if he hadn't *allowed* it, he had killed Diablo as certainly as if he'd slit his throat with a knife. Swilling rum, spitting, slobbering down the front of the absurd cotton sweater, his hands shaking, telling them he'd always taken care of him like a brother, they were partners, he'd never done anything to harm him, never. But on Friday night he'd killed him as sure as if he'd, oh dear God, he'd killed him, oh sweet Mary, he'd allowed the thing he loved most in the entire world to be slashed and torn . . .

Carella was beginning to get it.

. . . to shreds, he should have stopped it the moment he realized . . .

So was Hawes.

. . . how it would end, the moment he saw that the other bird was stronger, he should have stopped the fight, climbed into the ring, snatched his prizefighting rooster away from the ripping steel talons of the bigger, stronger bird. But no, instead he'd watched in horror, covering his face at last, screaming aloud like a woman when poor Diablo was slain.

"I killed him," he said again.

And now he confessed that he'd suspected from the start that the other bird was on steroids, the sheer size

246

of him, a vulture against a chick, poor brave Diablo strutting into the ring like the proud champion he was, battling in vain against overwhelming odds, giving his life . . .

"I was greedy," Santiago said, "I had ten thousand dollars bet on him, I thought he could still win, the blood, so much blood, all over his feathers, *madre de Dios*! I should have tried to stop the slaughter. There are owners who jump into the ring during a fight, without the permission of the fence judge, there are strict rules, you know, but they break the rules, they save their beloved birds. I was greedy and I was afraid of breaking the rules, and so I let him die. I could have saved his life, I *should* have saved his life, forgive me, Mary, mother of God, I took an innocent life."

"What *else* did you take?" Carella asked.

Because all at once this was still the tale of a gun and a dead old woman, and not a sad soap opera about a dead chicken. People ate chicken every Sunday.

"Take?" Santiago asked drunkenly. "What do you mean?"

"You drove Diablo uptown in a limo, didn't you?"

"He was a champion!"

"You stole a black Caddy . . ."

"I borrowed it!"

". . . from Bridge Texaco. A limo that . . ."

"I *returned* it!"

". . . was in for a new engine."

"He was a champion!"

"He was a bird who needed a ride uptown."

"A hero!"

"Who made a mess all over the backseat."

"A *mess*? A champion's feathers! *Diablo's* feathers!"
Diablo's shit, too, Hawes thought.

"How could I bear *touching* them?" Santiago said, and began weeping again. He tilted the rum bottle to his lips, but it was empty. He wiped his nose on the sleeve of the pink sweater.

"Did you find a gun in the glove compartment of that car?" Carella asked.

"No. Hey, no. No."

"Did you *know* there was a gun in the glove compartment?"

"No. What gun? A gun? No."

"A .38 Smith & Wesson."

"No, I didn't know that."

"Didn't see the gun, huh?"

"No."

"Didn't know it was in the glove compartment."

"No."

"That's good, Jose. Because the gun was used in a murder . . ."

"A murder? No."

"A murder, yes."

"And if we can trace that gun to you . . ."

"If your fingerprints are on that gun, for example..."

"I didn't shoot anybody with that gun."

"Oh? You know the gun we mean, huh?"

"I know the gun, yes. But . . ."

"Did you steal it from that glove compartment?"

"I borrowed it."

"Same way you borrowed the limo, huh?"

"I *did* borrow the limo. And I borrowed the gun, too."

"Why?"

"To shoot the bird who killed Diablo."

"So this was after the match, huh?"

"*Sí.*"

"You took the gun from the car *after* the match."

"*Sí.* To shoot the bird."

"*Did* you shoot the bird?"

"No. The cops came. I was going back in the theater when I saw all these cops. So I ran back to the garage."

"With the gun."

"With the gun, *sí.*"

"What did you do with the gun then?"

"I sold it."

The detectives looked at each other.

"That's right," Jose said. "I sold it."

Carella sighed.

So did Hawes.

"Who'd you sell it to?"

"A man I met at a club up the street."

"What club?"

"The Juice Bar."

"What man?"

"I don't know his name."

"You sold a stolen gun to a man you didn't even *know*?"

"We were talking, he said he needed a gun. So I happened to have a gun. So I sold it to him."

"You sold him a gun you'd just stolen."

"I had just lost my best friend in the whole world."

"What's that got to do with stealing a gun and selling it?"

"I *also* lost ten thousand dollars."

"Ah. So how much did you get for the gun?"

"Two hundred and fifty dollars."

"That's cutting your losses, all right," Hawes said.

"My greatest loss was Diablo."

"What'd he look like?" Carella asked.

"He was a white bird, large in the chest, with . . ."

"The man who bought the gun."

"Oh. He was a tall blond guy."

"Blond guy with a blue coat and a red scarf, yeah," Anna said. "Tall blond guy. Sure. Matter of fact, he was in here *twice*."

This was beginning to get interesting.

Georgie hoped it wouldn't get *too* interesting.

"The first time was Friday night around midnight," Anna said. "He was meeting a guy named Bernie, comes in here all the time. Scar on his right cheek, I think he's a bookie."

"The blond guy?" Tony asked.

"No, Bernie."

"Did you happen to get his name?" Priscilla asked.

"I just told you. Bernie."

"I mean the blond guy."

"No, I didn't. Matter of fact, the first time I laid eyes on him was Friday night."

"When was the next time he came in?"

"Yesterday," Anna said. "Around twelve noon. Met with Bernie again. They sat right over there," she said, and pointed to a table. "Money changed hands. At least yesterday, it did. On Friday, they were just talking. He seemed very angry."

"The blond guy?" Priscilla asked.

"No, Bernie."

"He was angry yesterday?"

"No, he was angry Friday. Yesterday, he was all smiles."

"So as I understand this," Georgie said, interpreting for Priscilla, "on Friday night the blond guy and Bernie the bookie just sat over there and talked, and Bernie was pissed off about something, is that correct?"

"Yes," Anna said.

"But money changed hands yesterday and Bernie the bookie was all smiles. Is that also correct?"

"Matter of fact, yes," Anna said.

"You know what this indicates to me?" Georgie said.

"What?" Priscilla asked.

"A man paying off a marker."

"That's what it looks like to me, too," Tony said, nodding sagely.

Priscilla nodded, too, and then turned back to Anna.

"But you never got the blond guy's name," she said.

"Matter of fact, I didn't" Anna said.

"And you don't know Bernie's last name."

"Just his first name."

In which case, let us be on our way, Georgie thought.

"But maybe Marvin knows," Anna said.

Matter of fact, he did.

Three black guys who looked like they were homeless bums were warming themselves up around a fire in an oil drum on the corner of Ainsley and Eleventh. Ollie felt like arresting them. He was cold and he was tired after a full eight-hour shift, not to mention trotting here and there around the city afterward trying to get a line on who iced the hooker and her two black buddies. Three-thirty in the fuckin morning, he *really* felt like arresting them.

"You guys," he said, approaching the blazing oil drum. "You know arson's against the law?"

"Nobody committin no arson here, suh," one of the men said. He was a grizzled old bum looked like that black guy in the prison picture, whatever it was called, *The Scrimshaw Reduction*, about this black guy who used to drive around this old Jewish southern lady before he got sent up. The old bum standing with his hands stretched out to the fire looked just like that guy in the picture. The other two looked like ordinary black bums you'd see standing around any fire three-thirty in the morning. Nobody looked at Ollie. They all just kept staring into the flames, hands reaching toward them.

"So is this your usual corner here?" Ollie asked. "This lovely garden spot here?"

He was being sarcastic. This was an unusually filthy stretch of Ainsley Avenue. Because of yesterday's storm—and because this was Diamondback, where nobody gave a damn about refuse collection, anyway—overflowing garbage cans stood against the tenement walls and marauding rats the size of buffalo were boldly shredding stacks of black plastic bags. The noise of the rats was frightening in itself. Over the crackle of the fire in the oil drum, Ollie could hear their incessant squealing and squeaking and scratching. He felt like shooting them.

"Everybody hard of hearing here?" he asked.

"This's our regular corner here, yessuh," the one from the *Scrimshaw* picture said. Ollie didn't know who he hated most, the ones who bowed and scraped or the ones with attitude. There wasn't much attitude around this fire tonight. Just three cold homeless bums afraid to go crawl into their cardboard boxes lest one of their brothers did them in the night.

"You happen to be here Saturday night around this time?" he asked. "Little later, actually?"

None of the men said anything.

"Hey!" Ollie shouted. "Anybody *listening* to me here?"

"What time would that've been, suh?" the older bum said. Doing his Uncle Tom bit for the benefit of the dumb honkie cop.

"This would've been six o'cock in the morning, suh," Ollie said, mimicking him. "This would've been a taxicab letting out a white blonde in a short skirt and a red fur jacket who was being met by three white guys in blue parkas and a black guy in a black leather jacket. So were you here at that hour, *suh*, and did you happen to see them?"

"We was here," he said, "and we happen to see em."

Carella and Hawes got to The Juice Bar about five minutes after Priscilla and the boys left. Marvin the bartender and Anna the hatcheck girl both felt it was déjà vu all over again. Just a few minutes ago, three people who might have been under-covers had been here asking about a tall blond man, and now here were two more very *definite* detectives flashing badges and

253

asking about the same tall blond man. They told Carella and Hawes exactly what they had told Priscilla and the boys.

So now five people were looking for a bookie named Bernie Himmel.

The cops had an edge.

At this hour, The Silver Chief Diner was mostly populated with predators. The morning shifts would not begin till eight, and any honest person with a night job—office cleaners and hospital personnel, transit employees and cops, night watchmen, bakery crews, cabdrivers, short-order cooks, hotel workers, toll takers—was still busy earning a living. Here in the diner, there were mainly prostitutes and pimps, burglars and muggers, dealers and users, the occasional noncriminal sprinkling of drunks, insomniacs, or writers with blocks. Ollie separated the wheat from the chaff at once. The minute he walked in, every thief in the joint recognized him for what he was, too. None of them even glanced in his direction.

He went straight to the counter, took a stool, and ordered a cup of coffee from a redheaded girl in a pale green uniform. Her name tag read SALLY.

"You serve Indian food here?" he asked.

"No, sir, we sure don't," Sally said.

"Native American food?" he asked.

"Nor that neither," she said.

"Then how come you call yourself the Silver Chief?"

"It's spose to be like a train," she said.

"Oh yeah?"

"That's what it's spose to be, yes, sir."

"What part of the South you from, Sally?"

"Tennessee," she said.

"You serve grits here, Sally?"

"No, sir."

"You serve hominy?"

"No, sir."

"How about a nice hot cup of coffee then? And one of those donuts there."

"Yes, sir," she said.

Ollie looked the place over again. Each time his gaze fell upon someone who'd been out victimizing tonight, eyes turned away. Good, he thought. Shit your pants. Sally came back with his coffee and donut.

"I'm a police officer," he said, and showed her his shield. "Were you working here on Saturday night around this time, a little bit later?"

"I was," she said.

"I'm looking for a blond girl was wearing a black mini and a red fur jacket."

He didn't mention that she was dead.

"*Fake* fur," he said. "Fake blonde, too."

"We get lots of those in here," Sally said, and with a faint tilt of her head indicated that lots of *those* were in here right this very minute, sitting at tables hither and yon behind Ollie.

"How about Saturday night? Remember a blonde in a red fur jacket?"

"I sure don't," Sally said.

"How about three white guys in blue hooded parkas?"

"Nope."

"Or a black guy in a black leather jacket."

"We get thousands of black guys in black leather jackets."

"These three white guys would've been peeing in the gutter."

"Where?"

"Outside there," Ollie said, jerking his head over his shoulder toward the front windows of the diner.

"This weather?" Sally said, and laughed.

Ollie laughed, too.

"Need Willie warmers, *this* weather," Sally said.

"Black guy would've run out the diner, told them to stop peeing."

"Can't blame him," Sally said, and began laughing again.

Ollie laughed, too.

"How do you know all this fascinating stuff?" Sally asked.

Ollie figured she was flirting with him. Lots of women preferred men with a little girth, as he called it.

"Three black guys outside told me," he said.

"Oh, *those* three."

"You know them?"

"They're out there every night."

"Yeah?"

"Yeah, they're crazy."

"Yeah? Crazy?"

"Yeah, they just got out of Buenavista a few months ago."

"Buenavista, huh?"

"Yeah. What they do, these mental hospitals, they medicate all these psychos till they're stabilized. Then they let them loose on the streets with prescriptions they don't bother filling. Before you know it, they're acting nutty all over again. I saw a man talking to a mailbox the other day, would you believe it? Holding a long conversation with a mailbox. Those three guys out there stand around that fire all night like it's some kind of shrine. The one who looks like Morgan Fairchild . . ."

"*That's* his name!" Ollie said, and snapped his fingers.

"He's the nuttiest of them all. Anything he told you, I'd take with a grain of salt."

"He told me these three white guys were peeing in the gutter when this black man in a black leather jacket came running out of here to stop them."

"Naw," Sally said. "Don't believe it."

"Were you working here alone on Saturday night?" Ollie asked slyly.

He spent the next fifteen minutes talking to another waitress, the short-order cook, and the cashier, who was also the night manager. None of them had seen three white guys in hooded parkas peeing in the gutter. And whereas all of them had seen half a *dozen* black guys in black leather jackets, none of them had seen one running out into the street to prevent mass urination.

Five minutes after Ollie left, Curly Joe Simms walked in.

There was no one named Bernie Himmel or Bernard Himmel listed in any of the phone directories for the city's five separate sectors. On the off chance that Marvin the bartender had got Bernie the bookie's family name wrong, they even checked all the listings under HIMMER and HAMMIL, but found no matching first name. There were two listings for B. HEMMER, but these turned out to be women, big surprise, who did not appreciate being awakened at a quarter to four in the morning.

"So that's it," Georgie said. "Let's forget it for now. Go home, get some sleep."

"No," Priscilla said.

She had just had an idea.

The computer listed a Bernard Himmel, alias Bernie Himmel, alias Benny Himmel, alias Bernie "The Banker" Himmel, a thirty-six-year-old white male who had taken two prior falls for violation of Section 225.10 of the state's Penal Law, titled Promoting Gambling in the First Degree, which read:

A person is guilty of promoting gambling in the first degree when he knowingly advances or profits from unlawful gambling activity by 1) Engaging in bookmaking to the extent that he receives or accepts in any one day more than five bets totaling more than five thousand dollars; or 2) Receiving, in connection with a lottery or policy scheme . . .

And so on, which second provision did not apply to either of Bernie's arrests and subsequent convictions.

Violation of 225.10 was a class-E felony, punishable by a term of imprisonment not to exceed four years. The first time around, Bernie was sentenced to one to three and was back on the street again, and at the same old stand again, after serving the requisite year. The next time, he drew two to four as a so-called predicate felon and was paroled after serving the minimum. The address he'd registered with his parole officer was 1110 Garner Avenue, not a mile away from The Juice Bar, where apparently he'd set up business again.

Carella and Hawes got to Garner at four A.M.

If Himmel *was* in fact taking bets again, then he was breaking parole at best and would be returned to prison to serve the two years he still owed the state. If, in addition, he was once again arrested and charged and convicted, then he would technically become a so-called *persistent* felony offender, and could be sentenced for an A-1 felony, which could mean fifteen to twenty-five years behind bars. Neither Carella nor Hawes had ever heard of anyone in this city or this state taking such a fall on a gambling violation. But Bernie the Banker Himmel was still looking at the two years owed on the parole violation, plus *another* two to four as a predicate felon with a new gambling violation. Such visions of the future could make any man desperate. Moreover, only two mornings ago, Carella and Hawes had knocked on a door and been greeted with four bullets plowing through the wood. They did not want to provoke yet another fusillade.

Without a no-knock arrest warrant, they were compelled to announce themselves. Gun-shy, they flanked the door. Service revolvers drawn, they pressed themselves against the wall on either side of it. Carella reached in to knock. No answer. He knocked again. He was about to knock a third time when a man's voice said, "Who is it?"

"Mr. Himmel?"

"Yes?"

"Police," Carella said. "Could you come to the door, please?"

Still standing to the side of it. Hawes on the other side of the jamb, facing him. Cold in the hallway here. Not a sound from inside the apartment. Not a sound anywhere in the building. They waited.

"Mr. Himmel?"

No answer.

"Mr. Himmel? Please come to the door, sir." They waited. "Or we'll have to go downtown for a warrant." Still no answer. "Mr. Himmel?"

They heard footsteps approaching the door.

They braced themselves.

Lock clicking open.

The door opened a crack. A night chain stopped it. The same voice said, "Yes?"

"Mr. Himmel?"

"Yes?"

"May we come in, sir?"

"Why?"

"We'd like to ask you some questions, sir."

"What about?"

"Well, if you'd let us in, sir . . ."

"No, I don't think so," Himmel said, and slammed the door in their faces. The lock snapped shut. They waited. In a moment, they heard the unmistakable sound of a window going up.

Carella took a calculated risk.

He kicked in the door.

He would worry later about convincing a judge that a reliable witness had seen a paroled gambling offender accepting money from a suspected murderer in an underground club that served booze illegally after hours. He would worry later about convincing a judge that slamming a door shut on two police officers merely here to ask questions, and then locking that door, and then opening a window were acts that constituted flight, than which there was no better index of guilt, tell that to O.J.

Meanwhile, the wood splintered, and the lock sprang, and the chain snapped, and they were inside a studio apartment, looking at a wide-eyed girl in bed clutching a blanket to her, the window open on the wall beyond, the curtains billowing on a harsh cold wind. They rushed across the room. Carella poked his head into the night.

"Stop! Police!" he yelled down the fire escape.

Nobody was stopping.

He could hear footfalls clanging on the iron rungs of the ladder below.

"I didn't do anything," the girl said.

They were already out the door again.

12

In the movies, one cop goes out the window and onto the fire escape and comes thundering down the ladders after the fleeing perp, passing windows where ladies in nightgowns are all aghast, while the other cop runs down the steps inside the building, and dashes around into the backyard so they have the perp sandwiched between them, All right, Louie, drop da gat!

In real life, cops know it's faster and safer, especially if the perp is armed, to come down the inside steps while he's outside descending to street level on narrow, often slippery metal ladders, especially when the temperature outside is three above zero. Carella and Hawes were a beat behind Bernie the Banker Himmel. They rounded the rear corner of the building just as he was climbing a snowcapped wooden fence separating the backyards.

This was a beautiful night for a little jog through the city. The clouds had passed, the sky above was a black canopy studded with stars and hung with an almost full moon that washed the terrain with an eerie glow. All was silent except for the sound of their footsteps crunching on crusted snow, their labored breaths puffing from chapped lips. They followed Himmel over the fence, right hands cold against the walnut stocks of their pistols, left hands gloved, coats flapping loose, mufflers flying behind them as if they were World War I fighter pilots. Himmel was small and Himmel was fast, and both Carella and Hawes were large and out of shape, and they were having a tough time keeping up with him.

In the movies, detectives are always lifting weights down at the old headquarters gym, or shooting at targets on the old firing range. In real life, detectives aren't often in on the big action scenes. They hardly ever chase thieves. They rarely, if ever, fire weapons at fleeing suspects. In real life, detectives usually come in *after* the fact. The burglary, the armed robbery, the arson, the murder has already been committed. It is their job to piece together past events and apprehend the person or persons who committed a crime or crimes. Sometimes, yes, a suspect will attempt flight, but even then there are strict guidelines limiting the use of force, deadly or otherwise. The LAPD has these guidelines, too; tell it to Rodney King.

Here in *this* city, tonight or any other night, gunplay was the very last thing Carella or Hawes wanted. The second least desirable thing was brute force. Besides, the way this little chase was developing, Bernie the Banker would be out of gun range at any moment. All three of them had now emerged from the barren backyards onto deserted—well, almost deserted—city streets, Himmel running ahead through narrow paths shoveled on icy sidewalks, banks of snow on either side of him, fast out-distancing Carella and Hawes who followed him and each other through the same narrow sidewalk burrows, knowing for damn sure they were going to lose him.

And then, three things happened in rapid succession.

Himmel rounded the corner and disappeared from sight.

A dog began barking.

And a snowplow went barreling up the street.

"This is what I'd like to know," Priscilla said.

Georgie yawned.

Tony yawned, too.

"If this tall blond guy delivered the key to the locker. . ."

"Well, he did," Georgie said. "We know he did."

"Then he had to know my grandmother, right?"

"Well . . . sure."

"I mean, she had to have given him the envelope with the key in it, am I right?"

"That's right."

"So why are we wasting time looking for this bookie, is what I'd like to know? When all we have to do is go to my grandmother's building and see if anyone *there* knows the blond guy."

"Good idea," Georgie said. "Let's do it in the morning when everybody's awake."

"It *is* morning," Priscilla said.

"Priss, please. We go knocking on doors at this hour . . ."

"You're right," she said.

Which astonished him.

Bernie Himmel was astonished to see a large black dog standing there like some fuckin apparition on the narrow path cleared through the snow. He stopped dead in his tracks. Ahead of him was the animal, snarling and barking and baring his teeth and blocking Himmel's escape route through the snow. Behind him, somewhere up the street, he could hear the roaring clang of a snowplow rushing through the night. He did what any sensible man would have done in the face of threatening fangs dripping saliva and slime. He leaped over the snowbank on his left, into the street, just as the plow came thundering by.

Where earlier there had been an evil growling monster guarding the icy gates of hell, now there was an avalanche of snow and ice and salt and sand pouring down onto Himmel's shoulders and head, knocking him off his feet and throwing him back against old snow already heaped at the curb, virtually burying him. He flailed with his arms, kicked with his legs, came sputtering up out of a filthy grey mountain of shmutz, and found himself blinking up into a pair of revolvers.

Fuckin Cujo, he thought.

The questioning took place in the second-floor interrogation room at five-thirty that Monday morning. They explained to Himmel that they weren't charging him with anything, that in fact they weren't interested in him at all.

"Then why am I here?" he asked reasonably.

He had been this route before, though not in this particular venue, which looked like any other shitty police precinct in this city, or even some he had known in Chicago, Illinois, or Houston, Texas.

"Just some questions we want to ask you," Hawes said.

"Then read me my rights and get me an attorney."

"Why?" Carella asked. "Did you do something?"

"You had my address, chances are you already been to the computer. So you know my record. So you want to ask me some questions. So I'll be back upstate tomorrow morning for breaking parole. I want a lawyer."

"This has nothing to do with breaking parole."

"Then why are you even mentioning it?"

"You're the one who mentioned it."

"Cause I'm six steps ahead of you."

"This has to do with a person you were talking to in The Juice Bar on Friday night . . ."

"I want a lawyer."

". . . and again on Sunday morning."

"I *still* want a lawyer."

"Give us a break here, Bernie."

"Why? You gonna give *me* a break?"

"We told you. We're not interested in you."

"I'll say it again. If you're not interested in me, why am I here?"

"This tall blond man you were talking to," Hawes said.

"What about him? *If* was talking to him."

Progress, Carella thought.

"We traced a murder weapon to him," he said.

"Oh, I see. Now it's a murder. You'd better get me a lawyer right this minute."

"All we want is his name."

"I don't know his name."

"What *do* you know about him?"

"Nothing. We met in a club, exchanged a few words . . ."

"Exchanged some cash, too, didn't you?"

The room went silent.

So did Himmel.

"But we're willing to forget that," Carella said.

"Then whatever I say is hypothetical," Himmel said.

"Let's hear it first."

"First let's understand it's hypothetical."

"Okay, it's hypothetical," Carella said.

"Then let's say the man is a big gambler. Bets on any event happening."

"Like?"

"Boxing, baseball, football, hockey, basketball, a man for all seasons. My guess is he bets the nags, too, but at one of the off-track parlors."

"Okay, he's a gamblcr."

"No, you weren't listening. He's a *big* gambler. And he's usually in over his head. Wins occasionally, but most of the time he doesn't know what he's doing. Fuckin greaseball can't tell the difference between baseball and football, how *would* he know how to bet? I give him thc odds, he picks whatever sounds . . ."

"What do you mean, greaseball?" Hawes asked.

"He's Italian."

"From Italy, you mean?" Carella said.

"Of *course* from Italy. Where *would* Italians come from, Russia?"

"You mean he's *really* Italian," Carella said.

"Yeah, really *really* Italian," Himmel said. "What's with you?"

"Never mind."

"You're surprised he's Italian, is that it? Cause he's blond?"

"No, I'm not surprised."

"He also has blue eyes, does that surprise you, too?"

"Nothing ever surprises me," Carella said wearily.

"You expect a wop to have black curly hair and brown eyes, you expect him to be a short fat guy. This guy's six-two, he weighs at least a buck ninety. Handsome as can be. Dumb Buck doesn't even know what the Super Bowl *is*, he bets a fortune on Pittsburgh, loses his shirt."

"When was this?"

"Two Sundays ago. Hypothetically."

"So, hypothetically, what was he doing in The Juice Bar this past Friday night?"

"Hypothetically, he was telling his bookie, in broken English, that he didn't have the twenty large to pay him."

"Is that what he bet on the Steelers?"

"Twenty big ones. Gave him a fourteen-and-a-half-point spread. Cowboys took it by sixteen."

"So what happened last Friday night?"

"The bookie told him to come up with the bread by Sunday morning or he was going to be *swimming* with the goddamn fishes."

"How'd he react to that?"

"Said he had to make a phone call."

"Did he?"

"Yeah, from the phone right there on the wall."

"What time was this?"

"Around one-fifteen in the morning. A few hours after the cops raided the Alhambra up the street from the club. Where they hold the cockfights."

"How'd you know that?"

"One of the owners came in. His bird had just got chewed up, he was practically weeping at the table. He told me he had a gun, he was thinking of shooting himself."

"His name wouldn't be Jose Santiago, would it?"

This city was full of mind readers.

"Yeah" Himmel said. "How'd you know that?"

"Lucky guess," Hawes said. "What time did *he* come in?"

"Santiago? Eleven-thirty, twelve o'clock. Right after the bust went down. I was sitting there waiting for Larry."

"Who's that?"

"The guy owed the twenty."

"I thought you didn't know his name."

"That was before everything got hypothetical."

"Larry what?"

"It's Lorenzo, but everybody calls him Larry."

"Lorenzo what?"

"I can't even pronounce it."

"Try."

"I'm telling you I can't. I wrote it down first time he placed a bet, it's one of those fuckin wop tongue twisters."

Carella sighed.

"Where'd you write it down?"

"On the slip."

"The betting slip?"

"No, a lady's pink slip, lace-trimmed."

269

The detectives looked at him. He knew he was being a smart-ass. He grinned. Nobody grinned back. He shrugged.

"Yes, the betting slip," he said. "Long since gone."

"Never wrote the name down again?"

"Never. Couldn't have if I wanted to. It was a mile long. Besides, I had his phone number. A man don't pay his marker, I give him a call, I say, Joey, you owe me a little something, am I right? It usually scares them."

"Did it scare Lorenzo?"

"He came up here to see me one o'clock in the morning, didn't he?"

"And made his phone call fifteen minutes later, is that right?"

"Yeah. We didn't have much to talk about after I mentioned him swimming with his little fishies."

"You didn't happen to overhear his end of the phone conversation, did you?"

"Yeah, but it was all in Italian."

"You think he called an Italian-speaking person, is that it?"

"I don't know who he called. I know he was talking Italian."

"What happened next?"

"He came back to the table, said he'd have the money by Sunday. Then he asked did I perhaps know where he could buy a gun."

"So you recommended Santiago," Carella said.

"Yeah, that's right," Himmel said, looking surprised.

"You didn't witness the gun changing hands, did you?" Hawes asked.

"No. But hypothetically, Larry bought it."

"What time did he leave here?"

"One-thirty or so."

"One more thing," Carella said.

"His phone number, right?" Himmel said.

Still six steps ahead of them.

At six-oh-four that Monday morning, the desk sergeant at the Eight-Eight called Ollie Weeks at home to tell him something had come up that might relate to the triple homicide he was investigating. He didn't know whether he should be waking Ollie up or not . . .

"Yeah, well you did," Ollie said.

". . . but some guy named Curly Joe Simms had called to say he was having a cup of coffee in the Silver Chief Diner on Ainsley, and a waitress named Sally told him a detective named Oliver Weeks was in there asking about three kids pissing in the gutter, and Curly Joe had seen these three kids with a person named Richie Cooper, who was a good friend now deceased. So if this detective wanted to talk to him . . ."

"What's his number?" Ollie asked.

The phone company told Hawes that the call from the wall phone of The Juice Bar at 1:17 A.M. on January nineteenth had been made to a telephone listed to a subscriber named Svetlana Helder at 1217 Lincoln Street in Isola.

This was puzzling.

Why had Larry Whoever called a woman who was murdered the very next night with a gun he'd purchased not five minutes after he'd got off the phone with her?

Meanwhile, Carella was dialing the number Bernie the Banker had given them. This was now a quarter past six in the morning. A woman's sleepy voice said, "*Pronto.*"

"*Signora?*" he said.

"*Sí?*"

"*Voglio parlare con Lorenzo, per piacere.*"

"*Non c'è.*"

In the next five minutes, in tattered Italian and shattered English, the woman—whose name was Carmela Buongiorno and who said she was the landlady of a rooming house on Trent Street, not five blocks from where Svetlana had been shot—told Carella that Lorenzo Schiavinato had been living there since October the twenty-fourth, but had moved out this past Sunday. She did not know where he was now. He seemed to be a nice man, was something the matter?

"*Che succese?*" she asked.

"What happened?"

"*Niente, signora, niente,*" Carella said.

Nothing, *signora*, nothing. But something had indeed happened.

Murder had happened.

And Lorenzo Schiavinato had purchased the murder weapon the night before someone used it on Svetlana Dyalovich.

They now had his full name.

They ran it through the computer.

There was *niente, signora*.

Niente.

* * *

Ollie figured Curly Joe Simms would turn out to be a bald guy and he wasn't disappointed. He made a note to mention to Meyer Meyer, up at the Eight-Seven, that he would start calling himself Curly Meyer. Curly Joe was wearing yellow earmuffs and a brown woolen coat buttoned over a green muffler. His eyes kept watering and he kept blowing his nose as he explained to Ollie that he was a night person, which meant that he only slept during the daytime. He was beginning to get a little drowsy right now, in fact, but he felt it was important to do his civic duty, wasn't it? Ollie was a little drowsy, too, but only because he'd just got up half an hour ago. At six forty-two in the morning, there weren't too many places open near the 88th Precinct station house. They met in the coffee shop of the Harley Hotel on Ninety-second and Jackson. The Harley was a hotbed dive catering to hookers and their clientele. A steady stream of girls walked in and out of the coffee shop while Ollie and Curly Joe talked.

Curly Joe was bothered that someone had drowned poor Richie Cooper.

"Richie was a close friend of mine," he said.

So close you didn't know he hated being called Richie, Ollie thought, but did not say. The man had come all the way over from Ainsley and Eleventh, six in the morning, he deserved a hearing, even if he was bald. Ollie ate another donut and listened.

Curly Joe sipped at his coffee and told him how on Saturday night he was sitting with Richie in one of the window booths at the Silver Chief Diner, both of them having coffee, when all at once Richie jumps up and yells, "Look at that, willya?"

"Look at what?" Curly Joe said.

"Out there. Those three guys."

Curly Joe looked.

Three big guys in hooded parkas were standing at the curb, pissing in the gutter. This was not such an unusual sight up here, so Curly Joe couldn't understand why Richie was so upset by it. But he certainly was annoyed, jumping up out of the booth, and putting on his black leather jacket . . .

"He was dressed all in black," Curly Joe said. "Black jeans, black shirt, black boots, the black jacket . . ."

"Yeah, go on," Ollie said.

. . . putting on the jacket, and tossing a couple of bucks on the table as his share of the bill, and then storming out of the diner and walking over to where the three guys were still standing there, shaking out their dicks. From where Curly Joe watched through the diner window, he saw, but could not hear, the conversation taking place between the four of them, Richie dressed all in black and appearing before them like an avenging angel of death. They almost all three of them peed on his boots, he was standing that close.

—*Now what do you call this?*

—*We call it pissing in the gutter.*

—*I call it disrespect for the neighborhood. That what the letter P stand for? Pissing?*

—*Join us, why don't you?*

—*My name is Richard.*

Big white guy zipping up and extending his hand to Richie.

—*So is mine.*

Second white guy holding out his hand, too.

—*Me, too.*

Third guy holding out his hand.

—*As it happens, my name is Richard, too.*

Richie holding out his hand, shaking hands with the three white guys, one after the other. And now there's a serious conversation at the curb, Richie probably explaining that what he did up here in Diamondback was sell crack cocaine to nice little boys like the three preppies here in their hooded parkas. In a minute or so, he begins leading them up the street, past the diner where Curly Joe is still sitting in the window booth, probably taking them to a place called the Trash Cat, which is an underground bar where there are plenty of girls all hours of the night, just like the Harley here.

They stop again not far from the diner, like at an angle to it, for another serious conversation Curly Joe can see but not hear.

—*You dudes interested in some nice jumbo vials I happen to have in my pocket here? You care for a taste at fifteen a pop?*

And now Curly Joe sees crack and money changing hands, black to white and white to black, and all at once a taxi pulls up to the curb, and a long-legged white girl in a fake-fur jacket and red leather boots steps out. She looks familiar but Curly Joe doesn't recognize her at first. The driver's window rolls down, he's got like a dazed expression on his face, as if he just got hit by a bus.

—*Thanks, Max.*

The girl blows him a kiss and swivels onto the sidewalk, a red handbag under her arm . . .

—Hey, Yolande, you jess the girl we lookin for.

. . . and Curly Joe recognizes her all at once as a hooker Jamal Stone fixed him up with one time when Jamal laid two bills on a pony and was a little short of cash. Her name was Marie St. Claire, she'd given Curly Joe the best blow job he'd ever had in his lifetime, did Ollie ever hear of a Moroccan Sip? So now there's another big conference at the curb, Curly Joe watching but not hearing, Richie's hands flying, *Six hundred for the three preppies here, whutchoo say? Two hundred apiece for the next few hours,* head bobbing, *you take me on, I'll throw five jumbos in the pot, whutchoo say, girlfriend?*—big summit meeting here on Ainsley Avenue—*We all go up my place, do some crack, get down to* realities, *sistuh, you hear whut I'm sayin?*

—*Well, I've been out since eleven last night, it's been a long one, bro. So maybe we ought to just pass unless we can sweeten the pot a little, hm?*

—*Whutchoo mean sweeten it? How sweet do you wish to sweeten it?*

—*If you'll be joining the party, I'll need ten jumbos . . .*

—*No problem.*

—*And a grand from the college boys here. Though you're all so cute, I might do it for nine.*

—*Make it eight.*

—*I can't do it for less than nine. Hey, you're all real cute, but . . .*

—*How about eight-fifty?*

—*It has to be nine or I'm out of here.*

—*Will you accept traveler's checks?*

—*Done deal.*

". . . and they all start laughing. They musta concluded their negotiation, don't you think?" Curly Joe said. "Cause next thing you know, she's looping her hands through two of the guys' arms, and they're all marchin off toward Richie's buildin, her in the red jacket, and Richie in his black leather, and the three kids with these hooded blue parkas got big white Ps and footballs on the back of them."

Daybreak is aptly named.

Unlike sunset, where colors linger in the sky long after the sun has dropped below the horizon, sunrise is heralded by a similar flush, but the display is brief, and suddenly it is morning. Suddenly the sky is bright. Day literally *breaks*, surprising the pinkish night, setting it to rout.

From the windows of the squadroom on the second floor of the old precinct building, they watched the day break over the city. It was going to be cold and clear again. The clock on the squadroom wall read seven-fifteen.

At a little past seven-thirty, the detectives began drifting in for the shift change. Officially this was called the eight-to-four, but it started at seven forty-five, because many uniformed cops were relieved on post, and detectives—all of whom had once pounded beats—honored the timeworn tradition. They hung their hats and coats on the rack in the corner, and exchanged morning greetings. Complaining about the vile coffee from the pot brewing in the clerical office down the hall, they sat nonetheless on the edges of their desks and sipped it from soggy cardboard containers. Outside the wind raged at the windows.

They double-teamed this one because it was now more than thirty-one hours since they'd caught the Dyalovich squeal and they were not very much closer to finding the person or persons who'd killed her. It was also two full days since they'd discovered the body of Yolande Marie Marx in the alleyway on St. Sab's and First. But whereas the Marx murder was officially theirs under the First Man Up rule, they had been informed that Fat Ollie Weeks of the Eight-Eight had caught a related double murder, and they were more than content to leave the three-way investigation to him. A hooker, a pimp, and a small-time ounce dealer? Let Ollie's mother worry.

So here they all were, those legendary stalwarts of the Eight-Seven, gathered in Lieutenant Byrne's sunny corner office at ten minutes to eight that Monday morning, Carella and Hawes telling the others what they had so far, and hoping that someone in this brilliant think tank would offer a clue or clues that would help them crack the case wide open.

"What it sounds like to me," Andy Parker said, "is you have nothing."

Parker was a good friend of Ollie Weeks. That's because they were both bigots. But whereas Ollie was also a good detective, Parker only rarely rose to heights of deductive dazzle. He was almost as big a slob as Ollie, however, favoring unpressed shirts, soiled suits, unpolished shoes, and an unshaven look he believed made him resemble a good television cop. Parker figured there were only two kinds of television cop shows. The lousy ones, which he called *The Cops of Madison County*, and the good ones, which he called *Real Meat Funk*.

As a detective, albeit not a very good one, Parker knew that the word "funk" descended from the word "funky," which in turn evolved from a style of jazz piano-playing called "funky butt," which translated as "smelly asshole." He was amused the other day when a radio restaurant critic mentioned that the food in a downtown bistro was "funky."

Not many things amused Parker.

Especially so early in the morning.

"Well, we do have the guy's name," Hawes said.

"What guy?"

"The guy who bought the murder weapon."

"Who you can't find."

"Well, he moved out yesterday," Carella said.

"So he's in flight, is that what you figure?" Willis asked.

He was poised on the edge of the lieutenant's desk like a gargoyle on Notre Dame cathedral, listening carefully, brown eyes intent. Byrnes liked him a lot. He liked small people, figured small people had to try harder. Willis had barely cleared the minimum-height requirement for policemen in this city, but he was an expert at judo and could knock any cheap thief flat on his ass in less than ten seconds. His girlfriend had been shot and killed only recently, by a pair of Colombian goons who'd broken into her apartment. Willis never much talked about her, but he hadn't been the same since. Byrnes worried. He worried about all of his people.

"Day after the murder, he powders," Kling said, "it's got to be flight."

Worried a lot about Kling, too. Never had any luck with women, it seemed. Byrnes understood he'd taken up with a black woman, a deputy chief in the department, no less, as if the black-white thing wasn't difficult enough. Byrnes wished him the best, but it remained to be seen. Next chapter, he thought. Life is always full of next chapters, some of them never written.

"Maybe he's already back in Italy," Brown said.

Scowling. Always scowling. Made it look as if he was angry all the time, like a lot of black people in this city were, with damn good cause. But in all the years he'd known Brown, he'd never seen him lose his temper. Giant of a man, could have been a linebacker for a professional football team, reminded him a lot of Rosie Grier, in fact, though Grier was now, what, a minister? He tried to imagine Brown as a minister. His imagination would not take him quite that far.

"Maybe," Carella said.

"Where in Italy?" Meyer asked.

"Don't know."

"What'd you find when you tossed her apartment?" Byrnes asked.

"Me?"

"You."

"Dead cat lying alongside her," Carella said.

"Skip the cat."

"Fish bones all over the kitchen floor."

"I said skip the cat."

"Savings account passbook in a dresser drawer, hundred-and twenty-five thou withdrawn the morning before she got killed."

"What time?"

"Ten twenty-seven A.M."

"Cash or bank check?"

"Don't know."

"What *do* you know?" Parker asked.

Carella merely looked at him.

"We know the guy's name," Hawes said.

"*If* he killed her," Parker said.

"Whether he killed her or not, we know his name."

"But not where he is."

"Check the airlines," Brown suggested. "Maybe he *did* go back to Italy."

"And we've got a clear chain of custody on the murder weapon," Carella said.

"Running from where to where?"

"Registered to a private bodyguard named Rodney Pratt, stolen from his limo on the night before the murder . . ."

"Who boosted it?" Kling asked.

"Guy named Jose Santiago."

"The famous bullfighter?" Parker asked.

This was a line he'd used before. The expression was his way of putting down anyone of Hispanic descent. Byrnes had heard rumors—which he tended to disbelieve that Parker was now living with a Puerto Rican girl. Parker? Sleeping with a famous bullfighter?

"The famous *cock*fighter," Hawes corrected.

"He fights with his cock?" Parker asked.

No one laughed.

Parker shrugged.

"So what do you figure?" Byrnes asked. "An interrupted burglary?"

"If the hun-twenty-five was in the apartment, yes."

"What'd *you* find when you tossed it?"

"Us?" Meyer asked.

"You."

"Dead fish stinking up the joint."

"Piss, too," Kling said.

"Cat piss."

"Are we back to the cat again?" Byrnes asked.

He was not noted as an animal lover. When he was ten, a pet turtle named Petie had suddenly died. Also a canary named Alice when he was twelve. And when he was thirteen, his mother gave away his pet dog named Ruffles. For peeing all over their apartment. Which apparently Svetlana Dyalovich's cat had been fond of doing, too. He did not want to hear another word about the dead woman's dead cat.

"Be nice if cats could bark, huh?" Parker said.

"Be nice if we could get *off* the goddamn cat," Byrnes said. "What else did you find?"

"Us?" Kling asked.

"You."

"Nothing."

"No money, huh?"

"Nothing."

"So maybe it *was* a burglar."

"The cat could explain those stains on the mink," Carella said.

"What stains?" Brown asked.

"The fish stains. They could've got on the coat that way."

"There were fish stains on the coat?" Brown asked.

Byrnes was watching him. Eyes narrowing, scowl deepening. He was looking for something. Didn't know what yet, but looking.

"If she fed the cat raw fish, I mean," Carella said.

"How do you know there were fish stains on the coat?" Byrnes asked.

"Grossman," Willis said. "I took the call."

"She was wearing a mink while she fed the goddamn cat?" Parker said.

"Are you saying the cat might've rubbed up against her?" Brown asked.

"No, these were near the collar," Carella said.

"Near the *collar*?"

"I took the call," Willis said again.

"Well, what'd Grossman say, actually?" Byrnes asked.

"He said there were *fish* stains on the coat."

"Near the *collar*?" Brown asked again.

"High up on the coat," Willis said, and opened his note-book. "These are his words," he said, and began reading. " 'Stains inside and outside, near the collar. From the location, it would appear someone held the coat in both hands, one at either side of the collar, thumbs outside, fingers inside'. Quote, unquote."

"I can't visualize it," Brown said, shaking his head.

"Okay to use this?" Willis asked.

"Sure," Byrnes said.

Willis picked up a magazine from Byrnes's desk, handed it to Brown.

"Hold it with your fingers on the front cover, thumbs on the back cover."

Brown tried it.

"That's how Grossman figures the coat was held."

"You mean there were fingerprints?"

"No. But he thinks somebody with fish oil on his or her hands held the coat the way you're holding that magazine."

Brown looked at his hands on the magazine. Everyone in the office was looking at his hands on the magazine.

"Didn't you say she was wearing a *wool* coat?" Kling asked.

"Yeah. When she went down to buy the booze."

"When was that?" Byrnes asked.

"Eleven o'clock that morning."

"The day she was killed?"

"Yes. Half an hour after she made the bank withdrawal."

"Something's fishy here," Byrnes said, not realizing he was making a pun, and not realizing how close he was, either.

When Priscilla and the boys drove up in a taxi at eight that morning, the superintendent of Svetlana's building was out front with the garbage cans, wondering if the Sanitation Department would ever start pickups again. Priscilla told him she was Svetlana's granddaughter, and he expressed his deepest sympathy, clucking his tongue and shaking his head over the mysteries and misfortunes of life. They chitchatted back and forth for maybe three or four minutes before he finally mentioned that Mrs. Helder's closest friend in the building was a woman named Karen Todd, who lived just down the hall from her.

"Probably there right this minute," he said. "Doesn't leave for work till about eight-thirty."

Georgie fell in love at once with the slender young woman who opened the door to apartment 3C. He guessed she was in her mid-twenties, a very exotic-looking person who reminded him of his cousin Tessie who once he tried to feel up on the roof when they were both sixteen. Tessie later married a dentist. But here was the same long black hair and dark brown eyes, the same bee-stung lips and high cheekbones, the same impressive bust, as Georgie's mother used to call it.

Karen was just finishing breakfast, but she cordially invited them into the apartment—batting her lashes at Georgie, Priscilla noticed—and told them she had to leave soon, but she'd be happy to answer questions until then. Although, really, she'd already told the police everything she knew.

Priscilla suggested that perhaps the police hadn't asked her the same questions they were about to ask.

Karen looked puzzled.

"For example," Priscilla said, "did you ever happen to notice a tall blond man visiting my grandmother's apartment?"

"No," Karen said. "In fact, I did not."

"How well did you know the old lady?" Georgie asked kindly.

Karen looked at the clock.

Then she gave them much the same information she'd given the police, telling all about her and Svetlana sipping tea together in the late afternoon, listening to her old 78s . . .

"It reminded me of T. S. Eliot somehow," she said again, and smiled at Georgie, who didn't know who T. S. Eliot was.

She told them, too, about accompanying Svetlana to her internist's office one day . . .

"She had terrible arthritis, you know . . ."

. . . and another time to an ear doctor who told her she ought to see a neurologist. Because of the ringing in her ears, you know.

"When was this?" Priscilla asked.

"Oh, before Thanksgiving. It was awful. She was crying so hard in the taxi, I thought her heart would break."

"And you're sure you never saw her with a tall blond man?"

"Positive."

"Never, huh?"

"Never. Well, not *with* her."

"What do you mean?"

"I don't think he went inside."

"Inside?"

"Her apartment. But one morning, when she was sick . . ."

"Yes?" Priscilla said.

"He brought fish for the cat."

"Who did?" Tony asked.

"A tall blond person."

"His name wouldn't have been *Eliot*, would it?" Georgie asked shrewdly.

"I have no idea what his name was."

"But he brought *fish* to her apartment?" Tony said.

"Fish. Yes."

"But didn't go in?"

"Well, actually, I don't really know. I was leaving for work when he knocked on her door. Svetlana answered, and he said . . . mm, yeah, that's right, wait a minute. He *did* give her his name, but I don't remember it. It was something very foreign. He had a foreign accent."

"Russian?" Priscilla asked.

"I really don't know. He said he was here with the fish for Irina."

"For Irina. So he knew the cat's name. Which means he knew my grandmother, too. But he didn't go in? When she opened the door?"

"Well, in fact I really can't say. I was already starting down the stairs."

"What *kind* of fish?" Georgie asked.

"I have no idea."

"Where'd he *get* this fish?"

"Well, I would guess at the fish market, wouldn't you?"

"What fish market?" Priscilla asked.

"Where Svetlana went for the cat every morning."

"And where's *that*?" Priscilla asked, and held her breath.

"Let's try a timetable on this thing, okay?" Byrnes said. He was getting exasperated. He didn't like little old ladies in faded mink coats smelling of fish getting shot with a gun stolen from a limo that had transported a fighting rooster uptown. He didn't like animals, period. Turtles, canaries, dogs, cats, fish, roosters, cockroaches, whatever.

"Where do you want us to start, Pete?" Carella asked.

"The gun."

"Belongs to a man named Rodney Pratt. Licensed. Keeps it in the glove compartment of his limo. Car breaks down Thursday night, he takes it to the nearest garage off the Majesta Bridge. Place called Bridge Texaco. Forgets the gun in the glove box."

"Okay, next."

"How do you know *he's* not the murderer?" Parker asked.

"We know," Hawes said, dismissing the very idea.

"Gee, excuse me for fucking *breathing*!" Parker said.

"Next," Carella said, "they work on the car all day Friday. One of the mechanics, guy named Jose Santiago, *borrows* the car, quote unquote, to drive his prize rooster uptown that night to a cockfight in Riverhead."

"Excuse me while I puke," Parker said.

"Puke," Kling suggested.

"A fuckin bird in the backseat of a *limo*?"

"So puke," Kling suggested again.

"Santiago's bird loses. He finds the gun in the glove box, decides to shoot the winning bird, changes his mind when the Four-Eight raids the place. He goes to a nearby after-hours joint called The Juice Bar . . ."

"I know that place," Brown said.

". . . where this tall blond son of a bitch we're trying to find is meeting with a bookie named Bernie Himmel who tells him he's gonna be swimming with the fishes unless he pays him by Sunday morning the twenty grand he lost on the Cowboys-Steelers game."

"*Swimming* with the fishes," Hawes corrected.

"What?"

"He stressed the word 'swimming.' "

"I don't know what you mean."

"He told Schiavinato he'd be *swimming* with the fishes."

"As opposed to what?" Meyer said. "Dancing with them?"

"I'm only telling you what I heard."

"Let me hear the rest of the timetable," Byrnes said.

"Okay. Saturday night, a quarter to twelve, we get a DOA at 1217 Lincoln Street, old lady named Svetlana Helder, turns out to be Svetlana Dyalovich, the famous concert pianist."

"I never heard of her," Parker said.

"Two to the heart," Hawes said.

"I saw that picture," Kling said.

"Was that the name?"

"I'm pretty sure."

"Next morning, around seven, we get a dead hooker in an alley on St. Sab's."

"Any connection?"

"None."

"Then why bring her up?"

"A policeman's lot," Carella said, and shrugged.

"He also called them the *blond* guy's fish," Hawes said.

"I'm lost," Parker said.

"So am I," Byrnes said.

"Himmel. The bookie. Bernie the Banker. He said they didn't have much to talk about after he mentioned Schiavinato swimming with his little fishies."

"I'm *still* lost," Parker said.

"Yes, can you please tell us what the hell you're driving at?" Byrnes asked.

"*His* little fishies. Not *the* little fishies, but *his* little fishies. *Schiavinato's* little fishies."

Everybody was looking at him.

Only Carella knew what he was saying.

"The cat," Carella said.

"Not the goddamn *cat* again," Byrnes said.

"She went out every morning to buy fresh fish for the cat."

"Where'd you say her apartment was?" Parker asked, suddenly catching on.

"1217 Lincoln."

"Simple," Parker said. "The Lincoln Street Fish Market."

"*Selling* fish," Meyer said, nodding. "As opposed to *swimming* with them."

13

At eight-fifteen that morning, the Lincoln Street Fish Market was not quite as bustling as it had been between four and six A.M. when fish retailers from all over the city arrived in droves. As Priscilla and the boys pulled up in a taxi, only housewives and restaurant owners were examining the various catches of the day, all displayed enticingly on ice—well, enticingly if you liked fish.

The market was a sprawling complex of indoor and outdoor stalls. On the sidewalk outside the high-windowed arching edifice fishmongers, wearing woolen gloves with the fingers cut off, woolen caps pulled down over their ears, and bloodstained white smocks over layers of sweaters, stood hawking their merchandise while potential customers picked over the fish as if they were inspecting diamonds for flaws.

It was a clear, cold, windy, sunny Monday morning.

"Where do we start?" Georgie asked.

He was hoping to discourage her. He did not want her to meet the man who'd dropped off that key to the bus terminal locker. He did not want her to learn that nobody had been in that locker except him and Tony here, who was backing away from the fish stalls as if his grandmother had cooked fish for him whenever he visited her on a Friday, which she had, and which he'd hated. He learned after her death that *she'd* hated fish, too. His mother, on the other hand, never had to cook fish in her entire lifetime because the church changed its rules. His mother was a staunch Catholic who practiced birth control and didn't believe in confession.

Priscilla looked bewildered.

She had never been to this part of the city before, certainly never to a fish market here, had never seen so much damn fish ever, and could not imagine how she could even *hope* to find a tall blond man among all these men wearing hats and smocks and gloves.

The bitter cold did not help.

Priscilla was wearing a mink, dark and soft and supple in contrast to the ratty orange-brown coat her grandmother had been wearing when someone shot her. The fur afforded scant protection against the harsh wind blowing in over the river. Georgie and Tony were wearing belted cloth coats and woolen mufflers, their fedoras pulled down low on their foreheads, their hands in their pockets, just like movie gangsters. Wind wailing around them, the three walked the four dockside blocks, studying the men behind each of the outdoor stalls and ice bins, searching for telltale blond sideburns at the rolled edges of ubiquitous woolen caps.

At the end of twenty minutes of close scrutiny, they were happy to be entering the long enclosed market. After the howling wind outside, even the indoor din seemed welcoming, fishmongers touting pompano and squid, sea bass and flounder, mackerel and shrimp, sole and snapper. They were coming down the center aisle, tall windows streaming wintry sunlight, stalls of iced fish on either side of them, Georgie blowing on his hands, Tony wearing a pained look in memory of his grandmother, Priscilla holding the collar of the mink closed with one hand because to tell the truth it was almost as cold inside here as it was outside, when all at once . . .

Behind the stall on the right . . .

Just ahead . . .

They saw a hatless man with muddy blond hair . . .

Standing some six feet two inches tall . . .

Wearing a white smock over a blue coat and a red muffler . . .

Bearing a marked resemblance to Robert Redford, and lifting a nice fat halibut off the ice to show to a female customer.

Hawes and Carella were just pulling up outside.

"Blond hair and blue eyes," Hawes said.

"Must be from Milan," Carella said.

"Or Rome. Rome has blonds, too."

"Redheads," Carella said.

A gust of wind almost knocked Hawes off his feet.

"Which first?" Carella asked. "Inside or out?"

Ask a stupid question.

Hawes reached for the doorknob.

At the downtown end of the enclosed market, four city blocks from where the detectives went in, Priscilla was just asking Lorenzo Schiavinato if he knew her grandmother Svetlana.

"*Non parlo inglese*," Lorenzo said.

Thank God, Georgie thought.

"He doesn't speak English," he translated for Priscilla.

"Ask him if he knew my grandmother."

"I don't speak Italian," Georgie said.

"I do," Tony said, and Georgie wanted to kill him.

"Ask him if he knew my grandmother."

Tony's grandmother was from Siciliy, where they did not exactly speak Dante's Italian. The dialect Tony now used was the one he'd heard at Filomena's knee while she was cooking her abominable fish. First he asked Lorenzo his name.

"*Mi chiamo Lorenzo Schiavinato*," Lorenzo said.

"His name's Lorenzo," Tony translated. "I couldn't make out the last name."

Small wonder, Georgie thought.

"Ask him if he knew my grandmother."

"Where are you from?" Tony asked.

"Milano," Lorenzo said.

Where they spoke *Florentine* Italian, and where the Sicilian dialect was scarcely understood. Lorenzo was, in fact, squinting his very blue eyes in an effort to understand Tony's Italian, which itself was a bastardization of the dialect his sainted grandmother had spoken.

It occurred to Georgie that the so-called "Italian" conversation between them was taking place in a fish market reputedly run by the mob, whose Italian was limited to a few basic words like "*Boff on gool*," which itself was a bastardization of the time-honored "*Va fa in culo*," better left uninterpreted in the presence of a fine lady like Priscilla Stetson.

Who now said, rather impatiently this time, "Ask him if he knew my goddamn *grand*mother."

In Sicilian Italian, Tony asked if Lorenzo perchance had known Priscilla's grandmother.

In Florentine Italian, Lorenzo asked who perchance her grandmother might have been.

"Svetlana Dyalovich," Tony said.

And Lorenzo began running.

From where the detectives were coming down the center aisle of the indoor market, checking out the men selling fish from stalls and barrels and bins and ice chests on either side of them, they saw a tall blond man running toward them, chased by Svetlana's granddaughter and the two goons who'd braced them at the club on Saturday night.

If the tall runner was, in fact, Lorenzo Schiavinato, then he was the one who'd bought the gun that killed Priscilla's grandmother. Despite what was known in the trade as "background"—the number of innocent bystanders at any given scene—the fact that Lorenzo had purchased the murder weapon was justification within the guidelines for Carella and Hawes to draw their own guns. Besides, the man was running. In this city, unless you were running to catch a bus, the very act was suspicious.

The guns came out.

"Stop!" Hawes shouted. "Police!"

"Police!" Carella shouted. "Stop!"

Lorenzo wasn't stopping.

A hundred and eighty pounds of muscle and bone plowed right through them, knocking Hawes off his feet, tossing Carella back onto a stall of very nice iced salmon, and causing a mustached man in a brown derby to throw his hands over his head in fright. Both detectives recovered at once, Carella first, Hawes an instant later.

"Stop!" they shouted simultaneously.

Hawes was in a crouch, pistol levered, holding his gun steady in both hands.

Carella was standing beside him, gun extended in both hands, ready to fire.

"Stop!" he shouted.

Lorenzo kept running.

Hawes fired first. Carella fired an instant later. Carella missed. Hawes did, too. He fired again. This time, his shot took Lorenzo in the left leg, sending him tumbling. Everywhere around them, the background was screaming. The mustached man in the brown derby was running in the opposite direction, away from the shooting, waving his hands hysterically in the air. He tripped over Georgie, who had thrown himself flat on the floor the moment he'd heard shots, the way his uncle Dominick had taught him to do. Lorenzo was trying to crawl away, dragging his wounded leg behind him. Hawes kicked him and then stepped on his back, holding him down while Carella cuffed him.

"Ask him if he knew my grandmother," Priscilla said.

"Few things we'd like to ask you, too," Carella said.

Everyone was breathing very hard.

Fat Ollie Weeks was asking the computer for any tri-state area high school, prep school, parochial school, Christian academy or so-called alternative school whose name began with the letter P.

There were fifteen such private schools in the metropolitan area alone.

Thirty-eight in the entire state.

Of the public schools, there were a hundred and forty-six, thirty of them beginning with the word "Port." Port This, Port That, more damn coastal towns than Ollie knew existed.

In the two neighboring states combined, there were thirty-nine private schools and a hundred and ninety-eight public schools that began with the letter P.

All of the public schools in this city were designated with the letters P.S. before the name, and so the computer belched out what looked to Ollie like more high schools than he could possibly cover in ten years of investigation. He limited the search to proper names alone and came up with sixty-three schools that had the letter P in their names.

Some of these schools were named for areas of the city, like Parkhurst or Pineview or Paley Hills. Others had been named after people. The computer did not differentiate between given names and surnames. The letter P appeared in Peter Lowell High, but it also appeared in Luis Perez High. But Ollie had been born and raised in this fair city, and he knew that kids never said they went to Harry High or Abraham High, but instead said they went to Truman High or Lincoln High. So he figured if the letter on those parkas stood for a person after whom a school had been named, then it sure as hell was the *surname*. Running down the printed list by hand, he limited the city's sixty-three public schools to a mere seventeen. He was making progress.

By the time he was ready to begin making his phone calls, his trimmed-down list seemed like a reasonable one.

Sort of.

The way the joke goes, a woman is telling another woman about her son in medical school, and she keeps referring to him as a doctor. The other woman says, "By *you*, your son is a doctor. And by your *son*, your son is a doctor. But by a *doctor*, is your son a doctor?"

By Byrnes, Carella was Italian. And by Hawes, Carella was Italian. But by an *Italian*, was Carella Italian?

Lorenzo Schiavinato asked for an interpreter.

The interpreter's name was John McNalley.

He had studied Italian in high school and college because he'd wanted to become an opera singer. He never did get to sing at La Scala or the Met because he had a lousy voice, but he did have a certain facility with language, and so—in addition to interpreting for the police and the courts, he also worked for many publishers, translating worthy books from the French, Italian and Spanish.

He still wanted to sing opera.

McNalley informed Lorenzo that he was being charged with murder in the second degree. In this state, you could be charged with Murder One only if you killed someone during the commission of a felony, or if you'd been earlier convicted of murder, or if the currently charged murder was particularly cruel and wanton, or if it was a contract killing, or if the victim was a police officer, or a prison guard, or a

298

prisoner in a state pen, or a witness to a prior crime, or a judge—all of whom, according to one's personal opinion, might deserve killing.

Murder Two was killing almost anybody else.

Like murder in the first, murder in the second was also an A-1 felony. In accordance with the new law, Lorenzo was looking at the death penalty at worst, or fifteen to life at best, none of which added up to a tea party on the lawn.

Naturally, he asked for a lawyer.

He was an illegal alien in the United States of America, but, hey, he knew his rights.

Lorenzo's lawyer was a man named Alan Moscowitz.

He was a tall angular man wearing a brown suit and vest, looking very lawyerly in gold-rimmed spectacles and shiny brown shoes. Carella disliked most defense attorneys, but hope springs eternal so maybe one day he'd meet one who wouldn't rub him the wrong way.

Moscowitz didn't understand Italian at all.

The melting pot realized.

They read Lorenzo his rights in Italian, and he said he understood them, and Moscowitz ascertained, through back-and-forth interpretation, that his client understood Miranda and was willing to answer whatever questions the detectives posed. The questions they posed had to do with shooting an eighty-three-year-old woman at close range in cold blood. Lorenzo didn't much look like a man who'd committed murder, but then again not many murderers did. What he looked like was a slightly bewildered Robert Redford who spoke only basic English like Me Tarzan, You Jane.

The back-and-forth, in English and Italian and then English again, went this way.

"Mr. Schiavinato . . ."

Very difficult name to pronounce. Skee-*ah*-vee-*nah*-toe.

"Mr. Schiavinato, do you know, or did you ever know, a woman named Svetlana Dyalovich?"

"No."

"How about Svetlana Helder?"

"No."

"Her granddaughter told us . . . did you know she had a granddaughter?"

"No."

"We've been talking to her. She told us several things we'd like to ask you about."

"Um."

"Mr. Schiavinato, did you deliver to Miss Priscilla Stetson at the Hotel Powell the key to a pay locker at the Rendell Road Bus Terminal?"

"No."

"Delivered it on the morning of January twenty-first, didn't you?"

"No."

"Miss Stetson says you did."

"I don't know who Miss Stetson is."

"She's Svetlana Dyalovich's granddaughter."

"I don't know either of them."

"Locker number one thirty-six. Do you remember that?"

"No, I don't."

"Where'd you get that key?"

"I don't know what key you're talking about."

"Did Svetlana Dyalovich give you that key?"

"Nobody gave me a key."

"Did Svedana Dyalovich ever come to your stall at the Lincoln Street Fish Market to purchase fish for her cat?"

"No."

"Early in the morning, this would have been."

"No."

"Every morning."

"No. I don't know this woman."

"Ever go to her apartment?"

"How would I? I don't know her. I don't know where she lives."

"Her neighbor down the hall told the granddaughter you went there to deliver fish one morning."

"I don't know her *or* her neighbor. *Or* the grand-daughter, either."

"Then you never went to 1217 Lincoln Street, apartment 3A, is that right?"

"Never."

"Mr. Schiavinato, I show you this weapon tagged as evidence and ask if you've ever seen it before."

"Never."

"Didn't you buy this pistol from a man named Jose Santiago . . ."

"No."

"On the night before . . ."

"No."

". . . Svetlana Dyalovich was murdered?"

"No."

"Didn't you telephone her a few minutes before you bought the gun?"

"No."

"Mr. Schiavinato, we have here a telephone company record showing that a call was made from a wall phone at a club called The Juice Bar at one-fifteen A.M. this past Friday night to a telephone listed to Svetlana Helder at 1217 Lincoln Street . . ."

"*Cosa*?"

The precinct's civilian stenographer read back the question. McNalley the interpreter translated it for Lorenzo and his lawyer. Moscowitz nodded that it was okay to answer it.

"I don't know who called this woman," Lorenzo said, "but it wasn't me."

"Weren't you in The Juice Bar that night at one A.M.?"

"No. I don't know this place."

"Uptown in Riverhead?"

"No."

"Harris Avenue? Uptown?"

"No."

"Mr. Schiavinato . . ."

Such a *damn* difficult name to pronounce.

"Mr. Schiavinato, do you know a man named Bernard Himmel?"

"No."

"Bernie Himmel?"

"No."

"Benny Himmel?"

"No."

"Bernie the Banker Himmel?"

"I don't know any of these people."

"Never placed a bet with him, huh?"

302

"Never. Any of them."

A good imitation of a Robert Redford smile.

Hawes wanted to smack him.

"Ever place a bet with him on the Super Bowl?"

"What is this Super Bowl?"

Smack the fucking smile off his face.

"Steelers against the Cowboys?"

"I don't know what any of this means."

"Twenty grand on the Steelers?"

"What is twenty grand?"

"You lost the bet. Because of the point spread."

"What is a point spread?"

"Twenty grand gone in a wink."

"What is a wink?"

"He sounds like *Jeopardy!*," Carella said.

"Please, Detective," Moscowitz warned, raising an eyebrow.

"Sorry, Counselor," Carella said, and raised his own eyebrow. "Mr. Schiavinato, didn't you lose twenty thousand dollars on the Steelers-Cowboys game?"

"I never had twenty thousand dollars in my entire life."

"You had it when you paid your marker, didn't you?"

"I don't know what a marker is."

"A promise to pay money you owed."

"I don't owe anybody money. I have an honest job. I do honest work."

"You owed Bernie Himmel the twenty thousand dollars you lost on the Super Bowl, didn't you?"

"No."

"You went to see him on Friday night . . ."

"No."

". . . and he told you he'd kill you if you didn't pay the money by Sunday morning."

"I don't know who you're talking about."

"Bernie Himmel. Your bookie. Bernie the Banker. You're a gambler, aren't you, Lorenzo?"

"Sometimes I bet on horse races. At the OTB. But I don't know this man you're talking about."

"Then you don't remember him telling you to get the money or you'd be swimming with your little fishies?"

"I don't know him. How could he tell me this?"

"After which you went directly to the wall telephone . . ."

"No."

". . . and called Svetlana Dyalovich. Why, Lorenzo? Did you want to make sure she'd be out of the apartment when you went there to burglarize it?"

"*Cosa*?" he said again.

The stenographer repeated the question. McNalley translated it. Moscowitz cleared his throat.

"Detective," he said, "my client has told you repeatedly that he did not know Svetlana Dyalovich, did not know her granddaughter, and never went to her apartment on Lincoln Street. Nor does he know a bookmaker named Bernie Himmel or a gun dealer named Jose Santiago. Now, if . . ."

"He's not a gun dealer."

"Excuse me, I thought he's supposed to have sold my client a gun."

"He *did* sell him a gun. But he's not a dealer. He pumps gas at a Texaco station."

"*Whatever* he does, my client doesn't know him."

Carella figured he kept calling him "my client" only because he couldn't pronounce his last name.

"So unless you have something *new* to . . ."

"How about a clear chain on the gun, Counselor?"

"You!" Moscowitz shouted, and pointed his finger at the stenographer. "Hold it right there." He turned to Carella. "Is this off the record?" he asked.

"Sure."

The stenographer waited. Carella nodded.

"Then let me hear it," Moscowitz said.

"We've traced the gun from its registered owner. . ."

"Named?"

"Rodney Pratt."

"To?"

"Jose Santiago, who stole it from the glove compartment of Pratt's car . . ."

"He's admitted this?"

"He has."

"And from there . . . ?"

"To Mr. Schiavinato here, who bought it from him for two hundred and fifty dollars."

"Well, this is where it begins to get speculative, Detective. But let's assume for the moment, arguendo, that my client *did* buy a gun from this man. How does that make it the murder weapon?"

"The bullets that killed Mrs. Helder and her cat were fired from it. We found them embedded in the door behind her body and the baseboard behind the cat. We recovered the gun itself in a sewer outside her building. The only thing we *don't* have is Mr. Schiavinato's fingerprints on the gun, and frankly . . ."

"Well, that's a very big negative, Detective. Anyone could have fired the gun."

"Perhaps your client . . ." Byrnes said.

He couldn't pronounce the name, either.

". . . can explain why he telephoned the victim minutes before he bought the gun that killed her."

"Why exactly *did* he call her, Lieutenant?"

The weak spot.

Byrnes knew it, Carella knew it, Hawes knew it, and now Moscowitz had zeroed in on it: Why had Lorenzo called Svetlana before buying the gun he later used to kill her?

"We think he was planning to burglarize her apartment," Carella said. "He called to find out when it would be safe. When she'd be home."

It still sounded weak.

"Are you saying he called to ask her when she'd be home? So he could run right over to burglarize . . ."

"Well, no, he didn't ask her flat out."

"Then how did he ask her?"

"I don't know the actual conversation that took place."

"But you think he was trying to determine when she'd be out of the apartment . . ."

"Yes."

"So he'd know when it would be safe to go in and burglarize it."

"Exactly."

"In Italian?"

"What?"

"This conversation. Was it in Italian?"

"Yes, it was. According to a witness."

"Because he doesn't speak English, you see."

"I suspect he speaks some English."

"Oh. And why is that?"

"He sells fish to English-speaking people, I'm sure he must speak at least a little English."

"We'll have to ask him, won't we?" Moscowitz said, and smiled sweetly. "In Italian."

Hawes wanted to smack *him*, too.

"How long was this phone conversation, do you know?"

"No, I don't."

"The phone company would know, I suppose."

"Yes, but . . ."

"Should we contact them?"

"Why?"

"Find out how long it took my Italian-speaking client to learn when his prospective victim would be out of the apartment so he could burglarize it."

He's trying his case right here in the interrogation room, Carella thought. And winning it.

"By the way, were there any signs of burglary at the scene?" Moscowitz asked.

"The window was open."

"Oh? This means a burglary was committed?"

"No, but Mr. Schievinato must have know there was money in the apartment . . ."

"Oh? How would he have known that?"

"He knew the woman. Talked to her every morning at the market. Even made a delivery to the apartment when she was sick one morning. She was a lonely old lady. She confided in him. And he took advantage of her trust."

"I see. By shooting her and killing her, is that it?"

"Yes."

"Why?"

"He was surprised during the commission of. . ."

"But I thought he called her to find out when she'd be out."

"Yes, but . . ."

"If he knew when she'd be out, how come he was surprised?"

"People come home unexpectedly all the time."

"So he shot her. Was this *after* he found this money he supposedly knew was in the apartment?"

"It had to've been. He paid off his bookie the very next day."

"Gave him twenty thousand dollars the next day, is that right?"

"Yes. Himmel told us . . ."

"A bookie," Moscowitz said, dismissing him with an airy wave of his hand.

"He had no reason to lie."

"Oh? When did bookmaking become legal?"

"We offered no deals."

"How about offering me one?"

"Like what?"

"We all go home. My client included."

"Your client is a murderer."

"Who stole twenty thousand dollars from an old lady, right?"

"Maybe more."

"Oh? How much more?"

"She withdrew a hundred and twenty-five from her bank the morning before she was killed."

Moscowitz looked at him.

"Let me get this straight," he said. "Are you now saying he stole a hundred and twenty-five thousand dollars from her?"

"I'm saying the money is gone. I'm saying twenty thousand of it was turned over to a bookie the following morning. I'm saying it's highly likely, yes."

"Stole all that money and then shot her, is that it?"

"Yes, that's it. That's what it looks like to us."

"Detective, I'll tell you what. This is so preposterous that I'm going to ask that you stop the questioning of my client right this . . ."

"It's Schiavinato," Carella said. "Skee-*ah*-vee-*nah*-toe."

"Thank you. All we're doing here is going over the same tired ground over and over again. You're wasting everyone's time here, and I think you know a grand jury will kick this right out the window in ten seconds flat."

"I think not."

"*We* think not," Byrnes amended.

"Either way, let's quit. Right now."

"Sure," Carella said. "In fact, I have a suggestion."

"And what's that, Detective?"

"Let's hold a little lineup."

Moscowitz looked at him.

"Let's drag Himmel and Santiago out of bed, and let's go wake up the man who saw your client kneeling over the sewer where we recovered the gun."

Moscowitz was silent for what seemed a very long time. Then he said, "What man? You don't have such a witness."

"Wanna bet, Counselor?"

"What I don't understand," Priscilla said, "is what happened to the other hundred and twenty."

"Me, too," Georgie said.

They were sitting in Lieutenant Byrnes's office, Priscilla in the comfortable black leather wingback chair behind the lieutenant's desk, the men on straight-backed wooden chairs across the room, near the bookcases. Outside the lieutenant's office was the squadroom proper. They could hear telephones ringing out there. Outside the grilled corner windows, there was the steady sound of traffic on Grover Avenue and the intersecting side street. Beyond the slatted wooden railing that divided the squadroom from the corridor outside, in a little room with the words INTERROGATION lettered on its frosted-glass upper panel, Lorenzo Schiavinato was still being questioned. The little digital clock on the lieutenant's desk, alongside a picture of a woman Priscilla presumed to be his wife, read 10:32 A.M. The day was beginning to cloud over. It looked as if it might snow again.

"He said she'd withdrawn a hundred and twenty-five from the bank, didn't he?"

"The cop, yeah," Tony said

"Told us a hundred and twenty-five, didn't he?"

"Carella, yeah."

"So how come there was only five in the envelope?" Priscilla asked.

"Which isn't exactly horseradish," Georgie reminded her yet another time.

He desperately wanted her to believe that the five was what the old lady had in mind when she said her granddaughter would be taken care of. He wanted her to get off that missing hundred and twenty. He knew where ninety-five of that was. It was in an envelope inside a shoebox on the top shelf of his bedroom closet, tucked into one of a pair of black patent-leather slippers he wore with his tuxedo on special occasions like New Year's Eve.

"What happened to the other hundred and twenty?" Priscilla asked again.

Georgie was still doing arithmetic.

Old lady took a hundred and twenty-five from the bank. But there was only a *hundred* in the locker. So where'd the other twenty-*five* go?

Lorenzo was weeping into his hands.

This was because he was Italian. It was also because his lawyer had advised him to tell him everything he knew about this old lady's death before the cops called in a lot of people who'd begin pointing fingers at him. Moscowitz listened without benefit of an interpreter as Lorenzo broke his tale in broken English.

It was a sad story.

After he heard it, Moscowitz told the detectives he had no doubt the crime had been committed, but there were unique and sympathetic circumstances surrounding it. In view of these unusual conditions, he had advised his client to tell his story in the presence of a district attorney, and was therefore requesting one now.

Which meant he was ready to cop a plea.

* * *

It was snowing outside by the time Assistant District Attorney Nellie Brand got to the Eighty-seventh Precinct. She felt cold and bedraggled even though she looked toasty warm and well-tailored in a brown suit, brown leather boots, a beige blouse, and a green headband that complemented, and complimented, her blue eyes and sand-colored hair.

She'd had an argument with her husband before leaving for work this morning, and her manner even with detectives she knew as well as those from the Eight-Seven—was unusually brusque. She knew Moscowitz, too, had in fact lost a court case to him not six months ago. Altogether, her mood did not bode well for Lorenzo Schiavinato, who looked too handsome by half and who had, by his own admission to his attorney, pumped two slugs into a little old lady. Nellie had already been briefed. An interpreter translating, she began the Q and A with the usual name/address/occupation bullshit, and then eased into a routine she'd followed a hundred times before. A thousand times. It was exactly 11:04 A.M.

Q: So tell me, sir, how long did you know the murdered woman?

Carella noticed that Nellie, too, had avoided using Schiavinato's name. He figured if the man ever got out of jail, he should change it to Skeever or something. But it also occurred to him that Nellie had called Svetlana Dyalovich "the murdered woman," and wondered if she was having difficulty pronouncing *her* name, too. Maybe everyone in the world should change his name, he thought, and missed part of Lorenzo's reply.

A:. . . at the fish market.

Q: Would this be the Lincoln Street Fish Market?

A: Yes. Where I work.

Q: And that's where you first met her?

A: Yes.

Q: When was this?

A: The middle of September.

Q: This past September.

A: Yes.

Q: So you've know her approximately four months. A bit more than four months.

A: Yes.

Q: Were you ever in her apartment on Lincoln Street?

A: Yes.

Q: 1217 Lincoln Street?

A: Yes.

Q: Apartment 3A?

A: Yes.

Q: When were you there?

A: Twice.

Q: When?

A: The first time to deliver fish for her cat. Svetlana was sick, she called the market . . .

Q: You called her Svetlana, did you?

A: Yes. That was her name.

Q: And that's what you called her.

A: We were friends.

Q: Did you visit your friend in her apartment on the night of January 20, two days ago?

A: I did.

Q: To deliver fish again?

A: No.

Q: Why *were* you there, sir?

A: To kill her.

Q: Did you, in fact, kill her?

A: Yes.

Q: Why?

A: To save her.

The way Lorenzo tells it, Svetlana is a nice old lady who comes to the market every morning to buy fresh fish for her cat, telling him every day—in almost perfect Italian . . .

Mica, lei parla Italiano bene.

Solo un pocotino.

No, no, molto *bene.*

Congratulating her on the way she speaks his native tongue, she shyly denying her facility with the language, telling him she needs . . .

Mi bisogna un po di pesce fresco per il mio gatto . . .

. . fresh fish for her cat every day, two fish a day, one in the morning, one at night. She feeds him only twice a day, but the fish must be absolutely fresh "because my Irina is very fussy," she says in Italian, with a girlish wink that tells him she must once have been a very beautiful woman. Even at her age, there is still something elegant about the way she walks, a long graceful stride, as if she is crossing a stage; he wonders sometimes if perhaps she was once an actress.

He first realizes she is in constant pain when, one early morning at the fish market, she can scarcely open her handbag to pay for her purchase. This is still September, and the weather is mild and sunny, but she is struggling nonetheless with the catch on the bag, and he notices for the first time the gnarled hands and twisted fingers.

She is having such difficulty with the catch on her bag that the pain contorts her face and she turns away from him in embarrassment, continuing her struggle in silence, her back turned to him. When at last she frees the stubborn interlocking metal pieces, she turns to him and he sees that tears are running down her face as she hands him the several dollars for the two fish.

"Are you all right?" he asks.

"*Puoi alzare la voce*?" she asks. "*Sono un po sordo.*"

Asking him to speak a little louder as she is a little deaf.

He repeats the question, and she answers, in Italian, "Yes, fine, I'm fine."

He learns one day, early in October, that she is originally from Russia and at once a stronger bond is forged, these two immigrants in a city of immigrants, he an Italian seller of fish, thirty-four years old and adrift in a foreign land, she a Russian expatriate in her eighties, a former actress, perhaps, or dancer perhaps, or perhaps even a princess, who knows, seeking fresh seafood for "*mio piccolo tesoro Irina.*"

My little treasure Irina.

She reminds him somehow of his gentle and cultivated Aunt Lucia who married a greengrocer from Napoli when Lorenzo was only twelve, breaking his heart when she moved to that beautiful but barbaric city so very far to the south.

Their daily exchanges are no longer than ten or fifteen minutes each, but during this time they each learn much about the other, and he finds that he looks

315

forward to her early morning visits to the market, a pretty silk scarf on her head now that winter is approaching, woolen gloves on her twisted hands, a worn blue woolen coat, he senses she was once a woman of elegance and taste who has now fallen upon hard times here in this harsh city.

One day he tells her why he left Milano.

"I am a gambler," he says. "I owed money."

"Ah," she says, and nods wisely.

"A lot of money. They threatened to kill me. In Italy, this is not an idle threat. I left."

"Do you still gamble?" she asks.

"Ehh," he says, and shrugs, and smiles ruefully, saying with the slight lifting of his shoulders and the faint grin, Yes, *signora*, every now and then, *che posso fare*? "And you?" he asks. "Do *you* have any bad habits?"

"I listen to old records," she says.

A week or so later, he learns that she once played piano on the concert stage, often performing at La Scala in Milan, which is where she learned Italian . . .

"But no! La Scala? *Veramente*?"

"Yes, yes!"

Excitedly.

"Not only in Milan," she says, "but also in New York and London and Paris . . ."

"*Brava*," he says.

". . . Budapest,Vienna, Anvers, Prague, Liège, Brussels, everywhere. Everywhere."

Her voice falling.

"*Bravissima*," he says.

"Yes," she says softly.

They are silent for a moment. He is wrapping the fish he recommended to her. "And now?" he says. "Do you still play?"

"Now," she says, "I listen to the past."

Just before Thanksgiving, she comes to the market one morning and tells Lorenzo she had been to see her ear doctor yesterday and he made some tests . . .

"Audiometric tests," she says. *"Non so il parole Italiano . . ."*

. . . she doesn't know the Italian word for the tests, they reproduce various sounds in each ear. The results weren't good, she tells him, and now she is fearful there may be something else wrong. She has lately begun to hear ringing in her ears, she is afraid . . .

Lorenzo tells her that tests aren't always accurate, and doctors often make mistakes, they think they're God, they think they can play with a person's emotions, but she keeps shaking her head and saying she knows the tests were correct, her hearing is getting worse and worse every day of the week. What if there comes a time when she can no longer listen to her own recordings? Then even the past will be gone. And then she might just as well be dead.

It is not until he delivers the fish to her, on the morning she got sick . . .

Q: What do you mean, sick?

A: Nothing serious. A cold. Although, for an old woman . . .

Q: When was this?

A: The beginning of the month.

Q: This month? January?

A: Yes.

317

Q: How'd you know she was sick?

A: She telephoned me.

Lorenzo, non mi sento tanto bene oggi. Me lo puoi portare i pesci?

Q: Phoned you at the market?

A: Yes. And asked me if I could please pick out two nice fresh fish for Irina, same as always, and deliver them to the apartment. I told her I would. She was a friend. I got there . . .

At eight-thirty that January morning, there is no one in the hallway when Lorenzo knocks on the door to apartment 3A. But just as Svetlana calls, "Yes, who is it?" the door to apartment 3C opens, and an exotic-looking woman with long black hair and dark brown eyes, and a mouth like Sophia Loren's, and high cheekbones and wonderful . . .

Q: What about her?

A: She was coming out of the apartment.

Q: 3C, did you say?

A: Down the hall.

Q: So what about her?

A: Nothing. I'm giving you all the details.

He tells Svetlana through the closed door that it's him, Lorenzo, and he's here with the fish for Irina. She calls to him to come in, the door is open. The girl from 3C has already gone down the stairs. Lorenzo goes into the apartment. It is a small apartment and frightfully cold on this day when winter has scarcely begun in earnest. Svetlana is sitting up in a double bed in the tiny bedroom, wearing a faded pink silk robe, covered with a blanket and a quilt that looks almost Italian. There is a dresser that is almost certainly

Italian, or so he believes, like one you might find on Sicilia or Sardegna, with ornate drawer pulls and paintings on the sides and top.

"*C'ho un mal raffredore*," she says, telling him she has a bad cold, and then gently warning him not to come near her, "*Non ti avvicinare.*"

Irina the cat is lying at the foot of the bed. She is a fat grey and black and white animal. She blinks up at Lorenzo as he comes into the room, and then catches the scent of the fresh fish wrapped in white paper, and is suddenly all upright ears and flashing green eyes and twitching nose. Like a jungle beast, Lorenzo thinks.

Svetlana asks if he would mind feeding Irina one of the fish. He needn't do anything but put it in Irina's bowl under the sink; Irina eats everything but the spine and the hard part of the jaw. Lorenzo goes out to the kitchen, unwraps the fish while the cat rubs against his leg. There is something about cats that makes him enormously uncomfortable. He never knows what a cat is thinking. He never knows whether a cat is going to lick his hand or spring for his throat. He puts the raw fish in the cat's bowl and backs away at once.

When he comes back into the bedroom, Svetlana asks him to sit for a moment, please, there is something she would like to discuss with him. He takes a chair near the dresser. Across the room, he can see into an open closet where old but stylish clothes, tattered and frayed, are hanging on silk-covered hangers the color of Svetlana's robe. She coughs, takes a Kleenex from a box beside the bed, blows her nose, and then says, "*Lorenzo, voglio che tu mi ammazi.*"

"Lorenzo, I want you to kill me."

14

He does not at first know how to react to this. Is this some sort of Russian joke? If so, Slavs have a very peculiar sense of humor. But is he supposed to laugh? No, she seems quite serious. She wants him to kill her. She would do it herself, she says, but she doesn't have the nerve. Besides, how does a person kill herself if she doesn't own a gun? Does she jump off the roof? Or turn on the gas? Or slit her wrists with a razor or a knife? Or hang herself from the closet pole? No, all of these seem too horrible even to contemplate. A gun is swift and sure, but where would she get a gun? Does Lorenzo know where to get a gun? And if he *can* get one, would he be so kind as to shoot her?

She is not smiling.

This is no joke.

In the kitchen, he can hear the cat demolishing the fish Lorenzo put in her bowl. The sounds are somehow obscene. Cats are too much like wild animals. One step backward and they would be in the jungle again, hunting.

Svetlana goes on to explain that she has been to see a neurologist who diagnosed a benign tumor on the nerve in her left auditory canal. Unless this is removed surgically, she will go completely deaf in that ear. But the chances of . . .

"Well, then of course you must . . ."

"No," she says, "you don't understand. Even if I *elect* surgery . . . this is what they say, Lorenzo, as if I would be electing a president, *elect* surgery, can you imagine? Even if I were to *choose* surgery, *agree* to surgery, even then . . ."

She shakes her head.

"I've waited too long, Lorenzo. The tumor is very large, they may not be able to save my hearing. The larger the tumor, the smaller the chance, is what he told me. The doctor. And with . . . with anything larger than three centimeters in diameter . . . with any tumor larger than that . . ."

And here she begins weeping.

"They might not . . . be . . . be able to save my facial nerves, either. Is what he told me. The doctor."

Lorenzo stands helplessly beside the bed.

"So what's the use? My hands are already dead, I can't play anymore. Should I now choose to live without being able to *hear*? Without being able to express feeling on my *face*? Whenever I played, my hands and my face said all there was to say. Do you know what they called me? A tornado. A tornado from the Steppes. A wild tornado. My face and my hands. A tornado."

Sobbing bitterly, the words coming out brokenly . . .

"What's left for me, Lorenzo? What? Why should I choose to live? Please help me."

Her hands covering her face, crying into them.

"Please," she begs. "Kill me. Please."

He tells her this is absurd.

He tells her that in any case, however slender the chances of success, she must undertake surgery, of course she must. Besides, a person shouldn't make decisions when she isn't feeling right, she's sick just now . . .

"See how pale you look!"

. . . she'll feel different about all this when her cold is gone. But she keeps shaking her head as he talks, no, no, no, insisting that she's given this a great deal of thought, truly, and he would really be doing her an enormous service if he would only find a gun and kill her.

"You're serious," he says.

"I'm serious."

"Svetlana," he says, "no."

"Why not?"

"Because we're friends. You're my friend, Svetlana."

"Then kill me," she says.

"No."

"Please, Lorenzo. Kill me. Take me out of my misery. Help me. Please!"

"No."

"Please."

"No."

"I'll pay you."

"No."

"I'll pay you ten thousand dollars."

"No."

"Twenty thousand."

"No."

"Lorenzo, please. Please."

"No Svetlana. I'm sorry no."

"Twenty-five. To kill me and to take care of Irina afterward. Take her home with you, feed her, care for her."

"I can't. I won't."

"I would pay you more, but . . ."

"No, Svetlana. Please. Never. Not even for a million. Never. Please."

But that is before he loses the money to Bernie the Banker.

What Bernie is telling him, if he correctly understands his very rapid English, is that he is going to kill Lorenzo unless he comes up with the money he owes by Sunday morning. Bernie is a Jew, he supposes, but he is beginning to sound very Italian with all this talk about swimming with the little fishes, very Italian indeed. Lorenzo has dealt with enough bookmakers, both Italian *and* American, to know that very often they won't necessarily kill you because then they will *never* get the money you owe them. On the other hand, having your legs broken or an eye put out is not a very cheerful prospect, either. He listens quite solemnly to what the little bookie is telling him, never doubting for a moment that Bernie himself or someone Bernie knows will hurt him very badly if he doesn't come up with the twenty thousand dollars he bet on those fucking Steelers, what are Steelers anyway, people who steal? The English language is sometimes mystifying to him, but he sure as hell understands what Bernie is telling him now. Bernie is saying "Pay me by Sunday morning, my friend, or you may have cause to be very sorry."

Is what Bernie is saying.

Which is when he calls Svetlana to say that if she still wants him to do what she proposed earlier this month. . .

"Yes," she says at once.

"Then I'm ready to do it," he whispers into the phone.

"When?" she whispers.

Both of them whispering in Italian like the conspirators they are.

"Now," he says. "Tonight."

"No. I have some things to do first."

"Then when?"

"Tomorrow night?"

"Yes, all right," he says. "Tomorrow night."

All of this in Italian.

Domani sera?

Sì, va bene. Domani sera.

"I'll call you tomorrow," he says.

"Good. Call me. But not in the morning. I'll be out in the morning. I have some business to take care of."

"Then when?"

"Early afternoon."

"I'll call you."

"*Ciao*," she says.

"*Ciao*."

Two old pals signing off. No mention at all of murder.

It is a little before eleven when he arrives at her apartment that Saturday night. She is wearing a flowered cotton housedress and scuffed French-heeled shoes. She tells him she went to the bank this morning to withdraw the money she promised him . . .

"I hate to take money for this," he says.

"I would not expect . . ."

"I'm in serious debt," he says. "Otherwise I wouldn't accept this."

"Take it," she says, and hands him an envelope. "Count it," she says.

"I don't have to count it."

"Count it. It's twenty-five thousand dollars."

He shakes his head, puts the envelope into the pocket of his coat. It is eleven o'clock sharp now.

"I had my hair done this morning," she says.

"It's very pretty," he says, admiring the finger wave. "You look beautiful."

"I would have put on a long black concert gown," she tells him, "but I want it to look as if an intruder surprised me. So there'll be no suspicion cast on you. We'll open the window. It will seem that someone came in."

"Yes," he says.

He is wondering what kind of man he is, to be willing to do this to a poor old deaf woman. What kind of man? But he keeps remembering Bernie's threat. And he rationalizes what he is about to do, telling himself that with the twenty-five thousand he can pay off the twenty he owes Bernie and with the remaining five can perhaps pick a good horse or two in next week's races, parlay the money into God knows how much, a fortune perhaps. Beside, he tells himself he is not really taking a life. He is only doing what Svetlana herself *wishes* him to do. He is helping her to die with dignity and honor. He is helping her to leave this world with her memories intact. For this, God will forgive him. This is what he tells himself.

They open the bedroom window.

Cold air rushes into the apartment.

She goes to the bedroom closet and takes from it an old mink coat.

"I want it to look as if I just got back from the store," she says. "So no one will suspect you."

His hand is beginning to shake on the butt of the gun in the pocket of his coat. He is not sure he will be able to do this now that the time is so close. He is not sure at all.

"Would you help me, please?" she asks.

He holds the coat for her as she shrugs into it. He can smell fish on his hands. There is always the stench of fish on his hands.

He is beginning to shake all over now.

From the table just inside the front door, she takes her handbag, begins searching in it, and at last finds what she's looking for, a white envelope with someone's name written on the front of it.

"Take this to the front desk at the Hotel Powell," she says. "My granddaughter's name is written on it. Ask the clerk to send it up to her suite. Make sure you say suite. She has a suite there, you know."

He nods, accepts the envelope.

"Promise me," she says.

"I promise," he says.

He slides the envelope into the left-hand pocket of his coat, the one containing the envelope with the twenty-five thousand dollars in it. The blood money. His right hand is in the pocket where the gun is. He is sweating now. His hand in the pocket is slippery on the handle of the gun.

It is now ten minutes past eleven.

The cat is in the hallway with them now. Looking up at them. First Svetlana's face, then his. As if expecting to be fed.

"Her carrying case is in the kitchen," Svetlana says. "On the table. She's used to it, she'll think you're taking her to the vet."

He looks at her, nods. Looks down at the cat. The cat is rubbing herself against his leg. It gives him the chills. He is sweating and shivering at one and the same time.

"Swear to me you'll take good care of her."

He says nothing for a moment.

"Swear," she says.

"I swear."

"Swear to me you'll feed her fresh fish every day."

"I promise."

"Swear."

"I swear."

"On your mother's eyes."

"On my mother's eyes, I swear."

The apartment goes very still.

In the kitchen, he can hear a clock ticking.

He looks at his own watch.

It is almost twenty minutes past the hour.

From the same hall table, Svetlana picks up a brown paper bag with a bottle of whiskey in it.

"I drink," she says in explanation.

"*Son' un' umbriaga*," she says.

"I'm a drunk."

"Everyone knows that."

As a matter of fact, he doesn't know this.

As a matter of fact, he doesn't know this woman at all.

But he is about to kill her.

"Are you ready?" she asks.

"Yes," he says.

She is standing just inside the door. The bag with the whiskey is cradled in her right arm. He removes the gun from his coat pocket. The cat keeps rubbing against his leg, purring. Sweat is beading his face, sweat is rolling down under the collar of his shirt, sweat dampens his armpits and the matted blond hair on his chest. His hand is shaking violently.

"Thank you for doing this," she says.

He steadies the gun in both hands.

"Take good care of Irina," she says, and closes her eyes.

The interrogation room went silent.

Q: Did you shoot her at that time?

A: Yes.

Q: How many times did you shoot her?

A: Twice.

Q: Did the shots kill her?

A: Yes.

Q: What did you do then?

A: I shot the cat.

Nellie looked at him.

"Why'd you do that?" she asked.

"I didn't want to take care of her. I know I promised Svetlana. But cats are not to be trusted."

Men, either, Nellie thought.

"So you took her money . . ."

"Yes, but only because I was afraid Bernie would do something bad to me."

"Did you pay him the twenty you owed him? Or did you stiff *him*, too?"

"I don't know what stiff means."

"Tell him what it means to stiff somebody," Nellie said to the interpreter.

"Ever leave a restaurant without tipping the waiter?" McNalley asked.

"I always tip waiters," Lorenzo said. "What does that have to do with Bernie?"

"She's asking did you go back on your word with *him*, too?" Moscowitz said. "Isn't that right, Counselor?"

"It's close enough," Nellie said. "Ask him" she told McNalley, who immediately translated the question.

"I didn't go back on my word with him or anyone else," Lorenzo answered. "I didn't *stiff* anybody, however you say it. I paid Bernie his money, and I did everything Svetlana paid me to do. Except for the cat."

"Except for the cat, right," Nellie said. "The cat, you shot in the head."

"Well."

"Well, didn't you?"

"Yes. I don't like cats."

"Gee, I love them" Nellie said.

And *I'm* the D.A., she thought.

"What'd you do with the other five thousand?"

"I bet it on the horses."

"Did you win?"

"I lost."

"All around," Nellie said.

* * *

All during lunch, Priscilla kept complaining about her cheap grandmother leaving her a mere five thousand clams. Georgie kept thinking about the ninety-five thou hidden in one of the black patent-leather dancing slippers in a shoebox in his closet.

First thing he did when he got back to the apartment was check the stash. There it was, in a spanking-clean envelope with a rubber band around it, as beautiful as when he'd put it there yesterday, bulging with money. He counted the money. He wanted to throw it up in the air and let it come down on his head. Instead, he put it back in the envelope and put the rubber band around it again, and put the envelope in one of the shoes, and then put the lid back on the box and put the box back on the top shelf. He closed the closet door. The phone on the kitchen wall was ringing. He went out to it.

It was Tony.

"When do we split the cash?" he wanted to know.

"I'll come by your place before we go to the club tonight," Georgie said.

"What's half of ninety-five?" Tony wanted to know.

"Forty-seven and change."

"How *much* change?"

"Five bills."

"Bring the change, too," Tony said, and hung up.

"What we've got here," Moscowitz said, "is a mercy killing, pure and simple."

"What we've got here, pure and simple," Nellie said, "is Murder Two. In fact, what we *may* have here, Alan, is murder for *hire*, which just may qualify for the death penalty."

330

"Oh, come on, Nellie, really."

"Man takes money to kill someone, that sounds to me like a contract killing."

"Woman gives a man money to assist her in committing suicide, that sounds to me like a mitzvah."

"What's a mitzvah?"

"You don't know what a mitzvah is?"

"No, what's a mitzvah?"

"How long have you been practicing law in this city?"

"Are you going to tell me what a mitzvah is?"

"It's a good deed."

"Man shoots a woman . ."

"She *asked* him to shoot her."

"That's a good deed by you?"

"That's a mitzvah. Nellie, this man isn't a criminal, he's . . ."

"Then what is he? An angel? He murdered a woman in cold blood. Shot her twice in the chest."

"She *wanted* to die!"

"How about the cat? Did she want to die, too?"

"Okay, I'll give you the cat."

"You'll give me more than the goddamn cat, Alan."

"What are you looking for?"

"Are the acoustics in here bad? I told you. Murder Two. Murder for hire. Lethal injection. That's what I'm looking for."

"This wasn't murder for hire, and you know it."

"He got twenty-five grand to kill her!"

"But *she's* the one who gave it to him. This wasn't some outside party who hired him to kill her. This was the victim herself who . . ."

"Victim, you've got it, Alan."

". . . who wanted to die, but didn't have the nerve to kill herself. She's arthritic, she's got a brain tumor, she's about to go stone-deaf, she's about to lose the nerves in her face, all she wants is *out*. My client helped her."

"Right, he's a Good Samaritan."

"No, he's a compassionate man who . . ."

"Who murdered her for twenty-five grand so he could pay off his bookie!"

"The best you've got here is Criminal Facilitation One. But this case is something that'll bring tears to a jury's eyes. Give him Facilitation Four, and we've got..."

"Facil . . ." She almost choked on it. "That's a class-A *mis*!"

"Okay, forget it then. Take a look at 120.30 instead. Promoting a Suicide Attempt. A person is guilty of promoting a suicide attempt when he intentionally causes . . ."

". . . or aids another person to attempt suicide," Nellie finished for him. "This wasn't an *attempt*, Alan! This was eminently successful. The woman is dead. And so's her cat."

"Lay off the goddamn cat, will you? We're talking about a woman in agony and pain, we're talking about a sympathetic man who . . ."

"You're talking about a lousy class-E felony, is what you're talking about. We're wasting time here, Alan. Let's roll the dice."

"All right, I'll grant you the suicide attempt was a success . . ."

"What suicide? He *murdered* her."

"Didn't you just say the *attempt* was successful? *Eminently* successful, weren't those your words? So what's it going to be, Nellie? Did the guy go in there and shoot her in cold blood, or did he merely help her commit suicide? You go for Murder Two, that's what the jury'll have to decide."

"Good, let them decide."

"Take a look at Michigan."

"Don't sing me Kevorkian."

"Gets kicked out each and every time."

"This isn't Michigan. And Kevorkian didn't shoot anybody."

"A jury might not see it that way, Nell."

"Don't call me Nell. I wasn't raised in the woods."

"Tell you what . . ."

"Sure, tell me."

"We're forgetting murder for hire, am I right?"

"Who said so?"

"Arguendo. And I guess you know that an affirmative defense . . ."

"Don't insult me, Alan."

". . . under 125.25 is that the defendant caused or aided another person to commit suicide."

"That's an affirmative defence, all right."

"Which happens to be the case here. An assisted suicide."

"So?"

"So you're absolutely right. You go for Murder Two, we'd be rolling the dice. And you just might lose."

"What do you suggest?"

"*Man* Two."

"No way."

"A person is guilty of manslaughter in the second degree . . ."

"I know the section."

". . . when he intentionally causes or aids another person to commit suicide."

"Man *One* is the best I can give you, Alan. Provided we agree on the max."

"That's too much to pay for a mitzvah."

"A mitzvah, my ass. Man One. The max, Alan. Eight and a third to twenty-five. Take it or leave it."

"Make it two to six."

"No."

"The poor bastard's a foreigner."

"Tough."

"He can't speak English, he looks like Robert Redford. You know what they'll do to him in prison?"

"He should've thought of that before he murdered the old lady."

"Come on, Nellie. You know he's not a killer. What do you say? The minimum, okay? Two to six, okay?"

"I'll give you a straight five to fifteen. And we'll oppose parole after five."

"You're a hard woman."

"I'll also throw in the cat. Have we got a deal?"

"A hard woman," Moscowitz said, shaking his head.

"Yes or no?"

"What choice do I have?"

"Good. Let's go home."

It was almost twelve-thirty when Carella and Hawes finished all the paperwork. They both looked bone-weary.

"Go home," Byrnes told them, "it's been a long night."

"Uh-huh," Carella said.

"Get some sleep."

"Uh-huh," Hawes said.

"You've still got a dead hooker on your plate," Byrnes reminded them.

To qualify, a school had to answer positively to two questions: "Do you have a football team?" and "Are your school colors navy blue and white?"

Didn't matter if he was talking to St. Peter's High or John Parker High. If he got an affirmative answer to both questions, he saddled his horse and rode on over.

By one o'clock that afternoon, Fat Ollie Weeks had personally visited all of the qualifying P schools in the metropolitan area and had struck nothing even faintly resembling pay dirt.

Only twelve of the blue and white schools had football teams. Only eight of those had parkas with a big white P on the back of them. Of those, only two had a white football logo under the letter P. Ollie talked to some sixty football players, all of them shitting their pants, trying to determine what each and every one of them had been doing this past weekend while a white hooker and two black dudes were respectively being eviscerated, drowned, and stabbed. These kids were used to TV violence, but man, this was real life.

The way Ollie looked at it, nobody in this country was *really* concerned about violence, anyway. If they were, they'd put the V-chip on football and hockey games. What *really* bugged Americans was sex. It was okay to talk about it obliquely on all those morning and afternoon TV programs, but show two people actually *doing* it, and, man, the house suddenly got hushed, and all at once everybody was running to protect the little kiddies smoking crack in the next room. Sex was The Great American Hang-up, legacy of those fuckin Puritans who came over from England. Speaking of which, he hadn't had any in a week and a half—sex, not Puritans—and here he was shagging ass all over the universe trying to find three football players who maybe had got a little bit sexy and violent *off* the playing field, and whose head hairs might just match those he already had.

He was back in the squadroom again by a quarter past one.

He checked his computer list again.

Began making phone calls again.

At two-fifteen that afternoon, he began driving upstate to a school named Pierce Academy, whose colors were blue and white and whose football team wore hooded parkas with a white letter P and a white football logo on the back.

At two-thirty that afternoon, Georgie looked up the name Karen Todd in the Isola directory and found a listing for a K. Todd at 1217 Lincoln Street. He dialed the number, and her answering machine told him she could be reached at work and gave him the number for St. Mary's Hospital.

He hadn't known she was a nurse, if she was a nurse.

This only whetted his appetite.

He dialed the number and was connected to a woman who said, "Records Office," immediately shattering a young boy's dreams.

"Karen Todd, please," he said.

When she came on the line, he told her who he was, and reminded her that he'd been to see her earlier this morning, did she remember, the tall good-looking guy, he actually said, with the black hair and brown eyes . . .

"I was with a blond woman and another man."

"Oh, yes," she said, "of course. Svetlana's grand-daughter, in fact."

"Yes," he said.

"I remember you, sure," she said. "Did you have any luck finding that guy who delivered the fish?"

"Oh, yes," he said. "The police have him. He killed her, I guess. Was what I could gather."

"No kidding? Wow."

"Yeah," he said. "Uh, Karen," he said, "do you think you might perhaps care to join me for dinner tonight?"

"Sure, why not?" she said.

From where Richard the First stood in the back row of the choir, he could see out over the heads of the two other Richards and all the other singers. Like a true monarch surveying his lordly domain, he looked down the center aisle of the church and beyond the transept to the huge oaken entrance doors. Late afternoon sunlight streamed through the leaded stained-glass windows on either side of the massive, vaulted space, illuminating it as if a religious miracle were in progress. Professor Eaton, the choirmaster, had just given them notes on how badly they'd sung the hymn

337

the last time around. They were now waiting for his hand signal to start the third chorus all over again.

Hand and head dipped at precisely the same moment.

"Keep Thou my all, O Lord, hide my life in thine . . .

"Oh let Thy sacred light o'er my pathway shine . . ."

The central portal doors opened.

A very fat man stepped into the narthex and looked up the aisle.

"Kept by Thy tender care, gladly the cross I'll bear . . .

"Hear Thou and grant my prayer . . ."

"Professor Eaton?"

The fat man.

Calling from the back of the church.

"Hold it, hold it," Eaton said, and turned with obvious annoyance toward where the fat man was coming down the aisle now, a lightweight trench coat open over his beer barrel belly. Under the trench coat Richard could see a plaid sports jacket, also unbuttoned, and a very loud tie. Now he was reaching into the back pocket of his trousers.

"What is it?" Eaton asked.

Now he was holding some kind of small leather case in his hand, a fob, whatever it was, the flap falling open as he waddled toward the altar. Sunlight caught glittering gold and enameled blue, sending shivers of reflected light into the echoing stillness of the church.

"Detective Oliver Weeks," he said. "There's some hairs I need to match. You got any singing football players?"

* * *

338

Georgie was expecting her at six-thirty. The arrangement was that she'd stop by at her own apartment to change clothes after work, and then come to his place for a drink before they went to dinner. That was why he'd gone downstairs to the liquor store to pick up a bottle of Canadian Club, because what she drank was Canadian Club and ginger ale, she'd informed him on the phone. He was downstairs for no more than fifteen minutes. The phone was ringing when he got back to the apartment. He put the brown paper bag with the booze in it on the pass-through between the kitchen and living room, yanked the wall phone from the hook and said, "Hello?"

It was Tony again.

"What time do you think you'll be here?" he asked.

"Sometime after dinner," Georgie said. "But I may be a little late."

"Like *how* late?"

"Maybe eleven, twelve o'clock."

"Why so late?"

"Well."

"Who is she?"

"Somebody."

"Who?"

"I'll tell you later. I got to go, Tony. She'll be here any minute."

"Bring me half of *her,* too," Tony said.

Smiling, Georgie put up the phone, and checked his watch. Six-twenty. Plenty of time to go look at the money again. It never failed to delight him, looking at all that money. Still smiling, he went into the bedroom.

The window was open.

The smile dropped from his face.

The drawers had been pulled out of his dresser and his shirts and socks and sweaters and underwear were strewn all over the floor and the bed. The closet door was open, too. Jackets and suits had been ripped from their hangers and thrown everywhere.

An open shoebox was lying on the floor.

Two black patent-leather shoes lay on the floor beside the box.

Both shoes were empty.

All of fifteen minutes downstairs, he thought.

This city.

Carella woke up at a quarter to seven that evening. The house was very still. He put on a pair of jeans and a T-shirt and padded around looking for someone. Not a soul was in sight.

"Fanny?" he called.

No answer.

"Dad?"

Mark, calling from his bedroom down the hall. He was sitting up in bed, reading, when Carella walked in.

"Hi, Dad," he said. "Have a good sleep?"

"Yes. How do you feel?"

"Much better."

"Let's see," Carella said, and sat on the edge of the bed, and put the palm of his hand on Mark's forehead.

"Where is everybody?" he asked.

"Fanny took April to ballet and Mom's out shopping."

"Shopping or marketing?"

"What's the difference?"

"About five hundred dollars."

"How can you tell my temperature that way?" Mark asked.

"Your forehead's supposed to feel hot at first. If it continues feeling hot, you've got a fever."

"I still don't get it."

"Trust me."

"So what's my temperature?"

"Ninety-eight point five. Wait," he said, and looked at his palm. "Five and a *half*," he corrected. "Either way, you'll be ready for school tomorrow."

"Good. Did you like school when you were a kid?"

"I loved it," Carella said.

"So do I."

"How's the book?"

"Crap."

"Then why are you reading it?"

"It's the best Mom could find at the supermarket."

"Speaks well for our culture."

He tousled Mark's hair, kissed him on the cheek, and was heading into the living room when Fanny came through the front door.

"Well, look who's up and about," she said. "Wipe your feet, April."

April shuffled her feet on the hall mat, put down her black tote bag with the ballet school's name and logo on it, and sat on the hall bench to take off her boots.

"How's Mark?" she asked.

"Better."

"Good," she said.

"Better get dinner started," Fanny said, and went off into the kitchen.

Carella watched his daughter, her head bent, as she struggled with the zipper on the left boot. Of the twins, she was the one who most resembled Teddy. The same black hair and dark brown eyes, the same beautifully expressive face. Mark favored his father, poor kid, Carella thought.

"How was dance?" he asked.

"Okay," she said, shrugging. "Where's Mom?"

"Shopping."

"Did you sleep good?"

"Well," he said.

"Well what?"

"Not good," he said.

"That's too bad," she said, and suddenly looked up at him. "Dad?"

"Yeah?"

"The other day, when Mark was feeling so awful, you know?"

"Yeah?"

"And I thought he might die?"

"He wasn't going to *die*, honey."

"I know, but that's what I *thought*."

"Well, don't worry, he's okay now."

"Yeah, but that's not what I'm trying to say, Dad."

She seemed suddenly distraught, her brow furrowed, her eyes troubled. He sat beside her on the bench, put his arm around her, and said, "What is it, darling?"

"When I thought he was going to die?"

"Yes?"

"I wished I would inherit his guitar."

And suddenly she was crying.

"I didn't want him to die," she said.

"I know you didn't."

Tears streaming down her face.

"But I wanted his guitar."

"That's all right, honey."

Sobbing bitterly.

"Am I a terrible person?"

"No, darling, you're a wonderful person."

"I love him to death, Dad."

"We all do."

"He's my very best brother."

"In fact, he's your only brother," Carella said.

April burst out laughing, almost choking on her own tears. He held her close, and said into her hair, "Why don't you go say hello to him?"

"I will," she said, "thanks, Dad," and rushed out of his arms and out of the room, yelling, "Mark! Wake up! I'm home!"

The old house was still again.

He went into the living room, and turned on the imitation Tiffany lamp, and sat in the comfortable easy chair under it, thinking about Mark's guitar and Svetlana's cat and the dead hooker with the plastic bag over her head.

When Teddy came home some five minutes later, he watched her as she eased the door shut with her hip, and then put two shopping bags brimming with groceries on the chair near the mirror. Watched her silently in her silent world as she took off her coat and hung it in the closet, thinking that here in this violent city where he plied his daily trade . . .

Here in a universe that seemed to grow darker and darker each day until every day threatened to become eternal night ...

Here there was Teddy to come home to.

He almost called her name out loud.

But she hadn't yet seen him, would not have heard him in any event. He kept watching her. She turned toward the living room, seeing him at last, surprised, her eyes widening, a smile blossoming on her face.

He rose and went to her.

The publishers hope that this large print book has brought you pleasurable reading. Each title is designed to make the text as easy to read as possible.

For further information on backlist or future titles please write or telephone:

In Australia, and New Zealand customers should contact:

Australian Large Print Audio & Video Pty. Ltd.
17 Mohr Street
Tullamarine Victoria 3043
Australia

Telephone: (03) 9338 0666 Fax: (03) 9335 1903
Toll Free Telephone: 1800 335 364
Toll Free Fax: 1800 671 411

In New Zealand:

Toll Free Telephone: 0800 44 5788
Toll Free Fax: 0800 44 5789

In the British Isles and its territories, customers should contact:

ISIS Publishing Ltd
7 Centremead
Osney Mead
Oxford OX2 0ES
England
Telephone: (01865) 250 333 Fax: (01865) 790 358